"I looked you up last night. Guess what I discovered?"

"That I've never been married?"

"No, that you—" June paused as his words sunk in. "You've never been married?"

"Wouldn't want to make any woman a widow. So, what startling thing did you learn about me?"

She shook her head. Once again Dean had thrown her off balance. How could he possibly know she'd tried to determine his marital status? "Forget it."

"Maybe I don't want to forget it. Whatever it was sure ruffled your feathers." He grinned, obviously amused by his bird reference.

"Ha-ha," she said, not finding him funny.

"Hey. I seem to remember you inviting me on this little jaunt. Did I misunderstand?"

She sighed. "No. I thought you would enjoy yourself. That was before I knew you preferred to hunt birds with that high-powered rifle you're so damned good with."

"Ah," Dean said, noting June's face had flushed a delightful pink in her anger, making her even more attractive. "Got it now."

Dear Reader,

I've loved birds since I was a little girl. When my mother couldn't find me, she knew my nose was either buried in a book or I was watching birds at my feeder. Maybe it's the wonder of flight, maybe it's their showy colors (in the bird world, males are usually the most colorful), or perhaps it's their lively songs. Whatever it is, I'm still a birder and lead bird walks on Sunday mornings during the spring and fall migration seasons in Miami.

Bird numbers are declining all over the world because of habitat loss and other stresses. However, there are strategies anyone can employ to help, backyard feeders being one. Why not participate in citizen science and help with the Christmas bird count? Check out a free bird walk in your area. You might find a hobby that will fascinate you for the rest of your life.

Her Cop Protector is a story I loved writing since it features birds, a hot cop and a mystery. Subtropical South Florida provided a steamy setting for a sexy romance. I hope you'll enjoy reading June and Dean's story as much as I loved telling it!

I love to hear from readers. Email me at sharonhartley01@bellsouth.net.

Stay present!

Namaste,
Sharon

SHARON HARTLEY

Her Cop Protector

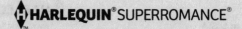

HARLEQUIN®SUPERROMANCE®

Recycling programs
for this product may
not exist in your area.

ISBN-13: 978-0-373-60914-7

Her Cop Protector

Copyright © 2015 by Sharon S. Hartley

Printed in U.S.A.

Sharon Hartley writes contemporary romances that revolve around cops and the fascinating but dangerous people who inhabit their world. After creating plots where the bad guys try to harm the good ones, she calms herself by teaching yoga, cultivating orchids and hiking in the natural world. An avid birder, during migration season Sharon leads weekend bird walks in South Florida. Please visit her website at sharonshartley.com.

Books by Sharon Hartley

HARLEQUIN SUPERROMANCE

To Trust a Cop
The South Beach Search

This book is dedicated to all the beautiful
birds stolen from their homes who
don't survive the journey.

CHAPTER ONE

WHEN JUNE ENTERED the air-conditioned chill of the North Beach Pet Shop, dozens of colorful birds came to life with raucous squawks. *Well, no wonder.* She glanced up at the bell rigged to clang whenever the front door opened. *An early warning system.*

To her left, a tall man in his forties behind the counter nodded at her. Colorful tattoos curled around both of his biceps. Piercings in both ears and his left nostril. "Let me know if I can help you," he said.

"Just looking," June said, in her best attempt at portraying a bored browser. She'd gotten good at that.

He returned to reading a magazine. Was this guy the owner or an employee? That would make a huge difference in his reaction in the next few minutes.

She sniffed the air to detect any foul odors. Mostly old cedar chips from the bottom of cages. Not too bad. At least this shop kept the smuggled birds in fairly decent conditions.

June snuck a glance to the rear wall, where the birds continued their noisy protest in floor-to-ceiling cages. A majority of monks. Some yellow-headed amazons and a few macaws. Exactly what the informant had reported. Birds flapped obviously clipped wings in futile attempts at liftoff. A few made it off perches and slammed into the wire barrier blocking their escape with a disappointed shriek.

June bit her bottom lip and looked away. After the

initial rush of sympathy, familiar anger mushroomed inside her chest, making her heart rate ramp up. *No good, June. Remain calm if you want to help.* Inhaling deeply, she lifted a container of dog shampoo from the display next to her and pretended to study the ingredients.

Remember, these birds are the survivors, she reminded herself, allowing the breathing technique time to work. Triple or quadruple this number didn't survive the journey.

She strolled toward the right side of the store, where an assortment of puppies romped or dozed in five-by-five wire cages stacked one on top of the other. A honey-colored cocker spaniel eyed her hopefully as she approached. When he reared up on his hind legs, she reached through the wire and stroked his soft head. This immediately gained the attention of a feisty Jack Russell terrier who pounced over to nudge the spaniel out of the way.

Too bad she couldn't save these furry sweeties. Their lives were equally sad, but disgustingly legal, products of puppy mills all over the country. She tested the air again. Definitely less pleasant on this side of the shop, but lingering disinfectant made the smell tolerable.

She glanced back at the clerk. He kept his head down and remained focused on his reading, so she continued toward her target: the birds. She needed evidence. Even from a distance of six feet she could see that their legs were banded, supposed proof of being bred in captivity. But she knew better. The barbarians now created counterfeit bands to thwart the Fish and Wildlife Commission's attempts to curb smuggling.

As if counterfeit bands could make this group of wild birds appear tame.

Of course, FWC didn't approve of her unorthodox methods. Even less of her trips to South America with the Tropical Bird Society to stop poachers at the source. Bird smuggling was hardly a high priority to the US government. They were much more worried about drugs. FWC didn't have enough manpower or budget to stop thousands of birds from being murdered each year.

She reached inside her jeans pocket, fingers tightening around her phone. She needed one good peek at a counterfeit band for confirmation. She'd take photos, enlarge them and she'd have her proof.

The door clanged behind her, signaling the entry of another customer. Her heart tripped into a faster pace again, but maybe this arrival would provide a distraction from her own activities.

The clerk murmured a greeting, and the newcomer, a male, grunted a reply as June leaned closer and peered at the leg of a magnificent scarlet macaw who glared back at her with haughty disdain. The bird stepped away with a short cackle.

"Hold still, my beauty," June whispered, focusing on the leg band, looking for the telltale signs of the fake markers, a bruised leg and missing scales—yes, there. Definitely bogus. She nodded to herself. But she already knew that.

With another sideways look at the clerk, she raised her phone, positioning her body to hide her actions. The second customer—a man—stepped next to her. She ignored him and raised the camera. *You're in the wrong place at the wrong time, buddy. Sorry.*

The customer said something during her first click, but he whispered his words and she couldn't stop gathering evidence to ask him to repeat himself. She kept clicking, gathering images of as many captives as possible.

"Hey" came a rough shout from behind her. "What the hell you think you're doing?"

June ignored the clerk. Beside her the new guy spoke again—the inflection sounding like a question—but his words were lost in the resumed squawking of agitated birds roused by the hostility of the clerk hurrying toward her.

"Damn it, lady. Stop taking photographs."

June didn't stop until a rough hand closed around her upper left arm and squeezed hard.

"Hey," she said, trying to pull away. "That hurts."

"It's gonna hurt a lot more if you don't hand over that camera."

She glared at him—but went still when she met his dark eyes. Fear flared in her belly as the man tightened his grip. This was precisely what Agent Gillis had warned her about. She shouldn't have come alone when Jared got sick and canceled.

She slid the phone into her pocket. "Let go of me or I'll file an assault charge."

"I don't think so, lady. You just give me your phone."

"Or what?"

"Or else you'll be very sorry. These are my birds, and I don't want you taking photographs."

So he was the owner. Bad luck, but explained his vigilance. June again tried to wrench out of his grasp, but he only squeezed harder. She swallowed, the pain in her arm now making it difficult to concentrate. She pushed away the stirrings of panic. Would this man really hurt her?

Hell, yes. The jerk's greed caused the murder of hundreds of smuggled birds.

"I'll scream," she said.

"And who do you think will care?"

Before she could answer, a brilliant red bird swooped over her head. She ducked instinctively, as did the shop owner.

"What the—" the owner shouted, finally, blessedly, releasing his grip.

The macaw flapped madly, but clipped wings made it impossible for him to go far.

Rubbing her arm, June turned in time to watch the new customer fling open the last cage and urge its prisoners to flee.

"What are you doing?" the owner shouted.

As if in answer, birds streamed out of confinement. Triumphant screeches resonated through the shop as feathered creatures in hues of green, blue, red and yellow attempted flight, but most only hopped awkwardly around shelves and the filthy floor of the shop.

The front door clanged again, and June focused on the back of the liberator as he rushed outside. A flight-worthy yellow-headed parrot zoomed for the opening. *Oh, no.* Fearing he'd be crushed by the closing door, she held her breath. But vivid green wings flapped through safely and disappeared into a patch of blue sky, no doubt headed for the closest tree.

"Shit," the owner moaned.

With a sigh, June withdrew her phone again and called the police.

DETECTIVE DEAN HAMMER heaved himself out of his police cruiser into heavy tropical air. Shaking his head, he eyeballed the peeling paint of the mom-and-pop pet shop in the seedy business section of North Miami Beach—a long eight miles from South Beach. He'd been busted not only off his beat, but off his regular gig. His lieutenant's cute idea of punishment. Yeah, real cute.

"Hey, Hawk," his temporary partner—a fresh-faced rookie whose training was also part of his exile—asked across the roof of the vehicle, "when was the last time you responded to a disturbance at a pet shop?"

"Yeah, well, that would be never, Sanchez."

Sanchez grinned. "Do you think the pets inside are rioting?"

"Funny. If you learn one thing while working with

me, Sanchez, you need to be ready for anything on a call."

Sanchez nodded and glanced toward the shop's facade. "Yeah, I know, I know."

You just think you know, rookie. Dean patted the Kevlar vest under his shirt and moved toward the entrance. "Things can go south in a heartbeat."

"And you must be prepared," Sanchez mimicked. "I bet you won't need your Remington M24 here, though."

"God, I hope not," Dean said as he jerked open the door. *A sniper gun at a pet shop?* A giant cowbell clanged overhead as he entered.

"Jeez," Sanchez breathed behind him over a cacophony of shrieking birds. "What the hell happened here?"

Good question, Dean thought, focusing on dozens of colorful parrots hopping and leaping in aborted flight attempts around the shop. No bodies. No citizens bleeding. No apparent robbery.

Damn if Sanchez hadn't nailed it. The birds had staged a riot and broken out.

A man, presumably an employee, chased the animals with little success. As soon as he got close to a parrot, the bird squawked and deftly hopped away. He'd managed to capture a few, though, since cages in the rear of the shop housed parrots. Dean looked for and spotted a surveillance camera on the back wall.

"Be careful where you walk," the man shouted. "Don't step on any of them."

"Uh, right," Dean said, his attention zeroing in on the only other person in the shop, a tall, knockout blonde in her midtwenties who stood by the cash register yacking on a cell phone.

"And arrest her," the bird chaser said. "She's responsible for this."

Arrest her? Dean's mood lightened. He'd like to interrogate this one, her sophisticated beauty reminding him of the Russian models who frequented Ocean Drive.

"You the owner?" Dean asked the man.

After a pause where he seemed to consider his answer, he said, "Yes. David Glover."

"Did she release the birds?" Sanchez yelled over the bird noise.

"I did not," the woman replied. She lowered her phone and gave the owner a look that would freeze lava.

"But your partner did," the owner shouted.

"I don't have a partner," she said.

"Yeah, right. Like you never saw the guy before."

"Never. And you're the one who should be arrested."

"For what?"

The blonde turned to Dean. "I called the authorities."

"You bitch," Glover said. "Only because I was too busy with—"

"Hold on, hold on," Dean interjected, the squawking of both human and bird now giving him a major headache. "Sanchez, help this guy round up the birds while I interview this nice lady."

The blonde nodded and dropped her phone into a large purse slung over her shoulder, its strap pressing between very nice breasts.

Sanchez grinned. "Good thing you warned me to be ready for anything."

"You're a real comedian, Sanchez." Dean pointed a finger at the owner. "We'll talk after you get your merchandise under control."

The blonde smiled. "Let me know how that turns out," she said to the owner.

Dean suppressed a laugh and interrupted the owner's heated response. She had a point. The shopkeeper wasn't dealing well with his escapees.

"You got an office in the back I can use?" he asked.

Dean noted Glover's second hesitation. Apparently the man had secrets to protect. "I won't look at a thing," Dean said, holding up his arms.

"Yeah, go ahead," Glover said and resumed chasing his birds, sidestepping around a growing accumulation of bird droppings.

The blonde smiled again, obviously finding the owner's frustrated lunges for his elusive birds hilarious. Glad to escape the noise, Dean ushered the woman toward the back. He liked the way she moved—her legs seemed to glide over the floor and she held herself with perfect graceful posture.

Inside the tiny dump of an office, he motioned for

her to sit in a chair facing a messy desk. He also sat and removed his interview notebook.

"Why aren't you in uniform?" she asked.

"Because I'm a detective."

Her eyes widened. "They sent a detective?"

Dean nodded. "Bird riots demand the full attention of the Miami Beach Police Department."

"Ha-ha."

"What's your name, ma'am?"

"June Latham."

"Address?"

After he got the basics, he said, "So, why don't you tell me what happened here this morning, Ms. Latham?"

"This pet shop markets illegally captured wild birds."

Dean glanced up from his notes. "How do you know?"

"Their leg bands are counterfeit." She shifted her weight to one hip and crossed a slim, shapely leg. "I came here to gather proof for Fish and Wildlife."

Dean rubbed his chin, thinking. "So you liberated these illegal birds so they could fly free again."

"Of course not. Releasing them without a safe harbor plan could harm them." She bit her bottom lip and looked down. "Actually, I should go help that clod before he harms one. He has no idea how to handle birds."

"And you do?"

"Yes." She leaned forward. "Can you arrest him?"

"Like he said, for what?"

"For selling illegal—"

"I think you know I can't do that."

She sat back and crossed her arms. "An arrest would teach him a lesson."

"Not my job." Although, considering his forced time with rookie Sanchez, maybe lessons *were* his job. "So, who released the birds? That's the crime I'm investigating."

"I don't know who he was. Some customer in the shop. I never saw him before."

"Give me a description."

She shrugged. "I barely looked at him. Maybe fifty or sixty, bald. Taller than me, maybe six feet. Really thin."

"Not bad for barely looking at him," Dean said. "So, what happened?"

"When that jerk grabbed my arm— Hey, that's a crime." She sat up straighter. "Assault."

"Do you want to file charges?"

She leaned back, glancing toward the outer room. "Let me think about that."

"Go on. The owner grabbed you…"

June Latham rubbed her arm with long, graceful fingers. Dean followed her movements, noting with disgust a red mark where someone had taken a stranglehold on her body. No question the area would bruise. He also noted well-toned biceps and triceps and wondered where she worked out.

"He wanted my phone. He wouldn't let go of me.

We argued. Suddenly a macaw flew over my head. When I turned, I saw this customer opening all the cages and urging the birds to escape."

"So you maintain you had nothing to do with releasing the birds."

She raised her chin. "I never lie."

"Good to know," he said, closing his notepad, believing she told the truth today. But everybody lied on occasion. "You're free to go." Review of the video surveillance would reveal if there had even been a crime.

She didn't move. "You're not going to do anything about the smuggled birds, are you?"

"I wish I could." See, now, there was a lie. Although he'd love to score points with this tall, blonde goddess, he was a homicide cop, not a bird savior.

"Do you know that wildlife smuggling is the third largest illegal trade in the world economy? Only drugs and weapons are bigger."

Actually, no, he didn't know that little factoid. But of course she didn't lie. "So take your proof to Fish and Wildlife."

"You know the birds will be gone by the time they act."

"I can't help that."

"You could impound the birds as evidence."

Dean assessed the woman before him. So here he had a true bleeding-heart activist. A rare breed these days, thank God, because they were nothing but a giant pain in the ass. "When I talk to Mr. Glover, will he admit the birds are illegal?"

"No."

"Then it's your word against his."

"But remember I have proof," she said, holding up her phone. "And I repeat, you could take the birds into protective custody pending investigation."

A bunch of shrieking, pooping birds in the Miami Beach Police Station? Yeah, that'd get him out of his lieutenant's shit can.

Dean handed her his card. You never knew. Maybe she'd call. "Let me talk to the owner. I'll document your allegations in my report, but that's the best I can do."

"That's the best you can do?" Disdain laced her words. "Really?"

Dean stood. Not likely she'd be calling. "You're free to go, Ms. Latham."

"But the birds aren't." With a final frosty glare, she moved toward the door.

JUNE DESCENDED FROM the rear exit of a county bus at her stop on Brickell Avenue. The monstrous vehicle belched poison out its exhaust pipe, changed gears with a low rumble and lurched north toward downtown Miami.

She removed her cotton sweater, thankful for the hot August sun to thaw out her supercooled skin. Bus drivers in Miami always kept their AC at arctic levels, since hot air blasted their faces at each stop. Her shoulder muscles relaxed as she breathed the salty fragrance from nearby Biscayne Bay. Dwarfed by scores of surrounding condo towers, she walked the landscaped path toward the Enclave's entrance. At least she was home.

What a disastrous morning. And she'd accomplished nothing.

Actually, she'd succeeded in something: stressing out an already traumatized group of birds.

She rubbed her arm, which still ached where that horrible man had squeezed. And the gorgeous raven-haired cop, Detective Hammer, had seemed more interested in ogling her than doing his job. Picturing his handsome face with its I've-seen-it-all-before expression, she wanted to dismiss him from her thoughts but couldn't. There had been something about him, something darkly vital that warned her as surely as the noisy bell at the pet shop.

Of course she'd email her photos to Agent Gillis, but by the time Fish and Wildlife noticed, the birds could be shipped to California.

Would Glover harm them? She hated to think he'd dispose of living creatures to avoid a fine. But why wouldn't he? He obviously didn't care that intelligent animals had been wrenched from their jungle homes, shipped under dreadful conditions a thousand miles away and then cooped up inside a tiny prison. And to think she'd even helped round up the darlings and placed them back in jail so Glover couldn't break a wing, the whole time acutely aware of the detective's intense blue eyes scrutinizing her movements. Hammer had even helped her corner one African gray parrot.

So she'd only made matters worse for the birds. Maybe she should listen to Agent Gillis and stop her commando raids to gather proof. Unless…well, maybe Glover wouldn't be so quick to deal with poachers next time one approached him. That was something, wasn't it?

Something, not much. But no, she couldn't stop. She had to try.

The condo's automatic doors whooshed open, and she entered the chilly elegance of the Enclave's lobby.

"Why such a sad face, Junie?"

Jerked from her tumbling thoughts, she nodded to Magda, the condo's dark-haired, eagle-eyed concierge seated in her usual spot behind the sleek oak counter.

"My goodness," Magda continued in her lilting accent, "you look like the condo association made you get rid of Lazarus."

Alarm shot down June's spine. Nothing happened in this thirty-story building that Magda didn't know about first. "Has there been another meeting? What have you heard?"

Magda held up long, manicured fingers. "I was kidding."

June blew out a breath. Not funny, but Magda couldn't know how worried she was about that rumor. Among others. "Good."

Magda leaned forward, resting on her forearms. "So, what's wrong, sweetie?"

"Just a rotten morning," June said. The less said about her investigative activities, the better.

"Were your buses late again?" Magda persisted.

"Actually, the system stayed on schedule today."

Magda shook her head. "I don't know how you manage to get around Miami on a bus."

"You just have to make that commitment," June said and then added with a grin, "and allow enough time."

"I need my car. Will your uncle be at the Labor Day party this year?"

"He hasn't decided." June removed her key from her purse and stepped to the bank of mailboxes on the wall left of Magda's position. "The weather's been great in New York, so he's not sure he wants to come when it's so humid here."

"So, when was the last time you drove the Cobra?"

June paused in removing mail from her slot. When had she last driven Uncle Mike's antique gas-guzzler? She'd promised to fire it up at least once a week. She grabbed mail and stuffed it inside her bag. "Thanks for the reminder. Guess I'm going down to the dungeon later."

Magda's face wreathed in a maternal smile. "I know you hate the parking levels."

"What would I do without you, Maggie Mae?"

Magda blushed, looking pleased. "Oh, you do fine, Junie."

"The jury is still out on that. Will I see you at the pool later?"

"Of course," Magda replied, buzzing June through the security door to the elevators.

Stepping inside a waiting car, June punched PH and swiped her fob to allow the elevator to ascend to the thirtieth floor. She closed her eyes as she was gently swept upward—like the wings of a bird flying up to her private aerie in the sky.

No, she reminded herself, opening her eyes. Her uncle's aerie. A temporary refuge. She must never forget this luxury didn't belong to her. Not anymore. Not for a long time.

And really nothing had ever been hers. Greed had been her parents' downfall. Had she once been like them? She couldn't remember.

What did it matter anyway? Nothing she remembered from her idyllic childhood had been real.

CHAPTER TWO

DEAN RUBBED EYES strained from watching grainy surveillance video and leaned back in his chair. He'd played the bird-shop security video four times since returning to the station. It backed up June Latham's version of events.

She and the mystery man hadn't entered the premises together. He'd released the birds while the owner confronted June. She never spoke to the guy before he rabbited out of the store.

Dean lifted his mug from the table and swigged cold coffee. Why the hell did the guy open those cages? Maybe he got religion from the sight of Ms. Latham and decided to help her cause. Dean snorted. That was as likely a reason as any. Who knew why citizens did anything anymore?

And why did he give a fig about June and her smuggled birds? He'd told his rookie the review was good training. Yeah, right.

"I don't see a crime to investigate," Sanchez said beside him.

"Not by the woman," Dean said.

"Glover won't be happy."

Dean nodded, remembering the shop owner's sputtering outrage when June walked free. Hell, even if he tracked down this bird liberator, what would be the charge? A misdemeanor—malicious mischief or some such nonsense. Hardly worth the police's time. "He'll get over it."

"Do you think Glover's birds are illegal?"

"Who knows?" Dean shrugged. What he really meant was *Who cares?* "Not our jurisdiction. But I told the woman I'd send my report to Fish and Wildlife."

A grinning Detective Lloyd Miller entered the viewing room with a steaming mug and glanced at the scene frozen on the monitor. Dean knew what Miller saw. Escaped parrots covering the floor and shelves of the North Beach Pet Shop.

"Whoa, Hawk. So the rumor is true. You got yourself a serious situation here. Birds on the lam, huh?"

"Haven't you got somewhere else to be, Miller?"

"And here I come with a sincere effort to help your new case," Miller said with an injured air. "My seven-year-old daughter has a little green parakeet named Birdie Bird. I'm offering her expert assistance with this bird caper."

Sanchez snickered.

Dean gave Miller the finger. He should be used to the mocking. The entire station had been riding him since the lieutenant busted him back to patrol. Didn't matter what case he caught, his fellow officers loved to remind him how low he had sunk.

Miller sat down and raised his mug toward the viewing screen. "I say blast those felonious birds from the air with your rifle. Tough shot, I know, but you're just the man for the job."

"Are you really as good a shot as they say?" Sanchez asked.

"Oh, he's good," Miller replied. "State champion. And very quick on the trigger, right, Hawk?"

Dean squeezed his mug, staring at his trigger finger. Best not to react. The less he said in response to this schoolhouse shit, the quicker the shit would end.

"It's why we call him Hawk," Miller added.

"I've never taken a shot that wasn't righteous," Dean told Sanchez.

"Not even the Wilcox kid?" Sanchez asked.

Dean leveled a look at the rookie. Damn rumors. "The Wilcox 'kid' was eighteen going on thirty-five with a rap sheet three miles long. He threatened his two young hostages with a semiautomatic."

"And you took him down?"

"Something like that," Dean said, shoved paperwork on the bird-shop case into a file. He'd been right to take that shot. He didn't regret a damn thing he'd done that day—only Lieutenant Marshall's decision to punish him for acting before the captain's go-ahead. But his lieutenant hadn't been on scene. Marshall didn't see what Dean saw through his scope.

Had he been too quick? No frigging way. The way he saw it, only the bad guy died that day. He should have gotten a commendation, not reassignment.

Lieutenant Marshall entered the viewing room carrying a slip of paper. Dean sat up, glad he hadn't made his thoughts verbal.

"Your lucky day, Hammer." Marshall handed Dean

the assignment sheet. "We got a body in the Sea Wave Hotel on Ocean Terrace, and I got nobody else to send. Take Sanchez. And don't shoot anyone."

DEAN TURNED ONTO Ocean Terrace and drove past a boarded-up art deco hotel on North Beach. If you asked him—and of course no one ever would—he considered its design as good as anything on South Beach. Not for the first time, he wondered why the beautiful people flocked to Ocean Drive seven miles south but avoided Ocean Terrace. Same beach, same architecture. But a homeless population wandered here instead of gorgeous European models.

A sleek twenty-five-story high-rise towered over the smaller historic gems, its shadow momentarily blocking the relentless August sun. Someone had tried to turn the neighborhood before the great economic bust. It'd happen eventually. Someday this area would become a gold mine for a brilliant developer with good timing.

But right now the only thing open was a half-assed surf shop instead of a celebrity-owned gourmet restaurant.

Across the street, Dean noted a large woman, hair covered with a bright yellow turban, sitting on a wheeled walker facing the dunes. Huge tortoiseshell sunglasses hid most of her face. Her head swiveled as she followed the police cruiser.

He also spotted a cart decorated with wooden and beaded jewelry on the wide sidewalk close to the dunes. Where was the owner? He or she would have to be found and interviewed.

"There it is," Sanchez said, pointing to a three-story structure with faded pink and aqua paint. The roof featured a stair-step roofline, leading to a spire at the apex. Neon signage announced they'd arrived at the Sea Wave Hotel.

"I see it," Dean said. Maybe five or six onlookers stood behind the crime-scene tape that blocked entrance to the hotel's lobby. Filthy clothing, backpacks and a couple of shopping carts told Dean these were street people.

He continued his assessment as he braked to a stop in front of the Sea Wave. Not many people around. Pitiful few tourists—but of course South Florida was in the middle of the mean season.

The heat enveloped him like a wet sponge when he exited the air-conditioned cruiser. Not even 11:00 a.m. and already sweltering. He smelled the ocean—and damn if he couldn't actually hear the crash of waves. You didn't get that on Ocean Drive.

"Jeez, it's hot," Sanchez said.

"That's why we live here, genius," Dean said, still evaluating the scene. The subject hotel sat in the shadow of two larger properties, the one to the right part of a well-known hotel chain and better maintained.

Dean stared at the dirty glass block and one oversize porthole window in the hotel's facade. A series of streamlined balconies wrapped around the sides of the structure. Satisfied he understood the setting, he stepped onto the hotel's wide, covered porch, where he was met by a young male uniformed officer whose badge read Robert Kinney. Dean had seen him around but didn't know him.

"You first on the scene?" Dean asked.

"Right," Kinney said with a nod.

"What have we got?"

"Body on a balcony on the second floor. Gunshot wound to the head."

"Who called it in?"

"Multiple 911 calls. A single shot was heard at 7:18 a.m."

Damn early in the day for a murder. "Any witnesses?"

"No."

"What else?"

The officer checked his notes. "The vic is one John Smith from Tulsa, Oklahoma."

"John Smith? You're kidding me, right?"

Kinney shrugged. "The room is registered to John Smith. Room twenty-two."

"Okay. My partner and I will check the scene. You and other officers begin interviewing bystanders and determine if anybody saw anything."

Dean entered the lobby and scanned its contents. Along the south wall, a sparse breakfast buffet on a long table. Straight ahead, stairs covered with filthy carpet led to a hall and rooms. To the right of the stairs was the front desk, where the only other occupant, a thirtysomething heavyset clerk, leaned against the counter, watching him. The way the guy rubbed his dark beard told Dean the clerk was plenty rattled. A surveillance camera hung over the desk.

Dean nodded at the clerk and proceeded up the stairs, followed by Sanchez. The carpet, which Dean noted was full of sand, covered the same cracked pink terrazzo as the lobby.

The door to unit twenty-two stood open. Dean looked through the room onto the balcony, where the medical examiner, Dr. Owen Fishman, a good man he'd worked with before, looked to be finishing up with the body. Dean nodded to himself and he pulled on latex gloves and cloth booties over his shoes. Excellent. He'd have control of the scene soon. The forensics team was still maybe ten minutes out.

"Inventory the room," he told Sanchez. "And begin making sketches. We go in and out the same way each time we access the scene."

The smell slammed into Dean when he crossed the seedy motel room toward the balcony. The smell was always the first thing. That coppery smell of old blood—lots of blood—and spilled guts.

God help him. He'd missed it.

He was back. He had a murder to investigate. Maybe his lieutenant had been right to bench him for a while to make him remember how much he loved his job. Maybe he'd needed that reminder to follow the rules.

Dean moved onto the balcony, where the ME completed his initial exam.

"Got a time of death?" Dean asked.

"Good morning, Hawk," Dr. Fishman said with a grin. "So you're back?"

"Depends on how quickly I can close this case." Dean snapped a series of photos of the body with his phone.

"Well, we've got a mystery here."

"Let me hear it."

"I'm putting time of death approximately seven thirty. GSW to the head. I'd say the shooter was on the roof of the Night's Inn next door." Fishman motioned with his head.

Dean looked across a narrow alleyway to the Night's Inn. "You're saying a sniper took the vic out?"

"That's what I'm saying."

But why? Dean wondered, taking a good look at the man's face for the first time. This John Smith appeared to have lived on the streets for some time. Shabby clothes, no jewelry, dirty hair, unkempt.

So how did this down-and-out vic wind up on the balcony of a hotel, which although clearly not the Ritz, easily cost a hundred bucks a night? Definitely a mystery, Dean thought, feeling more jazzed every minute.

"The vic's obviously a vagrant," Fishman said, agreeing with Dean's thought process. "No ID."

"He pissed somebody off somewhere," Dean said.

The doctor rose. "Will I see you at the autopsy?"

"You got it."

Fishman grabbed his medical kit. "So, who would go to the trouble to set up a difficult shot on this guy?"

"That's what I'm here for."

"Hawk," Sanchez yelled.

Dean looked over and saw the forensics team had arrived and were suiting up to process the scene. He snapped a series of photos of the room, then exited to give the new arrivals space, careful to travel the same way he'd entered to avoid any more contamination than necessary.

"Come with me, Sanchez," he said to his rookie. "We're going to talk to the desk clerk."

The clerk remained where Dean had last seen him, leaning against the desk counter watching the police activity. He straightened when Dean and Sanchez approached, a guarded expression on his bearded face.

"I'm Detective Dean Hammer, and this is Officer Ruben Sanchez." Dean stuck out his hand for the clerk to shake it.

"Walt Ballard," the clerk said, rubbing his hand on his jeans before shaking Dean's.

"Were you on duty when the shot was fired?" Dean asked. He withdrew his spiral pad to make notes.

"Yeah. I start work at six a.m."

"What can you tell me?"

"I'd just started a new pot of coffee for the breakfast buffet when I heard this *pop*. I knew right away it was a gunshot."

"You familiar with guns?" Dean asked.

"Not really, but—well, it was a strange, scary sound. Not normal, you know. Nothing I heard around here before."

"What happened next?"

Ballard shrugged. "Couple of screams from up-stairs. Another guest came down, a guy, and told me there'd been a shooting. I called 911."

"Did you go up?"

Ballard shook his head. "No, sir. I went nowhere near that room. I didn't want to get shot."

Dean believed him. "What can you tell me about this John Smith?"

"He checked in yesterday at noon. Polite enough, but secretive, like. Nervous, you know what I mean? Looking around constantly."

"You ever see him around here before?"

"Never."

"Did he have ID?"

Ballard hesitated. "He paid cash."

Dean gave the clerk a hard look. "You don't require ID?"

"If a prospective guest has cash, we let him stay. This time of year it's tough for the owner to break even."

"Did he have luggage?"

"One small airline carry-on type with wheels. Black."

Dean nodded. That was what he'd seen in the room. "Did he have a vehicle? Ask about parking?"

"No."

"Did you see anyone suspicious that morning?"

"No one but our regulars wanting a handout when I shut down the buffet."

Dean stared at Ballard, looking for obvious tells that the man was hiding something. "Didn't you think it odd that a vagrant had cash to pay for the room?"

"What do you mean?" Ballard looked confused. "John Smith might not be his real name, but he wasn't any vagrant. Believe me, I know the type. There's plenty in this neighborhood."

Dean withdrew his phone and brought up a photo of the body. He shoved the phone in Ballard's face. "That John Smith, the guy you checked into room twenty-two?"

Ballard's eyes widened. He looked as though he'd hurl.

"Jesus," he breathed. "Oh, man. Oh, shit."

"That's not John Smith?"

"No, sir, that's not John Smith. That's Rocky. He's homeless, a regular, hangs around here all the time. Sweetest guy ever. I let him sweep up and eat leftovers from the buffet when I shut it down."

"So, what seems to be the problem with Killer today?" June asked Mrs. Callahan, the elderly owner of the tiny Yorkshire terrier shivering uncontrollably on the examination table. June stroked her hand across the dog's soft head, and he raised pleading, liquid eyes to her face.

Killer really didn't want to be here. But then most dogs hated a trip to the veterinarian, knowing precisely where they were the second they entered the door and certain they were in for some cruel torture—like an injection via a long, sharp needle.

"I just don't know what to do," Mrs. Callahan answered. "He won't stop trying to eat his rear end."

"It's okay, sweetie," June murmured to the dog. "I won't hurt you." She ran a gentle hand across the dog's bluish-gray fur to comfort him, then backstroked to look for problems and found an angry, inflamed area.

"We've got a hot spot back here," June said. "Have you checked for fleas?"

"My Killer does not have fleas," Mrs. Callahan stated, peering over her thick glasses.

"Are you treating him with preventative medicine?" The dog twitched beneath June's hand, then licked her fingers.

"Oh, I don't believe in chemicals."

"I see," June said. "But he's got fleas. Lots of them. That's why he's scratching."

Mrs. Callahan's face flushed. "Are you sure?"

"I'm afraid so." June parted Killer's fur to expose pink skin, and two or three of the hateful biting beasties scurried for cover.

Mrs. Callahan's mouth popped open. "Oh, no. Poor Killer. I—I swear I looked and didn't see any."

The woman looked so distressed and embarrassed, June smiled at her. Both Mom and patient needed comforting today. And Mom might need new glasses.

"Dr. Trujillo will be in shortly, but don't worry.

She'll give Killer something to make him more comfortable."

"Thank you, Junie."

"You're welcome. Just be patient. The doctor is running a little behind this morning."

June stepped out of Killer's examination room just as Dr. Marisol Trujillo arrived. Her boss, the owner of Brickell Animal Hospital, wore her customary starched white lab coat over casual slacks, her smiling face framed by short hair that had turned a shade of soft gray at age fifty. Dr. Trujillo held a *cafecito* from Café Lulu in her right hand. June closed the examining room door, thinking that tiny foam cup contained enough caffeine to power a jet.

"Sorry I'm late, June," the doctor said in her lilting Hispanic accent. "*Dios Mio*, you know what traffic can be on US One."

"Actually, no." June stepped behind the hospital's counter and grinned at her boss. "Remember I walk to work."

"Don't rub it in. I know all about your light carbon footprint." The doctor took a sip of coffee and left bright red lipstick on the rim of the white cup. "Any emergencies?"

"No, we're good. Only Mrs. Callahan with Killer in room one."

The doctor sighed and moved toward her office at the rear of the hospital. "What is it this time?"

"Fleas."

Dr. Trujillo didn't pause. "Of course it is. I'll be right in."

"Killer is shaking so hard I think the fleas might jump off to save themselves from whiplash."

The doctor laughed and entered her office as the front door to the animal hospital opened. Knowing it couldn't be Elaine, Dr. Trujillo's receptionist, June glanced over to find Agent Donald Gillis, her contact with the Fish and Wildlife Commission, an old and dear friend of her parents', stepping into the waiting room.

Had he already been to North Beach Pet Shop? Had he rescued the birds? She'd emailed him her photos almost immediately, but realized it was much too early for him to have visited North Beach and returned. Plus, that didn't look like a pleased expression on his handsome, dignified face.

"Agent Gillis," June said.

Gillis nodded. "June."

"To what do I owe the pleasure?" Although she had a sneaking suspicion.

"Well, let's see. Something about escaped birds taking over a pet shop on North Beach?"

June sighed and sat down in a swivel chair. She'd kept such worrisome details out of her email and hadn't expected Gillis to hear about yesterday's disaster so quickly.

"Who ratted me out?" Had Dean Hammer actually contacted Fish and Wildlife? The idea improved her opinion of the guy, but there was no way Gillis could have seen any report this fast.

"Your buddy Jared posted the photos on Tropical Bird Society's Facebook page."

"Oh, great," June muttered. Jared was a Facebook junkie. "I didn't know you were a friend of our society."

"How else am I going to follow your dangerous activities?"

"I didn't do anything dangerous."

"Jared's post said you went alone."

Oops. June looked down to the desk. *Damn Jared and his Facebook fetish.* "He got sick. But it was broad daylight in a public place. I was fine." She met Gillis's eyes again, resisting the urge to rub the sore, bruised area on her left arm.

"We've talked about this, June. Confronting smugglers is a terrible idea."

"This guy wasn't the smuggler, just a greedy consumer of cheap, illegal birds."

"Please let my agency take care of it. It's our job."

"But you're too damn slow," June said. "And you know it. You should be on Miami Beach right now confiscating those poor birds instead of lecturing me."

"You could get hurt, June."

"I'm careful. I promise. Don't worry about me."

A small smile softened Gillis's face. "I promised your parents I'd look out for you."

June stiffened. "So you've told me."

"They were worried about what would happen to you if they went to prison."

"Uncle Mike took care of me."

"June. Your parents loved you very much."

"Yeah? Seems to me they loved their money more."

"I'm sorry you think that way."

She raised her chin. "Come on. Weren't you disappointed by what they did?"

Gillis looked away, so June knew she'd touched a nerve. He was trying to use guilt over her parents to make her cease her commando raids, when he had to have been hurt, embarrassed even, by their criminal activity.

"Everyone makes mistakes," he said.

"But some mistakes can't be undone."

Gillis remained quiet for a moment, and she wondered if he'd become lost in memories of good times. Gillis's deceased wife and her parents had been best friends. The couples frequently traveled and socialized together.

"Do any of their old employees ever contact you?" he asked in a wistful tone.

"You mean employees of Latham Imports?"

"Yeah. Your parents had some very loyal workers who took the criminal charges and the fire hard. I thought some might stay in touch."

"I haven't talked to any of them since the funeral, but Uncle Mike spirited me away." June shrugged, wishing Agent Gillis hadn't brought up her parents.

"Truthfully I try not to think about my life before the fire."

Gillis's eyes widened. "Oh, but, June, you—"

The phone jangled. Elaine, the receptionist, wouldn't be in until later. "I've got to get back to work," June said. "Are you going to check out the birds on North Beach?"

"The shop opens at ten a.m., and I'll be waiting."

"Thanks," June said, reaching for the phone. But she suspected the parrots were long gone by now; who knew where and under what conditions? If Detective Hammer had agreed to take them into custody for safekeeping, she wouldn't have to worry about where they disappeared to. But no, the man couldn't be bothered to even check out her photographic evidence.

As the image of the detective eased into her brain, she shook her head, knowing it wouldn't soon leave. His dark good looks crept into her thoughts way more than they should, especially considering how uncooperative he'd been with her investigation. Yes, the man was gorgeous in that bad-boy sort of way and in fabulous physical shape—to be honest, the sexiest man she'd seen in a long time—but she didn't get what she found so compelling about him, even if he had helped with the bird roundup.

But Gillis was right about one thing. She needed to be more careful. When she got caught gathering evidence, it only made circumstances more difficult for already stressed birds.

She looked at the bruise on her left arm, remembering how much it had hurt when Glover grabbed her and squeezed. She rotated her shoulder and felt a dull ache. No real harm done. Still, even if she wouldn't admit it to anyone but herself, she had been frightened.

From now on she'd only go on a raid when she had backup available.

CHAPTER THREE

DEAN STEPPED ONTO the roof of the Night's Inn and examined his surroundings, looking for signs of a sniper. A strong onshore breeze swirled around him, and the afternoon sun beat down on his shoulders. Heat shimmered off patches of black tar beneath his feet. He could see and hear the crashing waves of the Atlantic Ocean to his east. The high-rises of downtown Miami were visible far to the northwest.

He walked to the south edge of the structure. Below him, the vic's balcony jutted from the Sea Wave in plain view. The body had been removed—already on its way to the morgue—but dark blood stained the concrete floor. Yellow crime-scene tape flapped in the gusty wind in front of the hotel.

Beside him, a huge olive-green air-conditioning compressor provided good cover. He nodded. Perfect place to hide.

All the shooter had to do was hunker down beside the compressor and wait for the target to step onto the balcony. Dean examined loose gravel next to the machinery and, yeah, a disturbed area indicated someone had moved around up here. No clear shoeprints to make a mold.

How long had the perp waited for his victim? All night? No, the shooter had probably positioned himself just before daybreak, but time in the hide could stretch out forever.

Dean closed one eye and held up his thumb as if taking aim. He sucked salty, humid air into his lungs. *Wait for it*, he told himself and let out half his breath, finding the most stable part of the cycle. No tremors. The best time to take the shot.

No doubt that was what the murderer had done. Dean felt that certainty shimmering in the steamy air around him. But why? He needed to find out who this vagrant was, what he'd done that would make someone kill him.

Dean searched the roof, but found no evidence that would help him identify the sniper. Whoever he was, he—or she—was damn good. They'd left nothing behind to give them away. But that was what he'd expected. Someone skilled enough to make that shot would also be careful. Very careful. And cautious.

Satisfied with his examination of the roof, Dean descended stairs reeking of stale urine. Likely vagrants figured out a way to sleep here on rainy nights.

On the slow elevator ride back to the Night's Inn lobby, he decided to send Forensics to the roof to process the area, although he doubted they'd find any trace of whoever had shot Rocky—a name as likely to be fake as John Smith.

Damn, just who was this Rocky? Why did someone want him dead?

Motivation, he thought. *I need to find the motivation and then I'll know why, and that can lead me to the who.*

He hoped the desk clerk had the surveillance video

ready. They'd caught a break there, as the owner kept his lobby video a week because of a string of recent burglaries in the area. Dean hoped for a good image of John Smith and anyone else entering the Sea Wave in the past twenty-four hours. Although a shot of the perp was unlikely. His emerging profile of the shooter didn't indicate the man was stupid.

Sanchez met him on the terrazzo porch of the Sea Wave. "Anything?" he asked.

"Nada," Dean said. "Roof area was clean. Have you finished with the possible witnesses?"

Sanchez nodded. "Nobody saw anything suspicious."

"Talk to them again. Find out if anyone sleeps in the stairwell leading to the roof next door."

"You're thinking they could have seen someone heading up?"

"You never know. I'm going to check out the surveillance. Find me when you're done."

Dean entered the lobby. He spotted Ballard in an office behind the front desk and moved in that direction.

Ballard looked up from working with antiquated video equipment. "I'm not quite ready, Detective."

"What's the problem?"

"It's slow. I'm still looping back the twenty-four hours you wanted."

"How long?"

"Give me ten more minutes."

Dean nodded, but frustration gnawed at him. Time was ticking. The first forty-eight hours were critical.

He glanced outside to the ferocious glare of the tropical August sun and spotted the woman with the yellow turban by the dunes still perched on her walker. She was facing the hotels now, looking away from the beach, probably watching the police activity.

Time for a little chat.

She watched him approach, but her expression didn't change. When he got near, he could see his reflection in her huge sunglasses and suspected she had corrective lenses behind the dark ones. He noted a blue cooler in a wire shelf at the bottom of the walker.

"Afternoon, ma'am," he said.

"You a cop?" she asked.

"Good guess," he said and displayed his badge.

"Thought so. Someone got murdered, didn't they?"

"Why do you say that?"

"Been out here since daybreak. Heard the shot, then saw the body come out. Don't have to be a rocket scientist."

"You heard the shot?"

"Sure did." The woman pulled a tall can of beer from her cooler and took a long drink. Condensation rolled down onto her hands. She put the beer back in its nest of ice. "Was wondering when someone'd come talk to me."

Dean wondered how much she'd had to drink, hoping she hadn't started with beer at seven thirty. "Could you tell where the shot came from?"

She pointed toward the roof of the Night's Inn. "I seen the tip of the rifle right there."

Dean felt a smile form. He'd been right to talk to this woman. "Did you see the shooter?"

"Sure did."

Finally. Dean withdrew his notepad. "Male?"

"Male, but couldn't see his face, so don't ask me to make no sketch. He had a hat pulled down low. Couldn't even see the color of his hair."

"Age?"

"Couldn't tell. But he was tall and quick, like. Skedaddled out of there within a minute. Knew what he was doing." The woman nodded. "Just like in the movies."

Dean hoped her report wasn't a figment of the woman's imagination, a result of too many Hollywood movies and too many swigs of beer. "Why didn't you report seeing the gun?"

"Yeah, right." She shrugged. "No one believes an old lady."

"What's your name, ma'am?" He talked to his witness a few more minutes, but got no further useful information. She lived in a local apartment, so he could contact her later, if necessary.

Across the street, he spotted Sanchez reinterviewing the street peeps on the porch of the Sea Wave. Sweat ran down Dean's back, and he envied his partner's shade. With a sigh, Dean moved toward the woman with the beads, but a quick interview told him she'd set up her cart around 9:30 a.m. and hadn't even been in the area when the shooting went down. Dean shut his notebook and walked back to the hotel.

Ballard had the surveillance video ready to view in the small office, so Dean sat at the desk preparing himself for more eye strain. Jeez. What luck to have two cases in two days with video to sift through. But that was modern police work. Everything had gone digital and high-tech.

"Any way to speed this up?" he asked the clerk as the video rolled.

"The red button."

"Thanks. Say, you got any coffee left?" A shot of caffeine was just what he needed for the task ahead.

When Ballard returned with lukewarm brew, Dean murmured his thanks and continued reviewing the video. Most of it was a static view that captured the front desk and entrance to the guest room area. When a figure entered the frame, Dean slowed the stream to real time to try to make an ID, look for anything suspicious. He wanted to find when Rocky had gone through that doorway to his death, see who the man had talked to.

He'd been watching for over thirty minutes when Sanchez joined him. Dean paused the surveillance. "Anything?"

"Nobody saw a thing."

Maybe they did and maybe they didn't.

Street people didn't give up information without some cash motivation, which this case didn't yet warrant. And when they did reveal details, frequently the intel was fiction, brought into existence via a painful past and too much booze. The homeless were seldom reliable witnesses, but you couldn't discount their version of events immediately.

Dean nodded and rolled his chair to give the rookie more room to watch.

A quick blip on the left of the frame caught his attention. A man had entered and moved out of view toward the buffet table. Dean backed up and slowed the video down. All he could see was half a shoulder, but something about the man looked familiar.

He stayed out of the frame for two minutes, but then reentered and stood by the entrance to the hallway in full view of the camera.

Dean sat up straighter. *Holy shit.*

"Hey," Sanchez said in an excited voice. "That's the guy from the pet shop, the bozo that released the birds. He's even wearing the same ugly shirt."

Dean made a note of the time. Three thirty yesterday afternoon, three hours after the pet-shop incident.

As he watched, Rocky, the dead vic, sidled up to the bird liberator. The two spoke for several minutes. Rocky rubbed his abdominal area as if saying he was hungry. Seemed friendly enough, but Dean made a mental note to get a lip reader to watch the conversation. He needed a translation.

"Ballard," Dean yelled toward the front desk, pausing the video. "Come in here."

The clerk entered the office, eyebrows raised.

Dean indicated the monitor. "Who is this guy talking to Rocky?"

Ballard focused on the frozen image. "That's John Smith."

"The guy who rented the room?" Sanchez asked.

Ballard nodded.

"You're sure?" Dean asked, a shot of adrenaline charging him up far better than any caffeine. The first break in a case was often the most important.

"No question," Ballard said.

"Well, I'll be damned," Dean said. What were the odds?

There had to be a connection between the delightful June Latham and John Smith. He needed to find what it was. Maybe Smith was another bird nut. Ms. Latham said she didn't know him, but Dean now wondered about that.

He needed to have another conversation with her.

Dean checked the time. Just after three. He was almost done here. Should be no problem making it to the animal hospital where she worked before they closed at five.

JUNE STROKED HER palm across the velvety soft fur of a tiny black-and-white kitten in the cardboard box on a stainless-steel examining room table. The kitten arched his spine into her hand, obviously enjoying the attention. Three littermates, two more black-and-whites and one orange tabby, were extending their paws up the sides of the cardboard in a pitiful attempt at escape. They weren't quite strong enough yet, but the undersize feral mama watched her babies nervously from inside a cage next to the box.

"That's Oreo," Felicia Mayer said, the client who'd brought the litter in.

"They're adorable," June said. "Where did you find them?"

"Believe it or not, Mama chose my backyard to give birth in."

June glanced back to the mother, who now paced the cage, searching for her own escape. "Mama's no dummy. She knows where food is available."

Felicia, a dedicated cat lover, had founded Feline Rescue, an organization that trapped feral cats, had them spayed and then found safe homes. She used her ample powers of persuasion on Dr. Trujillo and other vets in the area to provide services at a reduced rate. June herself had donated more cash than she could afford to Felicia's cause.

Felicia smiled and stroked the tabby, the runt of the litter. "The kits seem pretty healthy, but I wanted Dr. Trujillo to check them out."

June estimated the kits to be four to six weeks old. Ready to be weaned. Oreo licked her finger with a rough tongue.

"You're already attached to them, aren't you?" June asked.

Felicia lifted the tabby and rubbed its fur across her

cheek. Mama cat whined, a mournful sound. "Yes," she said. "I couldn't help it. They're so cute and help-less."

"Are you going to keep all five?"

Felicia shrugged and shot a glance to the mother. "Probably. Unless I find really good homes."

"How many cats do you have now, Felicia?"

Felicia replaced the kit in the enclosure. "I feed about twenty, but they're all spayed."

June smiled at the thin, dark-haired woman who'd made it her mission to save every stray cat in South Florida. Considering her own work with birds, who was she to say a thing about Felicia's obsession with felines? "You're a good person."

Felicia sighed. "Maybe. Or maybe I'm just nuts."

June heard the front door chime, indicating an ar-riving patient. "Let me go see who that is. Just wait here. The doctor is finishing up with another patient and will be in to check the kits shortly."

"Thanks, June."

"Shall I have Elaine make an appointment to have Mama spayed?"

Felicia nodded. "This will be her first and last lit-ter."

June gave Oreo's fur another stroke and hurried to greet the new arrival, which according to the sched-ule should be Jessie, a goofy yellow Lab due for his annual checkup and the last appointment of the day.

But she heard a male voice say hello, and Jessie was always brought in by Sarah Weksler, a recent divorcee

"May I help you?" Elaine asked in her most professional voice, usually reserved for men, preferably widowers she hoped would invite her to dinner.

"Yes, ma'am. I'm Detective Dean Hammer and this is my partner, Ruben Sanchez. We need to speak with June Latham, please."

Elaine asked, "What's this about?" as June rounded the corner.

Hammer saw her and nodded slightly. "Police business," he said to Elaine, his gaze on June.

"What's going on?" June asked before Hammer could say anything else. Elaine was sixty years old, had worked for Dr. Trujillo since she opened her practice and never heard a rumor she didn't feel the need to spread. So now Dr. Trujillo would know two policemen had come to see her. Of course Dr. Trujillo would want to know why. She was on good terms with her boss, but the less said about her commando activities, the better.

"Ms. Latham," Hammer said. His dark eyes swept her body as she reached Elaine's side. "I'm hoping you remember we met yesterday at the bird riot on North Beach."

"Bird riot?" Elaine asked. "What bird riot?"

"There was no riot," June said, with what she hoped was a squelching glare at the detective. "Is this about the smuggled birds?" she asked when a burst of hope that Hammer had come because he'd arrested Glover slammed into her thoughts.

"Not exactly," Hammer said.

"Do you need my photographic proof of the counter-feit bands?"

"No, ma'am. I wonder if there's somewhere we could have a private conversation?"

"Private," Elaine murmured under her breath, making her voice loud enough to ensure that everyone heard. "Oh, my."

"Yes, ma'am," Dean said, turning the full force of his gaze on the receptionist. "I hope that's okay with you."

Elaine colored and looked away with a giggle.

Oh, please. June resisted the urge to roll her eyes at Elaine's reaction to Dean Hammer. Yeah, the guy was great eye candy, but way too sure of himself. She noted his partner followed the conversation with avid interest. As yesterday, the detective wore street clothes, a casual shirt, khaki pants and a tie, while the partner wore a Miami Beach Police Department uniform. Each of them had a holstered gun on his hip.

"I'm working," she said.

"But we only have one more patient," Elaine offered in a sweet tone. "I can show Ms. Weksler and Jessie into an examining room when they arrive."

Hammer gave Elaine a sharp salute. "Thank you, ma'am. The Miami Beach Police Department appreciates your cooperation."

"Anytime," Elaine said, girlishly fluffing her gray cloud of hair.

June hesitated, actually curious as hell to learn what this unexpected visit concerned if not the birds. But the way Hammer looked at her made her feel as if she were naked underneath her pink scrubs. "What if Dr. Trujillo needs me?"

"I'll come get you," Elaine offered.

June mentally shrugged away her irritation with the receptionist, who couldn't help who she was. Likely nobody found it easy to say no to the detective's overpowering presence. He had some innate ability to control everything around him.

"Let's go into examining room two," June said.

"You should use the doctor's office," Elaine suggested. "It'll be much more comfortable."

"But if—"

"June, you know she won't mind," Elaine said, interrupting June's objection.

"Of course. This way," June said, motioning with a sweep of her arm toward Dr. Trujillo's suite. *Well, why not? This is a private conversation.*

Once she was seated behind the doctor's mahogany desk, she realized she rather liked having some much-needed space between her and Detective Hammer. At least she hadn't been imagining his looks. He was just as vital and imposing as yesterday. Sitting behind the huge block of wood covered with stacks of paper made her feel more in control. She'd have to stand in an examining room.

She folded her hands in her lap and leaned back in the swivel chair while Hammer closed the door and took a seat beside his partner.

"This must be important for you to track me down out of your jurisdiction," she said.

"We're investigating a murder," Hammer said.

"A murder?" June swallowed hard and leaned forward. *A murder?*

"Yes. Of a human being," Hammer clarified. He raised his gaze from the blank sheet of paper on his open notepad to meet hers. "Not a parrot."

CHAPTER FOUR

"NOT FUNNY," JUNE SAID, meeting his direct stare. Why the lame stab at humor? Did he want to disarm her, put her at ease? Maybe distract her from the fact that two cops wanted to talk to her about someone's death?

"Why do you think I have any information about a murder?" she asked.

"Because the victim was killed in this man's hotel room." Hammer placed an eight-by-ten black-and-white photo of two men on the desk before her. "The one on the right."

June picked up the photograph and examined it. Two men were conversing, but what— "Oh, my God."

"You recognize someone?"

"One of them is the man who released the birds in the pet shop."

Hammer made a note. "You still say you never saw him before yesterday?"

"No. I swear. I don't know him."

"Please study the image carefully."

Stunned by Hammer's revelation, June scrutinized the photograph. The subjects didn't seem to know they were being watched, so maybe the shot was taken by a telephoto lens. Either that or a security camera. Before yesterday, she'd never seen either man before in her life. Or had she? She studied the image again.

"Where was this taken?" she asked.

"The lobby of a hotel."

"I'm sorry," she said. "I don't know who he is."

"His name is John Smith."

"That's a common name."

"And probably not real. What about the other man, the one on the left."

"He looks like—I don't know." She glanced up at Hammer and then his partner. "Like maybe he's a bit down on his luck."

"You're right. He was a street person."

"Was? You mean—"

"He's our victim."

June swallowed a bad taste in her mouth. "When did this happen?"

"This morning. That shot was taken late yesterday afternoon."

June looked back to the image, realizing the poor man had been murdered just hours after this photograph. How quickly life could change. She shook her head. But of course she already knew that.

"You're sure you don't know John Smith?"

"I'm sure." She replaced the photograph on the desk. "Both men are strangers to me."

"Too bad," the partner said.

"Have you remembered anything else about John Smith from the pet shop that might help us?" Hammer asked.

"Like what?"

"A tattoo, some jewelry, maybe a limp?"

She shook her head. "I was totally focused on the birds. I all but ignored him."

Hammer nodded. "Is it possible he's in one of your do-gooder organizations?"

"Do-gooder?"

"You know what I mean. Rescue groups."

"Of course it's possible, but—" June studied the photo again. When she looked up, Hammer watched her as if she were prey. "You think I'm lying, don't you? You think I know this John Smith."

"And just yesterday you told me that you never lie," he said in an intimate tone, one a date might use over a glass of wine.

She sucked in a breath and glanced at the partner, who returned her gaze without changing his expression. *Maybe my life is about to change again.*

"I have no reason to lie," she said.

"Ma'am, we're just trying to understand the facts," Hammer said, totally professional again.

Is he trying to confuse me? "I understand, but—"

"Don't you see how we find it odd that this man would release the very birds you're trying to rescue and you don't know him?"

"Yes, I admit it's strange. I thought it was bizarre yesterday, but I swear that's what happened. He did say something to me as I was taking photos, but I couldn't make it out and thought he might be trying to stop me."

The detective made a note, a sour expression on his face.

"Do you think I'm involved with this homeless man's murder?"

Hammer met her gaze and stared right through her as if trying to peer into her very soul. Unable to look away, June held her breath, wondering what he saw. Was he trying to decide if she were a murderess? Maybe that was why he'd been watching her so carefully. He didn't know her and wondered if he were dealing with a stone-cold killer.

Damn, she might not be perfect, but no one had ever suspected her of murder.

A light rap on the door broke the moment. "Come in," June said, relieved.

Dr. Trujillo cracked the door and stuck in her head. "Can I interrupt for just one minute?"

June jumped to her feet. "I'm sorry, Doctor. Do you need me?"

The doctor stepped into her office. Both policemen stood.

"Sit, sit," she said. "Sarah Weksler canceled, and I just want to get my cell phone." After throwing June a questioning glance, the doctor stepped out of the office with her purse. The policemen took their seats.

"Hope we haven't gotten you in trouble with your boss," Hammer said.

"Yeah, me, too," June replied. "But you didn't answer my question. Am I a suspect in this murder?"

"No, ma'am," Hammer said. "You're what we call a person of interest."

"Because you think I might have information to help you solve the case?"

"That's what we were hoping."

"I'm sorry," June said, "but I don't know anything about your John Smith."

Rising, Detective Hammer reached for the photograph. Her gaze zeroed in on the holstered gun strapped to his right hip.

"Thank you for your time, Ms. Latham."

"I wish I could be more help," she said, coming to her feet, thankful the interrogation was over.

Hammer handed her another business card, his warm finger lightly brushing hers in the transfer.

"Please think about your encounter with John Smith and give me a call if you think of anything else."

"But I don't—"

"Anything at all, ma'am. Our forensics team is analyzing the surveillance this photo came from. Would you agree to come into the station and watch the full video to see if that triggers any memory?"

June bit her lip and looked away from Hammer's piercing stare, thinking there must be more to his request than a simple viewing of a video. He had another reason to get her into the station. *What is the difference between a person of interest and a suspect?*

"Sometimes the smallest thing can be the break we need to put a guilty party behind bars," he prompted.

June sighed. "Okay, sure. When?"

"I'll be in touch when the evidence is ready for viewing. Thank you, Ms. Latham."

Hammer's partner nodded at her as they left Dr. Trujillo's office. June followed them out, more unsettled than she liked by her disturbing conversation with the detective.

What the hell was going on?

Dr. Trujillo and Elaine waited for her behind the reception desk. When the police officers had exited, Elaine pounced.

"Tell us everything."

June gave them a quick rundown of what had happened in the pet shop. "The police hoped I remembered something about the man who released the birds that could help them with their murder investigation."

"Oh, my goodness. You're a suspect?" Elaine grinned, looking as if the idea pleased her enormously.

"No. Or at least they say I'm not."

"What were you doing on Miami Beach?" Dr. Trujillo asked, her jaw set in disapproval. "Looking for smuggled birds?"

"Jared got a tip," June said simply. The less said the better.

"*Dios Mio*, Junie. You know how I feel about you doing that. You could get hurt," the doctor said.

"Is the tall one married?" Elaine asked.

"I have no idea," June replied quickly. His relationship status had never occurred to her. Detective Hammer's body language, hell, his whole persona, the way he openly checked her out, made her believe he was available. Available and looking. Looking very closely at her.

But married men flirted and cheated all the time. Of course she knew that. And she certainly wasn't interested in the domineering Detective Hammer.

"Just my type," Elaine said, fluffing her hair. "Serious hunk."

"I concur," the doctor said. "But don't you think he's a bit young for you, Elaine?"

Elaine shrugged. "Just saying."

"Well, let's close up, ladies," Dr. Trujillo suggested. "I think we've had enough excitement for one day."

"Heck, I wish handsome detectives would visit us every day," Elaine said as she pulled her purse from under a counter. "Lots more fun than a bunch of sick cats."

As June locked drawers and cabinets, she did as Hammer asked and thought about her brief encounter with John Smith, trying to remember anything distinctive about him to aid the police. Something about the still photo niggled at the back of her brain, some flash of familiarity. What was it?

She decided that feeling was most likely from seeing him in the pet shop two days ago. She didn't know him.

On her short walk home to the Enclave, she tried again. Trouble was, when she dredged up an image of John Smith, her thoughts immediately drifted to Detective Dean Hammer and his oh-so-penetrating gaze. Blue eyes and black hair. What a combination. She shook her head. The less she thought about Hammer, the better. She needed to put the whole incident out of her mind.

She paused as she entered the lobby, wondering if she should pay a visit to Uncle Mike's beloved Shelby Cobra. She'd drive it to the bird walk next Saturday, but that was a week away and she couldn't remember the last time she'd started that damn car. She sighed. Better do that now.

Steeling herself for a trip down to the dungeon, she waved at Magda behind the concierge desk and entered the stairwell. Unfortunately, because the Cobra was seldom driven, its assigned parking spot was on the lowest level. June trudged down three flights, her uneasiness growing with each step.

When she pushed open the heavy door to Tier C, she felt as if she'd entered a tomb. Dim overhead fluorescents gave every parked vehicle a looming, menacing aspect. The stale air reeked of petroleum products. Her quick steps echoed off thick concrete walls, an eerie sound. A suffocating sense of claustrophobia pressed her toward the oil-stained floor.

This was how parrots felt when locked up in a cage. Birds were wired to fly free, just as humans were made to see the sky and breathe fresh air.

She spotted the Cobra, its bright red paint covered as always by a green tarp, and hurried toward it, pulling her keys from her purse. She removed the tarp from the driver's side and inserted the key. Uncle Mike refused to alter his precious Cobra in any way, so no battery-powered clicker opened this antique beauty.

At a loud *boom* behind her, June whirled, fisting her hands until nails dug into her palms. Who— What was that?

But no one was there. She was alone. June unclenched her fingers. Probably something falling in the garbage chute. Damn, but the subterranean levels always made her jumpy.

She slid into the Cobra's driver's seat and ignited its powerful engine, which roared to life on the first try. Feeling her tension ease, she checked the fuel level. Over half-full. Good. No need to drive this—what did Mike call his baby? Oh, right. A muscle car. And not just any muscle car. For some reason this was a very special one, designed by some big-wheel car legend.

To her it was just another gas guzzler.

And when it came to muscles, the well-toned biceps on Dean Hammer's arms were much more to her liking, even if the man had done nothing but make her life miserable.

AT HEADQUARTERS THE next morning, Dean rewatched the video of the pet-shop riot in one of the viewing rooms. Sanchez sat beside him, also focused on the monitor.

Once again June Latham's recitation of the events matched what was revealed on the screen. Totally engrossed in snapping photos of the caged birds, she never fully looked at John Smith when he approached her.

"Do you believe her?" Sanchez asked.

"Yeah, I do. I don't think she knows John Smith, but I think he knows her. Look at this." Hammer backed up the video to where Smith approached June. "See? He says something to her right there."

"You're right." Sanchez leaned forward, but shook his head. "Can't make it out."

The surveillance continued to roll. When June didn't react to Smith's words, Smith either repeated them or said something new. The department's lip reader was currently viewing the Sea Wave lobby video in an adjoining room. He'd have him take a look at this one, too.

Glover moved into the frame. Dean made a derisive sound when the jerk grabbed June's arm.

"Glover is a real prince, isn't he?" Sanchez said.

"Watch Smith." Smith stepped toward the confrontation, appearing ready to intervene to help June. His face contorted into fury. He fisted and opened his hands repeatedly, even lifted his right arm as if to take a swing at Glover.

Now, that was interesting. Why would Smith react so strongly to Glover's treatment of a woman he supposedly didn't know?

"Wow," Sanchez said. "I didn't notice that before."

Dean hadn't, either, and that oversight pissed him off. He'd been too focused on the argument between June and Glover. Two days ago he hadn't cared about

John Smith's reaction. Shit. Two weeks on patrol, and the inactivity had caused him to lose his edge. To stay sharp, he needed to focus. To follow procedure.

Because he had a murder to solve, and right here was a clue. No question about it. He just had to figure out what the hell it meant. Just who was this mystery man Smith? What was his connection to June Latham? There had to be one.

Dean knew in his gut that Smith's appearance in the pet shop was no coincidence. He'd likely followed June in because he wanted to talk to her. What about? Birds?

A hit-man-style murder on North Beach?

Sanchez snickered when the video morphed into slapstick as parrots escaped their cages. Dean could almost hear their victorious squawks as they flapped their way to freedom. He paused the video.

"You still going to have Ms. Latham come in and look at the hotel surveillance?" Sanchez asked.

"Definitely. I have a few more questions for her."

"What about?"

"I'll let you know when I figure that out." A preliminary background check had revealed no wants, no warrants. She'd never been arrested, never even received a traffic ticket, which he found odd, although she had a current driver's license. Apparently a real solid citizen. Maybe too solid.

Rebel Simpson, the department's lip reader, entered the viewing room. "I'm done," he said, "but you're not going to like it."

"Give it to me," Dean said.

"It's strange. The victim asked Smith if he had any spare change. Nothing startling there." Rebel looked down at his notes. "At first Smith said, 'Sorry, man. Can't help you.' Then Smith seemed to get an idea. He said, 'I bet it's miserable hot living on the streets this time of year.' The vic agreed. Smith said, 'How would you like to sleep in my room tonight?'"

"Seriously?" Dean said. "So Smith is gay and was looking to hook up?"

"With a vagrant?" Sanchez asked.

"I don't think so," Rebel said. "The vic objects, says he doesn't roll that way. Smith insists no funny stuff, he's just a nice guy and there'll be a free meal in it for the vic."

"Yeah, right," Sanchez muttered.

"Why? Does Smith indicate the reason he's performing this great public service?" Dean asked.

"Smith says there's two beds in an air-conditioned room. The vic is obviously hesitant, but when Smith mentions a fifth of vodka, that clinches the deal and they head into the hallway together."

"For a nice romantic evening," Sanchez muttered.

Rebel shrugged. "All I know is what they said to each other. Weird, huh?"

"Doesn't make a damn bit of sense," Hammer said.

"It does if Smith is gay," Sanchez insisted.

"Did your interviews with the street people on North Beach indicate Rocky was gay?" Hammer asked.

"Nobody mentioned it," Sanchez said, shaking his head. "And yeah, I think someone would've."

"We may have to check that out," Dean said. "Rebel, have you got time to take a look at another surveillance video?" He motioned to the frozen image on the monitor. "It's short."

"Sure." Rebel positioned himself before the screen, and Dean backed up the pet-shop surveillance to where John Smith entered the frame.

"I want to know what this man said to this woman."

After watching the scene three times, Rebel sat back with a frustrated sigh. "This one is tough," he said. "The man is whispering, like he doesn't want anyone else to overhear him."

"You can tell that?" Sanchez asked.

"By the shape of his mouth," Rebel said. "And notice how the woman didn't react. She might not have caught what he said."

Hammer nodded. Again that matched what June Latham had told them.

"The only thing I'm confident of," Rebel continued, "is he says, 'June.' You know, like the month of the year. Sorry. I'm sure that doesn't help you at all."

CHAPTER FIVE

THE NEXT EVENING, June pushed open the door to her condo, incredibly glad to be home. Maybe now she could stop obsessing about Detective Hammer and his murder investigation.

It'd been a hectic day, full of her worry about traumatized patients, their demanding parents, a dead body.

She loved her job, and still hoped for acceptance to the veterinary school at the University of Florida, but today she wondered about that goal. It always seemed so ironic that Dr. Trujillo's mission was to help animals when most of her patients were terrified of her. June wasn't sure she wanted animals she loved cowering in the corner when she entered a room.

Lazarus shrieked from the balcony aviary, reacting to her arrival. June hurried over to check on him and found him hanging upside down from his favorite branch by one claw, his brilliant scarlet plumage iridescent in the late-afternoon sun.

"Hello, my lovely," she said.

Her answer was a loud guttural squawk.

"I'm glad to see you, too," she said. She slid open the glass door, stepping into the humid, oxygen-rich atmosphere of the aviary. Definitely warmer without the air-conditioning, but shaded and entirely pleasant. Probably very similar to the jungle in Peru where this macaw had been captured.

Lazarus flapped his huge wings and righted himself, but didn't take flight. He could have, though. She'd turned most of the balcony, which wrapped around the top floor of the thirty-story Enclave, into an aviary for the birds she rescued. She'd enclosed the space with parrot-proof screening and crammed it with trees, water features and interesting toys for her patients to amuse themselves. Lazarus was the only bird in residence right now, which was rare. She usually nursed at least two injured birds back to health at any given time. He'd be rehabbed enough to go to a permanent sanctuary somewhere soon, and while that thought should make her happy, instead it depressed her.

She was getting too attached. That happened when she cared for a bird too long. But she never kept a patient no matter how much she loved it, believing birds should always fly free when they were physically able.

While Lazarus squawked his encouragement, she changed the plastic floor protection and gave him a new supply of black oil sunflower seeds. She cleaned the huge aviary every day, not only for the health of the birds but to avoid complaints from the condo association wing nuts. There were some who didn't appreciate her rehab clinic.

When done, she stepped close to stroke the macaw's soft feathers. "Good boy," she murmured when he didn't back away. Only recently had he allowed her to touch him. Lazarus was definitely getting better.

She knew she couldn't save every bird, but this one at least should have a happy life from now on.

If Detective Hammer had agreed to confiscate the birds from the pet shop, she could have saved them, too. She flashed to his murder investigation and the photo of the dead man, something she couldn't stop doing since the interview in Dr. Trujillo's office yesterday.

Person of interest, indeed.

Lazarus made a chortling sound and ducked his head into her hand, wanting more, which pleased June.

"I know, Laz, I know. I need to stop thinking about that mean ol' detective."

The phone rang, and she stepped back inside to answer, sliding the door shut behind her with a last look at the preening macaw.

"Girl, whatever you're doing tomorrow night, cancel," a familiar female voice said after her hello.

June collapsed onto her sofa, settling in for a chat with her best friend from high school, Sandy Taylor. It'd been a while. "Why? What's going on?"

"A party at the Turf Club. And not just any party, the annual Labor Day costume gala."

"The Turf Club? You know I'm not a member anymore."

"Doesn't matter. You'll come as my guest. Donna is in town from Atlanta visiting her mom, so I'm rounding up the old gang for a mini reunion."

"Seriously?"

"Donna and Carole are both on board. You have to come."

"Well, I really don't *have* to," June said, not sure she wanted to and scrambling for an excuse. A reunion with her wealthy Pinecrest Prep friends could be fun—or it could be disastrous. A painful reminder of what she had lost.

"Yes, you do. Remember the outfits we wore Halloween our senior year?"

"How could I forget? We almost got suspended by Dean Holly when we entered the gym."

"That's the exact look I want all of us to rock tomorrow night."

"High-class hookers at the stuffy Turf Club? No way."

Sandy laughed, a carefree sound from a beautiful young woman with absolutely no problems. Funny how their lives had taken such different directions. They'd once been so close they pretended to be sisters.

"I can't wait to shake the place up," Sandy said. "You know it's just what that boring group needs."

June remained silent. No, she didn't really know. She hadn't stepped on the property since her parents were arrested.

"Come on, Junie. It'll be fun. Say you'll join us."

"What does your prim and proper husband say about this plan?"

"Paul will love the idea. He's always said he decided to marry me that very Halloween night."

"We did look good."

"We'll look even better now that we're not awkward teenagers."

"You were never awkward, Sandy."

"That's true. But I fill out the dress better now."

And there was the excuse June needed. "Sorry, but I didn't keep that costume."

"Of course not. I'm sending you one identical to mine."

"I can't let you do that."

"Oh, stop it with the false pride," Sandy said. "I want us to be twins just like in the old days."

"Sandy, really, I—"

"I need you to do this for me, Junie," Sandy said, an edge creeping into her voice.

"What's wrong?"

After a pause, Sandy said, "My perfect marriage is falling apart."

June sucked in a breath. So much for her envy of Sandy's glamorous life. "Oh, God, Sandy. I'm sorry. What—"

"It's not hopeless, but I need to spice things up with Paul, remind him why he fell in love with me."

"You don't need *me* to do that," June said softly.

"Yes, I do. Please, Junie. I know this will work."

"Do you want to talk about it?"

"Not on the phone. Maybe Saturday night. Please, please come. It won't be the same without you."

June remained silent. She had nothing special planned that night, but wasn't sure a costume ball at a swank club that was once her parents' favorite haunt was the most ideal way to spend her free time.

"We're all going in a limo," Sandy added, as if that final detail would clinch the deal. "We'll pick you up around eight."

"Okay," June said, not wanting to think how much tomorrow night would cost her friend. "Why not."

"Don't sound so glum. We're going to have a blast."

After receiving a few more details about the evening, including some gossip about their friends, June stepped back into the aviary. Lazarus gave a half-hearted squawk, but ignored her and kept eating as she sat in her own favorite perch, a sturdy cloth macramé chair suspended from the ceiling. From here she could either watch her patients or look out over the clear waters of Biscayne Bay and beyond Miami Beach to the Atlantic Ocean, a stunning vista that normally calmed her.

Unfortunately the view didn't have its usual effect. She took deep breaths and tried to wrench herself out of a long-gone past. But too much had happened. Too much was swirling around in her brain, too easily distracting her.

Why in the world had she agreed to accompany Sandy to the Turf Club? She'd avoided the place for ten years. Would anyone be around tomorrow night who remembered her parents? Probably not. She really ought to get over herself.

Lazarus tested his wings with a few quick flaps, flew the short distance to grab a hold of the chain holding up the swing and gazed down. June looked up as he waddled down the chain closer to her.

A bubble of excitement replaced her foreboding. Was Lazarus going to willingly approach her? She reached for a towel and placed it over her shoulder, holding her breath to see what he'd do next.

He cocked his head, squawked and flew back to his favorite branch.

She sighed. Almost. Laz was definitely making progress.

She pushed her foot against the balcony wall, forcing the chair into a gentle sway, her thoughts drifting back to her conversation with Sandy. If she could get through tomorrow night at the club, maybe that would be a step toward recovery for her, too.

One thing for sure. At least she wasn't obsessing about Detective Hammer and his murder investigation anymore.

DEAN STUDIED THE images of colorful tropical birds on the computer screen before him. He'd punched June Latham's name into a search engine, and one of the first hits was the Facebook page of the Tropical Bird Society, one of her do-gooder groups.

Rescue groups, he corrected himself. She'd objected to his use of *do-gooder*.

The page listed pet shops and vendors the group suspected of selling birds captured from the wild, so he created a fake profile, claiming to be vehemently opposed to this practice, and asked to join the group.

After acceptance, he posted a few times criticizing smugglers, receiving a lot of "likes." Before long, he received a private message with future dates of planned visits. John Smith could easily have tracked June to the North Beach location by doing the same thing.

TBS, the acronym most members used on postings, also had a standard web page where Dean found a schedule of their numerous activities, such as weekly outings to search for rare birds or to clean up various sites around the county. They seemed more of an environmental group than just a protector of birds. If he hit a dead end with this search, he'd get a roster of members to investigate.

So this was one way John Smith could have found June. He also could have tracked her cell-phone signal. The real question was why. Smith had clearly known her name before he released the birds. So why had he followed her?

More important, was there any connection to his dead body on North Beach?

The autopsy hadn't been much help. Forensics confirmed what he'd seen at the scene. Rocky had been in average health. The cause of death was one gunshot wound to the head. The ME found no obvious evidence that the vic had been gay, so John Smith's invite up to his room didn't appear to have sexual overtones. From the surveillance, the invite appeared to be a spur-of-the moment decision, so what had been behind it?

Something just didn't add up.

Dean scrolled through his list of search-engine hits, searching for more information about June, but didn't find anything pertinent. The woman definitely flew beneath the radar. Was that deliberate? Did she have something to hide? The name Latham kept popping up, though, Latham Imports, in connection with a fire and arson investigation from ten years ago.

Curious as to why the search engine kept linking June to the fire, Dean opened an old article from the *Miami Herald* entitled A Cautionary Tale About Greed, and read about a married couple, Carl and Eileen Latham. The Lathams operated a successful importing business, but the FBI, working in a joint task force with Fish and Wildlife, found cocaine in one of their shipments from Peru. The Lathams were wealthy and politically connected, and their photograph frequently appeared on the society page for having paid big bucks to attend this or that benefit, so the scandal created a huge sensation. Out on a bond, they of course insisted they were innocent and had no knowledge of the drugs hidden in their merchandise.

Friends rallied around them and their attorney promised a vigorous defense, but before the trial could begin, a suspicious fire destroyed the Latham Import Warehouse on the Miami River. The fire effectively ended the prosecution as the couple perished in the inferno.

Dean sat back, considering. This case was before his time as a detective, but he vaguely remembered hearing about it. Everyone wondered if the Lathams had set fire to their property to destroy evidence, but misjudged and caused their own death. Seemed too stupid to be true to him.

And why was Fish and Wildlife involved? He made a note to check that out, kept reading and found what he wanted at the end of the article.

"According to friends, the Lathams' only child, June Marie Latham, a junior at Pinecrest Preparatory Academy, will live with her father's brother, Michael Westbrook Latham, an investment banker in New York City."

So there was the connection to June. She'd been seventeen when her parents died and had gone to live with an uncle. Sad story, but Dean didn't see how the information helped his investigation. He needed to keep digging.

"Sanchez," he called.

"Yeah?" His rookie partner looked up from his own internet search for information on Rocky, their vic.

"Go to the Tropical Bird Society Facebook page. Research the profile of any friend or member who has posted to their site. I need to know who they are."

"You think maybe we'll find our John Smith?"

Dean shrugged. "Probably not, but we have to check it out."

"You got it," Sanchez said, his fingers moving over his keyboard.

Dean entered the name Michael Westbrook Latham

into the department's search engine. If June's parents were dirty, maybe her uncle was, too.

JUNE EXTENDED AN arm to the uniformed chauffeur, took a deep breath and exited the limousine into a warm summer night. Beneath the impressive portico of the Turf Club, lights and music blazed. She could hear the chatter of animated voices from inside the clubhouse.

"We're here," Carole squealed behind her in the stretch limo.

Less nervous than she expected, June stepped beside Sandy, the first of her friends out of the stretch, who looked regal in a light pink beaded sheath. June wore an identical dress, only hers was a very pale blue, and it molded to her body perfectly, revealing every curve. The hem was short, with a sexy slit up one side. The neckline plunged lower than she was used to, but she had to admit the effect was flattering. They each wore a matching headband across their foreheads with a feather plume jauntily waving in the back.

The costumes were expertly made and likely cost Sandy a fortune. Despite her misgivings, June loved the way she looked. She even enjoyed the subtle clicking sound the rows of dangling beads made as she moved.

But maybe that was because of the delicious dry, chilled champagne she and her three friends had enjoyed on the drive to the club. Truly their party had already started.

"I don't see Paul," Sandy murmured. "He said he'd meet us."

"He'll be here," June said, unsure where that confidence came from. She met Sandy for lunch once or twice a year, but hadn't spoken to Paul since her parents' funeral.

Dark-haired Donna scooted across the backseat and emerged in her bright red saloon-girl costume, an outfit with ruffles and a stiff petticoat. Carole came last in an emerald dress with a low-cut bodice.

"Well, don't we look fabulous?" Donna said with a smile.

"You know, we really do," June agreed, checking out her friends.

"Ready, girls?" Carole asked.

The four friends hooked arms and entered the grand ballroom together. To June it seemed as if everyone in the room turned to stare at her, but she knew that couldn't be true and was just her nerves kicking in.

"There you are." Paul Taylor approached, his eyes wide in what June hoped was appreciation of his wife's appearance. He gave her a quick hug, one without any real intimacy. His dark hair had begun to recede, so maybe an early midlife crisis was the problem with his marriage.

"Did you girls have a nice reunion?" he asked.

"We haven't been girls for a long time," Carole said.

"Still prickly after all these years, huh, Carole?" Paul asked.

Carole shrugged. On the limo ride over, Sandy had

revealed her suspicions about her husband's infidelity, which had infuriated Carole.

"It's been great to catch up," Donna interjected, always the peacemaker. "Thanks for sending the limo."

"You're welcome."

"Why aren't you in costume?" June asked, since Paul wore an ordinary business suit. An expensive one, expertly tailored, but one he'd wear to the office.

"I'm here as an attorney," he said in a defensive tone.

"Oh, how interesting," Carole said. "You *are* an attorney."

"Come on, Sandy. I need you to meet someone." Paul whisked Sandy away with a nod at the other three. Her feather bounced gaily as she hurried to keep up.

"What a jerk," Carole muttered.

"Don't make it any worse for her," June said.

Carole sighed. "It's just he— Oh, look. There's Laura Harris." Carole hurried in that direction.

"I need a drink," Donna said. "Let's find the bar."

"June Latham. What a pleasant surprise."

June let Donna go on ahead and turned to the speaker, a woman in her fifties dressed in a police officer's uniform, vaguely recognizing her as a member of her parents' large circle of friends.

"I'm sorry," June said. "Please remind me—"

"Sylvia Baker," the woman prompted, grabbing her hand and shaking vigorously. "I don't expect you to remember. It's been a long time."

June nodded, having no clue how long it'd actually been.

"How are you?" Sylvia asked. "Where have you been?"

"I'm good," June said.

"Look, Chuck," Sylvia said, grabbing a passing man dressed as the devil. "It's June Latham."

June found herself swept up into the festive melee, and despite her misgivings, the old guard seemed genuinely happy to see her. She didn't specifically remember anyone from her parents' generation, but they sure knew her.

"Oh, but you've turned into a lovely young lady."

"Your mother would be so proud."

"You have your father's smile."

Then a cloud would pass across faces as old friends recalled the scandal and hastily changed the subject. Everyone mostly tiptoed around the subject of her parents, and she didn't hear one snarky remark.

"But you just disappeared. Everyone thought you'd moved to Manhattan to live with your uncle," said a white-haired lady in costume as a cowgirl.

June heard variations of the same comment at least a dozen times. Ten years ago it was what she'd wanted everyone to think. Only Sandy, Carole and Donna knew she'd remained in Florida.

"Uncle Mike let me stay in Miami and finish my senior year."

"So you did graduate from Pinecrest Prep?" The lady's eyebrows dipped together in confusion. "I thought that—"

"Uncle Mike insisted I transfer to a public school. It was a compromise."

"Oh, I see."

But June could tell she didn't see at all. How did anyone explain the raw emotions of a seventeen-year-old whose life had just been kicked out from underneath her? Hell, she didn't understand it herself. All she knew was she had been terrified of New York City, which Mike insisted would be a fresh start. She'd imagined a freezing-cold city with giant buildings and no trees, which sounded like torture to a teenager who grew up in Miami diving into a swimming pool every day.

And, despite her humiliation, she'd needed the comfort of her friends.

But that was all behind her. Time to start avoiding the older generation.

"Excuse me," she said and stepped toward the bar.

Okay. She'd passed the hurdle of facing her parents' cronies, which hadn't turned out nearly as disastrous as she'd imagined. *Good job, June. You've satisfied their curiosity. Let the gossip begin.*

Now I deserve some fun.

She'd noticed plenty of guests her own age. New people to meet who knew nothing about her past. Who didn't care a flaming golf ball about her unsavory history. Even some good-looking men, a bonus she hadn't expected.

She knew the costume made her look damn good,

which boosted her confidence, and she ought to take advantage of that elusive feeling.

With champagne in hand, she looked for Sandy, wanting to make sure Paul hadn't upset her. June found her friend in a group that included her husband across the room. Sandy stood with her back to the floor-to-ceiling plate-glass windows that during the day revealed a beautifully maintained golf course. Tonight all that was visible was a subtly lit landscaped patio.

Husband and wife appeared to be getting along. June raised her champagne to her old friend. Sandy nodded and lifted a glass in return.

"It's uncanny how much you two look alike."

"My friend has a secret wish to be a twin," June said, extending her arm to a very nice-looking dude in a pirate costume. Not as hunky as Detective Hammer, but nice. "I'm June."

"Hi, June," he said, shaking her hand with a smile. "You don't remember me, do you?"

"Sorry. Do I know you?"

"Steve Hill. We were on the swim team together at Pinecrest."

"Oh, of course." She took a sip of champagne, recalling a gawky teenager who looked nothing like this tall man with sun-lightened brown hair.

"Do you still swim?" Steve asked. "I remember you were a freestyle specialist."

"Oh, I'll take a few laps in the pool where I live. How about you?"

"I swim competitively in a master's program."

"Good for you." That would explain his still-toned body.

"I remember you and Sandy used to dress alike in high school." Steve inclined his head in Sandy's direction.

"I know it's silly," June said, glancing back to where Sandy stood. "We're both only children and decided to be each other's sister."

The plate glass behind Sandy shattered at the same time as a loud *pop* reverberated through the room. Screams replaced lively chatter.

A red stain bloomed across the bodice of June's friend's exquisite pink dress.

In horrifying slow motion, Sandy, her face contorted in a grimace of surprise, fell facedown.

CHAPTER SIX

DEAN ARRIVED AT the Turf Club crime scene within thirty minutes of the first 911 call. He'd been in the station still working the North Beach murder with Sanchez, so he caught the case. His good luck.

Definitely a banner week for murders in the city of Miami Beach.

A uniformed patrolman working off duty met them at the front door.

"What have you got?" Dean demanded.

"One woman down," the cop reported. "ME is on the way."

Dean nodded, entered a huge, hushed ballroom ahead of Sanchez and thought he'd fallen down the rabbit hole. Helium-inflated balloons trailing festive streamers clung to the ceiling. Hundreds of guests dressed in outlandish getups stared at him. A pirate with an eye patch, a masked cancan girl, a helmeted astronaut.

Murder at a costume party. Just great.

Easy way for a murderer to hide.

"You got the shooter?" Dean asked as he moved through a parting kaleidoscope of colors and anxious faces. He didn't like to form theories before learning the facts, but wondered if someone pulled a pistol everyone thought was a prop.

"No one had eyes on the shooter."

"Not even one witness?" Sanchez asked.

"Not close range, then," Dean said.

"No," the patrolman said, shaking his head. "Sniper. From somewhere out on the golf course."

Dean halted his forward motion. "Sniper?"

"Yeah. One shot, one down. Looks like a hit to me."

Another sniper. And what were the odds?

Dean spotted the body, covered by what looked like a tablecloth, and moved toward it. "Anybody disturb the scene?"

"The husband rolled the body before I could get there, but it was obvious she was gone. One of the guests, a physician, confirmed she was dead. Then I made sure everyone stayed clear. Didn't let anybody leave, either, although a few might have snuck out."

"Good. We need to interview everyone here. Is there a manager?"

A man stepped forward. "I'm the manager."

"I'll need to see your surveillance video." Dean pulled on gloves and knelt beside the victim. He removed the bloodstained sheet and froze.

The dead-eyed face staring up at him was June Latham's.

He relaxed when he realized it wasn't her. But the description would be the same. White female, blonde, approximately twenty-six, hundred and twenty pounds, goddamn beautiful.

The dead woman lay on her back, but had hit the deck facedown. The husband had rolled her, but death was likely instantaneous. She wore a sparkly party dress now saturated with blood. Matching headband with a feather.

Beautiful young woman out for a good time and now dead way too young.

The vic had definitely been killed by a sniper. Dean glanced to the shattered window and shards of glass covering the plushly carpeted floor.

Couldn't be sure without forensics, but his gut told him it was the same weapon as North Beach. *Yeah, what are the odds?*

A tickle of excitement niggled the back of his brain. Somehow this case was connected to the North Beach hit. He needed to find that connection.

He snapped photos of the body but needed to wait for the crime-scene unit to process the scene. He'd gotten here fast. The primary detective didn't often arrive first, but the specialists should be here soon. He needed to locate the sniper hole on the golf course so Forensics could process that, as well. He glanced outside to a dimly lit concrete patio with attractive landscaping. Could he get lights on the area behind that patio? He wanted to check it out ASAP.

Dean recovered the body and rose. "No one goes out on that golf course until I give the okay," he said to the manager. "You're shut down until further notice."

"I understand."

"Do we have ID on the vic?" Dean asked.

"Sandra Taylor," the off-duty man reported. "Her husband is sitting right there, Paul Taylor."

Dean zeroed in on a white male in his late twenties or early thirties slumped at the closest table sur-rounded by friends. A bloody napkin lay on the table where he'd apparently cleaned his hands. His white shirt also contained blood spatter. The man stared at a glass full of ice and an amber liquid, then picked up the drink and took a long swallow. More blood stained his cuff. His hand shook.

He had that numb I-can't-believe-this-shit look about him. He'd turned his chair away from his wife's body.

The husband was always the first suspect, and this one appeared properly shocked. Interesting that he wore a business suit instead of a costume. Did he come straight from work? Important meeting on a Saturday? With who? Or maybe he didn't really want to be here?

"Where was the husband when the hit went down?"

"Standing right next to the victim."

"Got it," Dean said. *But he could have hired some-one.*

Dean focused on the support group surrounding the husband to look for reactions and realized a woman was staring back at him. His breath caught.

June Latham. June Latham with her hand resting on the husband's shoulder.

And damn if she wasn't any man's wet dream come to life. A pale dress clung to her curves, hugging and dipping in all the right places to make a man hungry. Made him hungry. Did other things to lower parts of his anatomy.

He couldn't tear his gaze away from her.

She exuded an aura of elegant old-money class and easy primal sex at the same time. Like a high-priced pro trolling these festivities on the hunt for a wealthy john. Was Ms. Latham living a double life? If so, she'd definitely come to the right club for that activity. The Turf Club's membership fees were the most expensive in the county. Both those fees and this woman were way out of his price range.

He didn't care about the club, but the thought of June being a pro initiated a spurt of anger.

She gave him a quick nod.

His gaze rose to her hair and a feather jutting out behind her head. He frowned. The dead woman sported a similar headband. In fact, June's dress appeared identical to the one worn by the vic. Even their hair was arranged in the same style.

What the hell was going on here?

Maybe he had fallen into a rabbit hole.

THE SIGHT OF Detective Hammer moving into the Turf Club Grand Ballroom and taking control of the chaotic situation mysteriously reassured June.

This man knows what he's doing. He'll figure out what the hell just happened. Why it happened.

As he directed his team, movements crisp and purposeful, she felt herself emerge from a block of ice that had frozen her since she watched Sandy collapse to the floor.

"Oh, my God," Paul said for the hundredth time.

June realized her hand rested on Paul's shoulder and gave a comforting squeeze, her gaze remaining on Hammer as he examined the body with his ever-present partner beside him.

Sandy's body. Beautiful, happy, perfect Sandy is gone.

Paul folded his arms on the table and placed his head on top. "Sandy. My God. Sandy. This can't be real."

She agreed with Paul. This couldn't be real.

Hammer rose, asked a question and turned to focus on Paul. Then Hammer's gaze caught hers, and everything else in the room receded. No question he recognized her, but of course he would. A look of speculation entered his eyes as he openly checked out her costume.

Speculation and hunger.

She shivered, but gave him a slight nod of recognition.

He spoke to the two uniformed cops with him. They nodded.

"Ladies and gentlemen." Hammer made his voice loud enough for everyone to hear. She hadn't realized how quiet the room had become until he spoke.

"I'm sorry for the inconvenience. Please be patient, but you'll need to wait here until interviewed by an investigator. More officers are on their way to speed up that process."

Then he turned back to her and motioned with his head slightly. She took that as a sign that he wanted to speak to her. With an apologetic murmur she knew didn't register with Paul, she moved toward the detective. The murmur of voices resumed in the room.

"Ms. Latham," he said in a professional, neutral voice that belied the feral expression in his eyes.

She nodded and swallowed, needing to moisten a dry mouth.

He frowned. "Are you okay?"

"Could I sit down?" she asked. She'd been standing next to Paul since Sandy...since the shooting. June closed her eyes against the memory of Sandy's shocked expression.

"Of course." Hammer pulled out a chair. "I'd like to ask a few questions."

"Thanks." June sat, positioning herself so she couldn't see the cloth-covered body.

She suspected her friend had been dead before she hit the carpet. And then Paul had totally lost it. And not just Paul. The entire room had filled with terrified screams. She'd gone to Sandy—to Paul, to pull him away from his wife, the sound of crunching glass beneath her feet ugly and loud.

It seemed foolish now, but she realized she'd remained next to Paul in an effort to somehow protect him, shield him from the evil that had entered this ballroom. Donna and Carole had done the same.

"Did you know the victim?" Hammer asked.

"Yes. She is—was—one of my best friends."

"I'm sorry for your loss," he said.

June wondered how many times he'd uttered those

exact words in his career. "Thanks. We came to the party together tonight."

Detective Hammer pulled out his notebook. "She didn't come with her husband?"

"No."

Hammer scribbled a note. Wait. Had she just incriminated Paul?

"We were having sort of a girls' night out with two other friends," June explained.

Hammer looked up. "Why? Any trouble in the marriage?"

June opened her mouth to deny that idea, but hesitated. The knot in her stomach tightened as she processed where Hammer was going with that question. Paul was a suspect.

"Maybe," she admitted. "I'm not sure."

Hammer jotted another note.

"But Paul had nothing to do with the shooting," she said. "They've been in love since high school."

"You went to high school with the victim and her husband?"

"For a while, yes. Believe me, Paul would never hurt Sandy." As she said the words, June wondered if they were true. Never kill her, no. What a ridiculous notion that Paul would pay someone to shoot Sandy. How best to convince the detective of that fact?

But Sandy's feelings had been hurt by her husband's recent distance. Indeed, that had been the point of their sexy costumes.

"I'm sure you're right," Hammer said smoothly. "Can you tell me what you saw tonight?"

"It was so fast," June murmured and related the surreal nightmare of how the window exploded, her friend collapsed and the room went crazy.

"Anything else?" he asked when she'd finished. He'd listened without interrupting, his face a complete blank.

"That's all I can think of."

"Did Ms. Taylor have any enemies?"

"Everyone loved Sandy."

He nodded, but the thought flashing through his brain was almost audible. *Apparently not everyone.*

"Did she work?"

"No."

"Kids?"

"No." June closed her eyes, worried Sandy sounded like a spoiled slacker. But she had wanted kids. She and Paul were waiting a few more years to start their family. "She volunteered a lot of hours at the Lowe Art Museum."

"It's good there's no kids," Hammer said softly. "Murder is hardest on children."

June opened her eyes at the sympathy in his voice.

"I guess so," she murmured.

"So you and the victim were close?"

Again June hesitated. The truth was she and Sandy had drifted apart since she left Pinecrest. Had she lied when she told Hammer Sandy had been one of her best friends? Months often went by without them speaking.

And now I'll never speak to Sandy again. Never hear her soft laugh. Oh, Sandy. I'm so sorry. So, so sorry. How did we let that happen?

She took a deep breath, wishing she could cry. Sandy's death was certainly a good reason for tears, but she hadn't cried since the fire. Not even at her parents' funeral.

"In high school we used to pretend we were sisters," June told Hammer, looking down at the table. "We even dressed alike sometimes."

"You're dressed alike tonight."

His tone had changed, and June glanced up. Hammer was staring at her feather again. Self-conscious, she removed the headband and placed it on the table.

"I know it's silly," she murmured. "Sandy had the costumes made."

"Anything else you can tell me? Can you think of any reason someone would want to murder your friend?"

June remained silent for a moment. What did she really know about Sandy's life lately? God, but that thought made her sad.

"To be honest," she said, "we weren't as close as we once were. I might not be the best person to ask."

"Is there any reason why someone would want to kill you?"

A jolt went through June at Hammer's question. "Me? Why would you ask that?"

"You seem to be a lightning rod for trouble," Hammer said.

"That's ridiculous. You don't even know me."

"I've been assigned three new cases in the last forty-eight hours. You have a connection to all of them."

She opened her mouth to reply, then shut it without speaking. He had a point.

"You and the victim here look a lot alike. You even had the same feather sticking out of your hair."

June's gaze fell to the headband on the table. Horror washed over her as she reasoned out Hammer's implication. "You think someone was gunning for me and shot Sandy by mistake because we were dressed alike?"

"So I really want an answer to my question," Hammer said, his blue gaze boring into hers. "Is there any reason someone would want to kill you?"

"That's crazy," June said.

"Maybe," Hammer said. "But when I saw your friend's face, for a second I thought it was you. Through a scope from a distance..." Hammer turned his head to look out over the dark golf course. "I don't know. Could happen."

June also turned to look. Just as she did, light flooded the area behind the clubhouse.

"Finally," Hammer murmured, then turned back to her. "Did you see the man who released the birds here tonight?"

"You think there's a connection?"

Hammer hesitated before he answered, "Probably not, but I can't overlook any possibilities."

"I didn't see him, but I wasn't looking for him. And with all the costumes, I would never recognize him."

"So, do you have any enemies?"

"None that I know of." She shrugged. "Maybe a few pet-store managers."

Hammer nodded. "I admit it's a long shot, but do me a favor. Think about it. Think about anybody you've made angry recently."

"Other than Glover, no one. Believe me, I'm usually a nice person."

"I believe you," Hammer said. "I'll also believe you if you tell me your dress is a costume—" his gaze fell to her bodice and slowly raked her body "—and not your working clothes."

"Working clothes?"

"I have to tell you, when I first saw you—"

"You thought I was working this party as a prostitute?"

Hammer raised an eyebrow. "Isn't that the theme behind the costumes?"

"Well, yes, but…but…" June hesitated, realizing she was sputtering. Should she be outraged or flattered? Sandy had indeed wanted to look sexy and outrageous to spice up her threatened marriage.

The detective held up his hands in defense. "Sorry, but this is a murder investigation. Hookers lead dangerous lives and are frequently targets."

"I'm *not* a hooker," she said. "You know where I work, for goodness' sake."

"Yeah, I didn't really think so. Definitely a costume." The briefest of smiles transformed his face as their eyes met. "I'm glad."

A tiny thrill traced June's spine despite tonight's tragedy. How could she help it the way the detective looked at her? She wanted to ask him why he was glad, but remained silent. She knew why.

"I don't suppose your friend is a working girl, either?" Now Hammer was all business again.

"No!"

He looked away as a group of people carrying heavy duffel bags arrived. June decided it must be the crime-scene specialists. With a pang, she remembered Sandy had loved all those television dramas that revolved around forensics experts solving mysteries at a crime scene.

And here they were at her own murder.

Hammer flipped his notebook shut, a signal he needed to move on to other tasks. "I'll be in touch if we need anything else."

"Thank you," she said, wanting him to stay. Talking to him, even if it was about Sandy's murder, kept her from thinking about the fact that her friend was really dead and what that meant.

He stood, but looked down at her, his expression softening. "Do you need a ride home?"

June glanced at the table where her friends still huddled. "No."

He placed a hand on her shoulder, his touch light and somehow comforting. "You sure?"

"I should go back to Paul," she said, grateful for the offer. Even such a small kindness felt good right now.

"Okay." He gave a slight squeeze and let his arm fall back to his side. "Don't forget to think about who you've made angry. It could be something minor, even a while back."

She nodded but didn't answer. Hammer moved away, striding toward the new arrivals.

She was sorry to see him go. His presence reassured her, made her feel as though someone competent would solve this unfathomable puzzle. How could anyone want to kill Sandy?

It wasn't a puzzle; it was a mistake. Sandy's murder had to be a mistake.

But what mistake? Was Dean Hammer's theory a good one? Was there someone out there who wanted *her* dead? If so, then who? Why?

She hated the idea that Sandy could have died in her place.

She thought hard, but decided that idea was wrong. The only feathers she ever ruffled were to protect birds. Otherwise, she kept her head down and stayed out of everybody's way. She didn't like being the focus of attention. She'd experienced way too much of that because of her parents.

The obvious answer was Sandy and Paul had gotten into something bad that had nothing to do with her. She knew from firsthand experience the universe was a cruel place that could trap unsuspecting victims in its unrelenting vise. Tonight was likely another example of how much she and Sandy had drifted apart. In a way, their friendship had become another casualty of her parents' criminal activity.

Hopefully Detective Dean Hammer would figure it out.

Feeling as if she'd aged eighty years, June rose and moved toward Paul. And where did this sudden confidence in the detective come from? A few days ago she'd considered him an arrogant macho man too lazy to help captured birds.

She glanced down at the feather on the table, her thoughts circling back to Hammer's theory of mistaken identity. She shivered.

Is someone trying to kill me?

CHAPTER SEVEN

AFTER EMPTYING A clip in the target, Dean stepped back, removed his ear protectors and changed the ammo in his Glock. He waited for the target to slide his way, the tangy odor of gunpowder swirling in the air around him. With the earpieces temporarily off, the shots of fellow shooters echoed loudly on the concrete walls.

He did some of his best thinking after a session at the Miami-Dade Police Gun Range. Focusing on the bull's-eye in the distance, squeezing off the rounds, accepting the blowback of the recoil and then checking the results were all so methodical. So clean. The routine and concentration sharpened his mind.

He usually enjoyed the camaraderie with fellow police officers, too, often scheduling a practice session with his younger brother, a Dade County SWAT officer. But not today. Today he wanted to lose himself in the practice, hoping for a breakthrough afterward.

On the long ride home, he often came up with a new theory in a case. A new angle to shake things up. He needed one because he'd run smack into a dead end on the recent sniper attacks.

The *Miami Herald* was all over the shooting at the Turf Club, their many articles in the three days since Sandy Taylor's murder hinting at Miami Beach Police incompetence. Of course it was a front-page story with bold, inch-high headlines. Beautiful Society Woman Murdered at Country Club by Mysterious Sniper.

The shark journalists hadn't made the connection to the homeless corpse on North Beach, but Dean knew it was just a matter of time.

With the target again in place, Dean replaced his ear protectors, took his stance and emptied the clip, every shot hitting in the center ring. He nodded, pleased. A blare horn sounded, signaling the end of this session, and he decided to pack it in. He'd been shooting for over an hour, and his arm ached, although not unpleasantly, from the work.

He slung his duffel over a shoulder and nodded at other law-enforcement officers as he exited. Most of these men and women knew him as the state champ, and he accepted their congratulations on good shooting.

But the praise didn't make him feel good today. It made him feel useless.

Because, damn, he was missing something. He needed to find the link that tied June Latham to two murders.

He chirped his vehicle open, tossed the duffel into the backseat and slid behind the wheel. There'd been no sign of John Smith, the mysterious bird liberator from the pet shop, on surveillance video at the Turf Club. That didn't mean Smith wasn't at the party. Almost any costume could have disguised his presence.

Dean gunned the engine and began the drive home,

his thoughts constantly sifting through the clues in his cases, searching for a link, a connection.

Using the bullet trajectory, he'd found the sniper's hiding place on the golf course within minutes. But other than a few partial shoe imprints that were unusable for evidence, Forensics came up empty there, too. Whoever the hell this sniper was, he was good. Likely had a military background. Because of that, Dean now thought of him as a man. Not that women weren't good shots—he'd been bested by plenty in competitions— but he'd never heard of a woman trained for sniper duty in the Middle East.

And his gut told him that was exactly where this shooter had come from. Shooting at a still target was one thing. Shooting at a live, moving human being was another.

Especially a gorgeous blonde laughing it up at a gala party.

He merged into the traffic flow on the Palmetto Expressway and set cruise control at the maximum speed.

His investigation into the Taylors revealed squeaky-clean citizens with no hint that either was involved in anything illegal. They lived in a McMansion in an expensive zip code, the mortgage wasn't underwater and both drove new German sedans. Hubby worked as an attorney and made a nice living defending insurance companies from the bogus claims of injured workers. He'd never even had a criminal client who might hold a grudge. No unusual transfers of money.

They took a luxury cruise once a year. Attorney Taylor spent most of his time at his law office. Even slept there sometimes.

As June had insisted, Sandy was a volunteer extraordinaire, devoting her free time—of which she had a lot—to good causes and expensive lunches. But of course someone had to spend the workaholic husband's money.

The husband had denied any trouble in the marriage. All the cops who'd witnessed the interview believed him. There'd be a second and likely third and fourth chat with attorney Taylor, but first Dean wanted to probe into Ms. Latham's hint about marital discord. She'd been too upset the night of the murder for him to explore what she'd meant by that "maybe."

Yeah, and now he'd circled back to the lovely June Latham. Every instinct he possessed screamed that she was at the center of the two murders. So, what about her was causing people to end up in the morgue? Her New York uncle had never been arrested. The only scent of criminal activity around her was a ten-year-old fire.

She'd remained strangely disconnected from the murder of her friend, answering his questions without a single tear. She'd also scoffed at the idea of being the intended victim of the country-club hit, but that could be because of fear. June apparently didn't like to display her emotions, so probably wouldn't admit to being afraid.

And he now suspected Rocky, the homeless vic

on North Beach, had been a decoy. Why would John Smith need a decoy?

Two people dead, and neither had been the original target. Lame. Really lame, especially for a shooter as talented as this one had to be. Could he have made two mistakes that bad?

Dean shook his head. That was the only explanation he had right now. The only thing that made sense, even if there was nothing in June's history to explain why someone wanted her dead.

Nothing on paper anyway. But maybe she had a jealous boyfriend. June didn't seem the type to tolerate a violent lover, but he'd learned anything could happen. Especially when a beautiful woman was involved.

Hell, maybe Sandy Taylor had been enjoying a little something on the side that lawyer hubby didn't know about. Made sense, considering the time he spent working. Dean decided to drop a few hints about wifely infidelity during the husband's next interview. Once the initial shock of death faded, he might look for any signs his spouse had taken a lover.

At his exit, Dean decelerated and left the expressway. He'd decided what to do next, but first he wanted to grab a shower.

He needed to visit June Latham in her home.

Any cop worth his badge could learn a lot about the good citizens based on where they lived. Were they neat? Messy? Were the rooms full of furniture or sparsely decorated? Bright colors? Closed drapes? Family photos on the walls?

He was certain she'd have a pet of some sort. Probably not a bird, though.

A good detective noticed details. Details supplied the pieces of a puzzle that made up a human being. When that human being was a person of interest in a case, solving the riddle became vital.

And, man, was June Latham ever a person of his interest.

Dean braked to a stop in the driveway of his duplex located in the Upper Eastside, an area full of old homes north of downtown Miami, and checked his watch. She should be home from work in about an hour, so the timing worked.

Solving mysteries was what he had been born to do, and did he ever look forward to unraveling the enigma of Ms. Latham.

In fact, he wanted to learn everything about her.

RELAXED IN HER swing inside Lazarus's aerie, June stared at the macaw, silently urging him to fly to the towel draped over her shoulder. As inducement, she held out his favorite treat, a huge medjool date.

But he squawked, turned his beak to preen brilliant feathers, haughtily ignoring her.

June sighed and lowered her hand.

She felt too good right now to nurse disappointment over a bird's rejection. After a miserably hot, humid walk home from the animal hospital, she'd indulged in a swim in the condo's huge pool, completing more laps than she had done in weeks, and the swim had refreshed and invigorated rather than exhausted her.

Her still-damp hair and bathing suit kept her cool, even though the temperature hovered somewhere near the nineties. A gentle breeze from the aerie's ventilation fan also helped, flowing gently against her skin, making her feel deliciously alive.

She pressed a foot into the concrete floor, sent the swing into a gentle sway and curled her legs under her. She closed her eyes and tried not to think.

Of course that was impossible.

The pool area had been crowded with other residents this afternoon, but as usual few ventured into the water for more than a quick soaking. Huddled under shade, they all watched her, commenting afterward on how much energy she had. She was the youngest person on the pool deck by at least thirty years. Maybe forty. Not many people her age could afford to buy at the Enclave. Even Sandy had been envious.

As intended, the swim washed her constant thoughts about Dean Hammer's investigation into Sandy's murder out of her mind. But then she'd exited the pool and all those sagging, pale, almost naked male bodies had made her wonder how Detective Hammer would look in a bathing suit. And now she was picturing how he would look completely naked.

What the hell was wrong with her?

She opened her eyes and stared at Lazarus. He

shook himself, quit fluffing his feathers and eyed her questioningly.

June proffered the date again and said, "Laz, no one at the pool looked anywhere near as good as my detective fully clothed."

The macaw emitted a harsh cackle, which June interpreted to mean *Since when is he* your *detective?*

"Good point," she said.

She knew many residents of the Enclave wondered about her relationship with Uncle Mike, probably because he visited so seldom. Various committees were always trying to get rid of the aerie, but she wasn't breaking any rules and kept it spotlessly clean. And since she was on the top level, no one could hear Laz's squawks.

Her phone rang, and June reached into a pocket to check the caller. Unavailable. Probably a robocall. She hesitated but decided to answer and request they not call back.

"This is Detective Hammer, Ms. Latham."

June lowered both feet back to the floor to stop her sway.

Before she could respond, he continued, "I'm in the area and wondered if I might come up. I have a few more questions."

"Right now?" She raised a hand to her wet hair. *Questions? About Sandy's murder no doubt.* She stared at Lazarus, and he stared back.

"Yes, ma'am. It won't take long."

"Where are you?"

"On Brickell, just about to turn into your driveway."

"Oh." She started to ask how he knew her address, but realized that was ridiculous. She'd given him her address at the pet shop last week. Even if she hadn't, the man was a cop and could learn everything about her. Probably already had done so.

"Do you want to leave my name with security or should I use my badge to get in?" he asked.

"I'll call down with your name." All she needed was a rumor about police visits circulating the building. The staff claimed to be circumspect, but they gossiped worse than the residents. It was the only way anyone could have learned about her aerie.

"Thank you," he said. "I appreciate your cooperation."

"See you in a few," she said.

She sat frozen for a second, her mind racing in a thousand directions.

His voice gave away nothing. She couldn't tell if he thought she was a murderer or had come to report the police had found a suspect in Sandy's murder. She didn't think they'd made an arrest. He could tell her that on the phone. Did he really think she was guilty of something worse than liberating a few smuggled birds?

A few more questions? What about?

Damn. Sexy Detective Hammer was coming to her home and she didn't know what to do first.

Call the guard gate, silly!

June called the front gate and left Hammer's name.

Next she phoned the concierge desk and asked Magda to allow Detective Hammer access to her floor. Had he known how tight security was in this building?

Obviously. That was why he'd called.

"You win, Laz," she said stepping close to the macaw. She gave him the date, which he accepted gently, but with an air of triumph. She stroked his head once, then hurried inside to change out of her bathing suit.

As Dean drove into the impressive entrance of June's building, he felt a vague sense that something was off-kilter. He'd known her address was in a high-rent district, but hadn't realized she lived in the Enclave, considered by many to be the most exclusive building in Miami. Definitely the most expensive.

Security was as excellent as advertised, the staff polite and well trained, requiring proof of identity for admittance. He presented his driver's license rather than his badge, but the alert guard eyed his unmarked police vehicle with a knowing look.

And he'd been forced to flash his police ID a minute later anyway, since the building had a mandatory valet policy. Police policy trumped condo policy every time, so he left his locked Crown Vic Interceptor at the curb beside an unhappy valet attendant on the phone with his supervisor.

He didn't know much about art or decorating—definitely not his area of expertise—but the tasteful elegance of the Enclave's lobby made him slow his quick steps over a polished marble floor to admire contemporary leather seating that actually looked comfortable. The spectacular crystal chandelier dangling from the high wooden ceiling probably cost two years of his salary. A graceful vase full of colorful exotic flowers no doubt set the condo association back a week of his wages. Quite the "wow" factor for arriving guests.

A gracious, uniformed brunette in her fifties, a concierge named Magda according to her badge, greeted him by name when he stated his purpose. She directed him to the correct elevator for the correct tower for Ms. Latham's unit and pressed a hidden button to allow him access.

As he ascended to the top floor, Dean decided even the carved wooden paneling of the elevator reeked of luxury. How the hell did June afford these swanky digs on a veterinarian's assistant's salary?

Her financials revealed no more than a couple hundred bucks in the bank. She didn't own any property, so he'd assumed she rented. She didn't even own a damn car, which explained why no traffic tickets. The idea that she could be a pro flitted through his mind again.

When the elevator opened into a small foyer with only two antique-looking doors, one discreetly marked Deliveries, he realized her unit comprised the entire floor. The entire top floor of the Enclave?

He needed to take a closer look at June's financials.

Dig a little deeper into what was driving her lifestyle, because whatever it was didn't float on the surface.

The main door swung open before he could knock. He lowered his arm. Of course the efficient Magda had trumpeted his arrival.

"Hi," June said with a welcoming smile.

"Ms. Latham." Dean tried not to gape at her, but damn, the woman looked spectacular as always in a pale blue sleeveless shirt and khaki shorts. He eyed her long, tanned legs and wondered if those perfect thighs felt as firm as they looked. He'd never considered himself a leg man, but hers could instantly alter anyone's preference.

Digging a little deeper into this woman was required? Man, oh, man, did he ever love his job.

"I think by now you should call me June," she said.

"With pleasure, June," Dean said. "I'm Dean."

He noted her damp hair and wondered if she'd just gotten out of a shower. He swallowed the images that idea conjured up. He needed to get a grip.

"So, Dean," she said, emphasizing his name and directing him toward a sofa in the center of the room. "You say you have more questions for me?"

"Yes. This shouldn't take long." He quickly assessed details inside the apartment as he followed her. Of course, he'd already learned plenty on the way in. The well-made, top-of-the-line furnishings inside the unit only confirmed that hers was no ordinary condo, even for Brickell Avenue's luxurious penthouses.

His gaze was drawn to a balcony that wrapped

completely around the floor—or at least as much of it as he could see. But instead of a view out to Biscayne Bay, he found a tropical rain forest full of trees and shrubs.

Intrigued, he moved toward the area and was met by a guttural squawk.

"That's Lazarus," she said, joining him by sliding glass doors.

"I take it Lazarus is a parrot?"

She shrugged. "In the parrot family, but technically a scarlet macaw."

He peered into the foliage. The afternoon light was fading, but he found a large, mostly red bird sitting on a leafy branch staring back at him with what had to be suspicion.

Well, right back at ya, buddy. Dean remembered a bird similar to this one from the pet shop.

"I'm surprised you keep a bird," he said. "I thought you didn't believe in that."

"I don't usually, but he's undergoing rehab."

"Rehab? Does he have a substance-abuse problem?"

"Very funny. He's suffering from a broken heart," she said.

Dean shot her a look. "A broken heart?"

June nodded. "Did you know parrots can live as long as humans?"

"Seriously?"

"Yes. That's why adopting one is a commitment most people shouldn't undertake. But Lazarus had a great life—well, at least for a captive bird. He lived with a wonderful caring owner for over twenty years, but the man had a heart attack and died. He lived alone, and no one came for three days. Lazarus was out of his cage and tried to protect his best friend's body from the rescue workers."

"Oh, man," Dean murmured, imagining the scene, which had elements of humor, but somehow he didn't feel like laughing.

"The beak of a scarlet macaw is a serious weapon, so there was quite the standoff. Of course Lazarus was finally captured, but unfortunately they broke his wing in the process."

"And then you stepped in?"

"My rescue group did. Dr. Trujillo treated him, and I'm nursing him back to health. His injuries are almost healed, but he still misses his old owner and doesn't trust anyone. I'm trying to win him over, but…"

She shrugged and trailed off, smiling at Lazarus with such affection Dean wondered how the bird could resist her. He noted June had a perfectly shaped mouth made for far more than just smiles.

"You've made him a beautiful home," he said, still watching her. "Will you keep him?"

"No," she said, with what sounded like regret. "But there's always another rescue to take his place. Sometimes I have two or three at a time. People buy birds and quickly learn they aren't the easiest animal to take care of. They're loud and extremely messy."

As if to prove her point, Lazarus shrieked, flapped huge, colorful wings and turned his back on them.

Dean laughed, deciding they'd just been dissed. No question this macaw was an interesting creature.

"So, does he speak human?" he asked.

"Lazarus comprehends a lot of English. Maybe about thirty words, but it's hard to get him to interact with me. Some researchers insist parrots are as intelligent as apes, which makes the way we treat them even sadder."

"What will happen to him?"

"He'll go to a sanctuary in North Florida and live out his life with others of his species."

"Doesn't sound too bad," Dean said, turning from the balcony to check out the rest of the unit. He admired June's rescue work, even if she went to extremes with it. Eying a closed door, he decided that likely led to a bedroom and wondered if the bird's area extended around the entire apartment.

"It'll be great for him," she said, still staring at the parrot. "But I'll miss him. Laz is the first rescue I've been tempted to keep. He's been so sad. It feels like a betrayal to send him away from his new home after all he's been through."

Her voice was so soft and wistful Dean intuited she related the bird's circumstances to her own when she'd lost her parents and been sent to live with an uncle in New York City. She probably just felt it on a gut level, not even consciously aware she made that connection.

"Shall we sit?" he asked.

"Oh. Sure." She smiled at him, looking a little sheepish. "Forgive me. I get carried away sometimes."

"No. Really?" he asked, pretending he hadn't noticed.

Her grin widened. "I guess you already know I'm a bit militant about birds."

"Well, you do seem quite fond of them." He was, too, actually. Just in a different fashion. But perhaps he'd better not mention that his most frequent interaction with birds was shooting turkey on hunting trips. Something told him she wouldn't appreciate that particular type of bird-watching activity.

"I'm assuming your visit is in reference to my friend's murder," she said, hesitantly sitting on the edge of a handsome leather sofa, one long enough for him to recline on. "You're here in an official capacity?"

Dean joined her and removed the notebook from his jacket pocket. "Of course."

"Are you always on duty this late?"

"A detective is almost always on duty." He inwardly groaned at how stiff that sounded.

"So, where's your partner?"

"He's off. He's a rookie, not a detective."

"Why do you have a rookie partner?"

"Pairing seasoned officers with newbies is part of a new training protocol instituted by the department." Or more accurately, a lesson instituted by a certain lieutenant to remind one particular detective there was good reason to follow the rules.

"You don't sound too happy about that new system."

"Actually, Sanchez is a good man. I don't mind

training him." Dean relaxed back into the leather, surprised by his admission. But it was true. He'd discovered he enjoyed showing his rookie the tricks he'd learned over the years. Might save the guy some hard lessons.

"Sometimes we learn what we're supposed to be doing in the strangest ways," she murmured.

Dean wanted to explore that comment. The faraway look in her brilliant blue eyes told him she'd been taught a lesson in a painful way. He suspected it had something to do with her parents.

But they'd drifted way off subject. He needed to guide the conversation away from him and back to his case.

"Tell me," he said, "does this apartment really take up the entire top floor?"

"No. Only the east-facing half. There's a separate elevator for the other side."

"Nice," he said. "The rent must be pretty high," he said, leaving an opening big enough for a flock of macaws to fly through.

She nodded. "No kidding."

When she offered nothing else, Dean caught her gaze and cocked his head. Time for the direct route. "So, June."

She arched her eyebrows, waiting for him to continue.

"I know how much you make each month. How do you pay for this private palace?"

CHAPTER EIGHT

JUNE GRINNED AT DEAN. Of course she'd known full well what he'd been getting at. Most first-time visitors assumed she either sold cocaine or was kept by a sugar daddy. Interesting how the detective tried the polite method first, but then just came right out and asked how the hell she managed to live in the Enclave rather than wondering about it.

"Fortunately I don't pay rent," she said. "This is my uncle's winter home. I sort of, well, house-sit permanently."

Dean checked his notes. "Your uncle is one Michael Westbrook Latham?"

"Right. He lives in Manhattan."

"The man who became your guardian after your parents' death?"

She eyed him warily, but he gave nothing away. "You know about my parents?"

"Considering your connection to two murders, you had to know we'd check you out."

She nodded. She had known that, had expected it. She wasn't proud of what her parents had done, but it had nothing to do with her. She had nothing to hide.

"So I guess I'm still a person of interest," she said.

"Yes, ma'am. You're a person of great interest."

June caught a change in his tone and with a thrill decided he was flirting with her. *Is it safe to flirt with a cop? Appropriate when being interviewed?*

"In two murders now," he continued.

"But not a suspect, I hope?"

"Not yet."

"Is that a warning?"

Dean managed an offended expression, but she knew it was an act. The man liked to play with her. Well, guess what, Detective Hammer? She could play, too.

"Should I have an attorney present for this conversation?" she asked.

He flipped shut his notebook, his eyes now dark and serious, his mouth set in a grim line. He hadn't liked that question. "You have an absolute right to counsel. Do you want me to leave?"

"No," she said, surprised at his laser-quick switch back to cop professionalism. "I'll answer your questions."

"If you'd rather come into my station tomorrow with a lawyer, we can do that. I thought you'd prefer to do it this way, but if I'm wrong—"

"You were right," she insisted. "Thank you. This is fine."

"You're sure?"

"Yes," June said. "I don't have any secrets." Obviously Dean had a lot more experience at this game than she. Or maybe this wasn't really a game. Maybe she just wanted it to be one because the guy sitting next to her was so unbelievably hot that, despite a week crammed with unusual events, including the murder of an old friend, Detective Dean Hammer had occupied most of her thoughts.

"Okay, then." He nodded and opened his notebook again. When he focused his attention back on her, he said, "Please understand our investigation is still on-going."

June rolled her eyes. "That's exactly what a police spokesperson always says on TV. Please just be honest with me."

A slow smile spread across his face, softening his eyes. "Yes, ma'am. I'll try. Have you thought any more about how you know John Smith?"

June sighed. "We're back to that again? I've told you I don't know that man. Never saw him before in my life."

"Well, see, here's the problem. He knows you. The video reveals John Smith tried to speak to you as you snapped your evidence. He called you by name inside the pet shop. Twice."

June stared at Dean. "That man knew my name?"

"Yes."

Uneasy, June thought back to that scary moment and shook her head. "Well, I didn't hear him. I was too nervous about what I was doing, I guess."

"Not only that, he got furious when the shop owner grabbed you. He definitely knows who you are."

"How could he know me?" she wondered aloud. "Did he follow me there?"

"That's precisely what I'd like to figure out," Dean said, meeting her gaze with a direct stare.

"I'm telling you the truth," she said, immediately realizing that was what all suspects told the police.

"Are you still willing to come to the station to look at the surveillance video?"

"Of course."

"Good. That could shake loose a memory."

As Dean consulted his notes, June placed a hand on her stomach, where dread flared to life. Maybe he didn't believe her. He sure looked grim. Oh, God, how had this happened? How had her activities to save birds dragged her into a police murder investigation?

"Have you given any thought to who you might have pissed off?" Dean asked. "Or who might be holding a grudge?"

"So you're still stuck on the idea that I was the target instead of Sandy?"

He shook his head. "I'm not stuck on any theory. I am here to gather information, and that's the truth."

June studied his face. Was he telling her the whole truth about this visit? She noted he was fresh-shaven at 6:00 p.m. Why? For her? Not likely. Maybe he had a date after this interview. He smelled faintly of a nice cologne, as though he was just out of a shower.

"I can't think of anyone who would want to kill me," she said finally. "And I *have* thought about that unlikely scenario."

"Fair enough." He consulted his notes. "The night of the murder, you indicated there might be trouble with your friend's marriage. Can you explain that comment?"

"I knew you were going to ask me about that. I said I wasn't sure, and I don't want to say anything to implicate Paul."

"Because you don't believe he had anything to do with his wife's murder?" Dean asked.

"That's right."

The detective waited for her to say more. Really not wanting to tell him Sandy's last confidence to her, June looked away from him. But she couldn't lie. This man would sniff out a lie before it left her mouth. And what if she was wrong about Paul? What if there had been more to Sandy's insecurity than Paul working too hard?

"One of the reasons we were dressed in those outlandish costumes was that Sandy wanted to rekindle the romance in her marriage. She wanted to remind her husband why he'd proposed."

Dean didn't answer immediately. "I don't mean to be insensitive in light of your loss, but I have to tell you, those dresses would definitely achieve that particular goal."

"Was that a compliment, Detective Hammer?"

He met her gaze and lifted his lips into an incredibly sexy smile. "Just a professional observation."

June swallowed. Now he had to be flirting.

"So," Dean continued, "her husband's attention was fading?"

"Paul worked a lot of hours."

"But why would you wear the same costume as your friend?" Dean raised his eyebrows. "In my way of thinking, a threesome isn't the best way to restart a marriage."

June felt heat rush into her cheeks, now suspecting he deliberately wanted her off balance. Probably an old cop trick to manipulate persons of interest into admissions they didn't want to make. "Don't be crude. We used to dress alike in high school. Silly little girl stuff, like a secret society."

"At—" He flipped through a few pages of notes, not the least chastened by her comment. "Pinecrest Preparatory Academy?"

"Right."

"Where the waiting list is long and the tuition expensive."

June nodded. "And the education top-notch."

"So, why didn't you finish there? You graduated from a different high school."

She tensed. Damn, he really had dug into her background. "Why would my educational history be part of your murder investigation?"

Dean leaned forward, his expression serious again. "I'm digging for a link, a connection between you and two dead bodies. No cop believes in coincidence, and we believe you're at the center of two murders."

"I don't see how."

Dean sat back, eyes narrowed, watching her. "For starters, the same gun killed both victims."

"Oh, my God," she said, the information slamming into her, shocking her as if she'd dived into an unheated pool on a cold day. She shook her head,

denying the facts. "You're sure?" she asked, knowing
the question sounded foolish. Of course he was sure.
He had forensics and ballistics and whatever else cops
used to convict criminals.

Dean said, "Yes. I'm very sure."

"That makes no sense. What connection could there
be between Sandy and a homeless man?"

He continued to stare at her. "You."

"Me?" June rose. "I see." But she didn't understand any of this. Realizing she was on her feet, she
walked toward the aviary, needing to hide her horrified reaction.

"That's why I'm asking these questions," he said.
"I'm sorry if it feels intrusive."

June stared blindly into the foliage, vaguely aware
of a chill and that she'd wrapped her arms around her
chest, seeking warmth.

She sensed that Dean rose and moved toward her.
"I apologize for upsetting you," he said. "But I'm trying to solve your friend's murder."

She didn't look at him. "If what you're saying is
true, I'm somehow responsible for Sandy's death."
She swallowed. "And the death of a man I don't even
know."

"No," Dean said in a kind voice. "I didn't say you
were responsible. I said you could provide a link to
help me figure out who is."

"Responsibility," she murmured. "That's such a
loaded word, isn't it?"

"What are you talking about?"

He sounded confused, but of course to cops everything was clear-cut, probably had to be for them to do their job. If someone broke a law, no matter why they did it, they were guilty. And then they were punished.

But did it matter who was responsible? Was she responsible even if she didn't know how?

June shivered. Dean stood so close she could feel the heat from his body, and she suddenly longed to turn into that warmth.

"Are you okay?" he asked. He reached out and touched her arm.

She shook her head, embarrassed to behave like a wimp in front of him. He probably thought she was about to cry. She never cried and didn't get it why this news so overwhelmed her.

"Hey, you're trembling," he said.

"I'm sorry," she managed. "This isn't like me."

Next thing she knew, he'd wrapped his strong arms around her and she was enveloped in a blanket of warmth. She stiffened, then relaxed against him, listening to the steady beat of his heart beneath a solid, muscular chest. He smelled even better up close. What a surprise that this macho cop would actually try to comfort her.

"You're chilled," he said. "Probably because of your damp hair."

"And you're warm," she whispered, feeling inexplicably safe in the shelter of his embrace. Something else that made no sense.

After a moment he said, "June, listen to me."

She closed her eyes. She liked hearing him speak her name and wondered why.

"You are not to blame for your friend's death."

She opened her eyes. *But am I responsible?*

"So you really don't consider me a suspect?" she managed, stepping away from him. She shot him a look and found him watching her, eyebrows drawn together. This guy obviously wasn't used to consoling anyone.

"Maybe that's enough questions for tonight," he said.

"No, I'm fine." She grabbed a sweatshirt off a dining room chair where she kept it handy for after swims. Dean's arms worked better, but he couldn't hold her all night, much as she might want him to.

She sat on the sofa again. "Let's finish."

He joined her. "Why do I get the feeling you're reading more into the ballistics report than you should?"

Refusing to think about responsibility, she looked down at her tightly clasped hands and tried to remember his last question. Oh, right. Why she hadn't graduated from Pinecrest with the rest of her class.

"My uncle wanted me to move to the city with him, but I begged him to let me stay in Miami." She shook her head, remembering their arguments. "There'd been so much change in my life I didn't want to leave my friends. He could easily afford the tuition of the prep school, but at the time he was running for a borough commission seat or something in New York on a platform supporting public education. So we compromised. I transferred to the public school and he let me stay."

"Where did you live?"

She shrugged and settled back into the sofa. "Here."

For the first time, the detective appeared surprised. "By yourself?"

"Hardly. This building is full of hundreds of people and a huge staff."

"Who aren't responsible for a child's well-being."

She eyed him. "You sound like my uncle. I was seventeen, not seven."

He stared back at her thoughtfully. "So, how many wild parties did you have, Miss June?"

"Only one when I turned eighteen. The thing is I had to swear my friends to secrecy. If their parents knew, they might have made trouble about my living arrangements."

"Sounds like your plan backfired," he said.

"It was good training. I learned how to take care of myself." But she had been lonely. Even frightened some nights. Worse, after a few months, she'd stopped hanging out with her old friends so much. She couldn't go to parties or someone's parents might see her. Life went on at Pinecrest without her. She'd been depressed over everything, so she was considered a freak at the new school, but eventually made new friends. She'd even joined the swim team so she could feel like a part of something again.

"Your uncle should have been shot," Dean said, as if he could read her thoughts.

She shook her head, willing the old sadness away. She'd needed the time alone. She'd been grieving her parents and her old life.

And now the hot cop was feeling sorry for her. She didn't want that. She'd rather he go back to flirting.

"Shooting him is harsh, don't you think?" she said, hoping to lighten the mood. She looked down, noticed her clasped hands and relaxed them. "At first Uncle Mike came every weekend, but gradually he realized I was doing just fine."

Dean raised his hand and cupped her cheek, his touch soft and gentle. She raised her gaze and met his probing blue eyes. "Were you doing just fine, June?"

She caught her breath, feeling suspended in time. This was crazy. She didn't know this man, not really, but the strange intimacy of the moment compelled her to be honest. Maybe it was the way he said her name. Maybe it was because he sat so close to her. She should put up her usual barriers, push him away.

But she didn't want to. Besides, she'd asked for honesty from him. Didn't she owe it back?

"Some nights were hard," she admitted.

He smiled as he stroked her cheek.

"You're some kind of special woman," he said.

She closed her eyes, certain he was going to kiss her, not wanting to think about why that wasn't a good idea.

DEAN STARED INTO June's lovely face and wondered what the hell he was doing. He had to get out of here before he did something he'd regret.

She had the most kissable mouth he'd ever been this near without tasting. And she was all but begging him to taste her.

But she was also hurting because of her friend and vulnerable because of painful memories he'd dragged out of her. He wouldn't take advantage of that.

Maybe another time, another woman, but not tonight. Not this woman.

June was still a person of interest in this case.

He dropped his hand from her smooth flesh. She opened her eyes, and he read disappointment there. He was behaving like a fool. Maybe he should stay.

"I should go," he said, unable to tear his gaze from hers.

"No more questions?" she asked, her voice breathy.

"Not tonight." Not wanting to, he came to his feet. She was like a powerful magnet, pulling him back to her. He had a lot more questions. For one thing, he wanted to probe into the relationship with her uncle. And she needed a warning.

She also rose, her arms wrapped around her chest.

"I do have a request, though," he said.

"Something else to think about?" she asked.

He hated to break what felt like a weird form of magic between them, but had no choice. "I want you to be careful."

She frowned, and just like that the mood evaporated. "What do you mean?"

"I want you to stay aware of your surroundings at

all times. Watch to see if you're being followed, if you see the same car frequently."

Her blue eyes widened. "My God. You think someone might try to kill me?"

Dean sighed. He hated doing this to her. Her behavior tonight had been persuasive, and his gut told him she hadn't had any advance knowledge of the murders. But doubts remained because he lacked proof. He was a cop. He relied on evidence. No way around the fact that his evidence so far revealed she was somehow connected to John Smith. When he figured out that connection, he'd find his perp.

And the perp could be gunning for her with a sniper rifle.

"I don't want to scare you—"

"I think that's exactly what you want to do."

"Sorry. All I'm asking you is to use common sense. Stay out of dark alleys, remain in public areas." Although a skilled sniper could find a hide almost anywhere.

She shook her head. "I can't do that. I'm conducting a bird walk on Saturday out into Matheson Hammock."

"Cancel."

"I can't. I won't. It's my turn, and they're depending on me."

"You're going bird hunting?"

"Not hunting. Watching. This is the beginning of the migration season and my bird society leads birders to look for warblers and such flying to the tropics for the winter."

"Warblers?"

"Small migratory birds. They're quick and hard to spot for most people. Plus, a La Sagra's flycatcher has been spotted in the area."

"A flycatcher?"

"Yes. La Sagra's is rarely seen here, and I'm hoping to add it to my list."

Dean thought about Matheson Hammock, a wilderness area south of Miami he remembered as full of rough, wet terrain.

"Hiking out into a forest is not a good idea," he said.

"You can't expect me to hide inside my apartment."

"Just until we catch the shooter."

He saw unease flicker through her eyes, replaced by resolve. "That's ridiculous. But I'll be careful. And there will be plenty of other people around on Saturday, if it makes you feel better."

"It doesn't."

"You can't tell me what to do."

Dean stared at her and she stared back. He might not have known her long, but understood she wouldn't back down from leading this great bird hunt. She'd had some tough breaks, and the circumstances of her life had left her with an overdeveloped sense of responsibility. She'd committed to the birding trip, so she'd do it no matter what he said.

Part of him admired her for that. Another part of him wanted to shake some sense into her.

He sighed. "I'm thinking all that time living alone made you too damn independent."

"Oh, really?" June placed her hands on her hips, looking so defiant he was tempted to grin. If only this were funny.

"Well, I'm thinking that badge makes you too damn bossy," she said.

Now he did grin. "Bossy?"

"You apparently think you can tell your persons of interest how to live."

"Yeah? Well, apparently this one isn't listening."

She lowered her arms and smiled back at him with that gorgeous mouth so ripe for kissing. He wanted to pull her into his arms again and kiss her into—what? Submission? No, definitely not submission. He liked a woman with a little fire in her. This one had plenty. Although she tried to remain aloof, he suspected strong emotion raged beneath that cool veneer. Wouldn't he just love to peel away her layers, along with her clothing? Yeah, he'd definitely like to kindle passion for something other than birds out of June.

"I think it's unlikely that this shooter person will follow me on a birding trip to Matheson," she said, dragging him back to reality. "If you knew the area, you'd realize there's nowhere for him to hide with a rifle."

"I do know the area." He took a step backward, then turned toward the door, reminding himself to get his sorry ass away from June Latham and her very kissable mouth before he complicated matters and

torpedoed her cooperation. It would be a huge mistake to start anything with her no matter how much
he wanted to. He needed to keep a clear head where
she was concerned or risk her life and the success of
this investigation.

He had two dead bodies in the morgue. She could
wind up the third.

And he still had those doubts.

"I've made you angry," she said.

"*Angry* isn't the right word," he said, with no inten-
tion of telling her what he was thinking. He chanced
another glance at her and found her smiling. Looking
pleased even, as if she'd thought of something good.

"Just be careful on this birding expedition," he said.

"You could come along," she suggested. "Keep me
safe."

That invitation held him at the door, although he
needed to make his escape before he weakened and
asked her to accompany him to Mary Brickell Vil-
lage for a drink. Or dinner. And then what naturally
came after.

"You mean go with you on your bird hunt?" he
asked.

"Sure," she said. "Why not? You'd enjoy it."

"What? You tramp through the mangroves peering through binoculars looking for tiny birds that eat
flies?"

She shrugged. "And some big ones. Predators, like
osprey. Hawks even."

Her grin widened, and she put an emphasis on

hawk that made him wonder if she knew that was his nickname.

"Sounds buggy," he said.

"Probably will be."

He shook his head. "Not my kind of hunting. I'll pass, but will be in touch about a time to look at the video."

She nodded, and he stepped out into the hallway. Dean waited until he heard her locks engage, then continued to the elevator.

His Crown Vic waited where he'd left it, and he tipped the valet attendant for his irritation.

As Dean accelerated out of the Enclave entrance, he noted the twenty- and thirty-story condos that lined Brickell Avenue. He slowed and looked up. He was worried about June's safety in the hammock? Shit. He pounded his steering wheel.

She walked to work five days a week along this street. A sniper could lie in wait on any of these roofs, fix her in his sights, take the shot, then vanish before anyone figured out where the bullet in the beautiful dead woman on the sidewalk had come from.

The golf course had been easy, but the shooter had made a mistake. Here the trick would be access to those roofs. There'd be security of course. Still, with enough time, no question it could be done. If John Smith or anyone else wanted to eliminate June badly enough, her lifestyle provided an easy target.

Or she could be involved with the murders and no one was after her at all.

CHAPTER NINE

STILL SMILING, JUNE leaned against her front door after Dean left, feeling exhilarated, more alive than she had in years—all because of a sexy Miami Beach cop who radiated deadly charm. Strange. She'd never gone for dangerous bad-boy types before. Her last boyfriend—good old "what's his name"—had been more the preppy type.

She couldn't figure Dean out. He flirted outrageously with her, and she was pretty sure cops weren't supposed to use that particular interview technique. But when she freaked over his ballistics report, he treated her with kindness, even tried to reassure her. And just now he'd tried to scare her with a warning someone might be trying to shoot her. Of course, he did that in hopes she *wouldn't* get shot, which was a nice thing, right?

His visit left too many jumbled, crazed thoughts streaming through her head. She didn't know what to obsess about first.

Far-fetched as it seemed, she had to consider Dean's theory that Sandy had been killed by mistake, that the sniper had been after her.

Oh, Sandy. I'm so sorry. June closed her eyes. But that thinking only led her back to the why. She couldn't imagine why anyone wanted her dead. Her pet-shop activities hadn't been all that successful.

Yeah, maybe a few owners held a grudge over losing birds but hadn't been mad enough to commit murder.

She swallowed. Or at least she didn't think so.

Should she be looking over her shoulder every second? Was she supposed to cower in the dark until the cops caught the killer? What if they never did? Sometimes cases remained unsolved, and this one seemed complicated.

She needed more information.

June pushed away from the door, walked to the desk in her bedroom and turned on her laptop. Over the past week, she'd been tempted to enter Dean's name in a search engine and see what popped. So far she'd resisted, telling herself she wasn't a cyberstalker, that she had no business thinking about Dean Hammer's hot bod.

"Resistance is futile," she murmured as she leaned over and typed his name.

She sat as a few hits materialized on the monitor. Not many. She clicked on the first three or four links, but got nothing on her particular Dean. Nothing? How could that be? She narrowed the search, but still a big fat zero. Frowning at the lack of any personal information regarding a Dean Hammer in Miami or Miami Beach, she tried the Miami Beach Police Department website.

There she learned that private information about police officers wasn't likely to be available on the web.

She probably should have realized that. Of course cops needed to protect their privacy from bad guys.

But the search engine produced a few obscure hits she hadn't checked out yet, and something about him could still show up. Seemed unlikely he'd managed to keep any mention of himself off the internet. As a cop, he could unearth her high school grade-point average if he wanted to know, and she couldn't even find out if he was married.

Oh, face, it Junie. That's what you really want to learn. You don't want to spend one more second lusting after a married man.

She'd assumed he was available that first day, but how many times had women been wrong about a man's marital status? He knew everything about her, and she knew squat about him. Which meant, although he suspected she was hiding something, there was no mystery left where she was concerned.

She clicked on a link that read "2013 South Georgia Turkey Shoot" and waited for the website to load. A bright red title appeared: "This year's winners!" A color photograph slowly materialized where a beaming Dean stood in the center of a group of mud-splattered, fatigue-clad hunters, all of whom held rifles crooked in one arm. With the other arm, each proudly displayed a carcass of a dead turkey.

Horrified by the ghoulish image, June quickly clicked to the next page and found more macabre photos of men delighted with themselves over killing innocent animals for entertainment. She shook her head, saddened to know Dean participated in this sort of travesty. She knew this lifestyle existed of course. She just couldn't understand it.

The last page contained lists of past shoots and winners. Dean had been the winner for three years running. He was also national champion with some particular rifle at a distance that seemed very long indeed.

June linked back to her search page and tried again. She found one more relevant hit, a photo of Dean in a dress military uniform, but maybe ten years younger. A gray-haired man in what looked like a high-ranking officer's uniform presented Dean a trophy shaped like a rifle.

Obviously he was an expert shot and likely learned his craft in the military. Good for him.

June continued looking until she logged on to the last search result, where she found Dean L. Hammer again, a musician in Ohio she'd learned way too much about, and shut down her computer.

She sat for a moment, mulling over what she'd learned about the detective. In the past, she'd tried to talk hunters out of their violent sport. She'd never had any luck and assumed she'd have none with Dean. Of course turkeys and ducks weren't endangered like tropical birds. She knew that, but she just didn't get how anyone could enjoy killing. Not unless you needed the meat to feed your family.

Target practice, sure. Okay. Shooting was a skill, an ability you could train for and improve. Like swimming. The more you practiced, the better you got.

Both were sports, though, useless as a life skill, since few people actually shot game in order to eat or swam fast to outrun a shark.

So Dean himself was an actual predator. She should have known. She'd heard Dean's partner refer to him as "Hawk." She shivered. Hawk. That suited him better than Dean.

Figured. A Cooper's hawk was one of her favorite birds to spot while birding.

And now her thoughts had circled to Saturday's birding trip, which she had committed to lead months ago.

Dean didn't want her to go, but June was sure no sniper would tromp into the wetlands with what she'd learned was an expensive weapon, the barrel of which could easily be seen through the mangroves. Plus, at least twenty pairs of eyes would be focused on the surroundings, constantly searching for the slightest movement in hopes of spotting an unusual bird. No matter what Dean thought, Matheson Hammock wasn't a good place to lie in wait to commit murder.

She slumped back into the chair, her soaring sense of excitement having crashed into disappointment. She liked the way Detective Dean Hammer made her feel. Scary, yes, but God, so alive and a part of the world. Last time she'd felt this way was—when? Maybe at a swim meet ten years ago when she'd finished ahead of an All-City sprinter.

Ten years? How sad was that?

But he was way too dictatorial. She didn't like a

man who thought he could tell her what to do, and Dean seemed to think he could order her around like some sort of commanding officer. Truth be told, that bothered her a lot more than his hunting.

She still didn't know if he was married or single, but that didn't matter now. She needed to resist her foolish attraction to Dean. Apparently she wasn't into the bad-boy type after all.

Too bad. Getting to know him better would have been the most fun she'd had in a very long time.

Restless, she moved onto the ten-foot section of balcony Uncle Mike had insisted be reserved for humans and free of rehabbing birds. Leaning against the cool, concrete wall, she admired the coral-tinged clouds that towered over the eastern horizon, the vast Atlantic Ocean below reflecting their vibrant colors. Miami Beach, a thin slash of land where lights slowly blinked on, interrupted that mirror effect. Closer, a darkening Biscayne Bay again reflected the colorful sky.

This was the view people expected when they visited the Enclave. She'd sensed Dean's surprise when he looked instead into Laz's aviary, and had almost brought him to see this spectacular panorama. She would have, except they'd have had to walk through her bedroom. She hadn't wanted to do that.

June swallowed. So maybe it wouldn't be easy to forget about Dean. At least not until he found the murderer and stopped contacting her.

The pull she felt to him was something other than just his looks. What? Something basic, elemental.

Visceral. Whenever they shared the same room, his presence resonated deep inside her. He eased his way into her senses until he dominated her attention and thoughts.

Maybe because she'd never had anyone so attentive, so focused on what she was saying. He teased her. She teased him back. Being with him was, well, fun, even though their conversations were deadly serious.

She just liked being near him.

She liked it even better when he touched her. She slid her palms down her arms, remembering when he hugged her close. He'd been sweet. He'd been warm. She'd longed to climb inside him and share that warmth.

But he was too hot. She'd get burned. She'd been burned enough already.

WHEN DEAN ARRIVED at his desk the next morning, he found a stack of cardboard boxes. A quick look inside told him these were the case files on Carl and Eileen Latham he'd requested from archives.

Looked as though he was going to spend his day revisiting June's history. Which was fine with him. Driving home from June's last night, he'd wondered if the murders in the present had their roots in the past. Maybe the evidence in these boxes would give him that link. Long shot, but he needed a break, was due for a break.

Still standing, Dean organized folders into chronological piles, oldest information on top. One stack for the fire and one for the narcotics case. Damn, but this would be tedious. Definitely not his favorite part of police work, but necessary. And he was on his own this morning, since Sanchez and the other rookies were with the department shrink for some new sensitivity training, which the lieutenant had darkly suggested Dean might need himself.

Sensitivity training? He didn't have time for that shit. Dean snorted and moved into the break room to pour a cup of caffeine. He was plenty sensitive, and he had two murders to solve.

Returning to his desk, he parked his ass in his chair and began sifting through the past, starting with the drug bust. The more he dug, the more he wondered about the case against the Lathams. Something didn't add up. Was it possible June's parents hadn't been the actual smugglers?

Just before lunch, Sanchez joined him. His rookie partner looked disgusted and a little dazed.

"How'd it go?" Dean asked, handing him a thick stack of paper he'd already reviewed. Two sets of eyes were always better than one.

"Bunch of crap," Sanchez murmured as he collapsed into a chair at his own desk across from Dean.

Dean grinned. "You're not enlightened?"

"I'm now aware of my prejudices. What's this?" he asked.

"The evidence on June Latham's parents' criminal case," Dean said.

"What am I looking for?"

"Any connection to our two murders. Names, places, anything that doesn't fit."

"Got it." Sanchez opened the first file and began to read.

Dean watched the young cop a moment. Sanchez didn't utter a single complaint about boring desk work. *This rookie just might turn out to be a good cop.* Was he observant enough, though? Good time to find out.

"Sanchez," Dean barked.

The rookie looked up.

Dean slid a grainy photograph across their adjoining desks. "Take a look at that."

Without comment, Sanchez reached for the photo, eyeballed it, then flipped it over. "This was shot twenty years ago." Sanchez turned the picture again and this time studied the image carefully. He chuckled softly. "Man, look at the women's hair. And the clothes."

Dean knew what he saw. Fifteen or so men and women in two lines, one standing, one sitting, grinning at the camera, obviously thrilled by the day's events. Balloons floated over a banner that read Grand Opening.

"What was the grand opening for?" Sanchez asked.

"Latham Import," Dean said. "Do you recognize any of those faces?"

Sanchez narrowed his eyes, still examining the photo. "Shit," he murmured. He lifted his gaze to Dean. "I don't know. He's younger, but that could be John Smith, first row center."

"Bingo," Dean said. "There's our connection. John Smith worked for Latham Import."

"You know, that fits," Sanchez said. "If Smith were a longtime employee of a family business, he'd know who June was. Especially since she was an only child."

Dean took a swallow of cold coffee. "But June wouldn't necessarily know him."

"She was probably what—six years old at the time of this grand opening? She wouldn't recognize a man she'd met occasionally twenty years later."

"If she'd ever even laid eyes on him. The trick now will be to determine his real name. I wonder where the old company records are kept or even if they're still in existence." Dean looked down at a photo of the charred remains of Latham Import's warehouse. If the records had been inside that rubble, nothing was left.

Something else to question June about.

"So, why would John Smith try to contact June in the pet shop?" Sanchez asked.

"What do you think?"

Sanchez sat back in his chair, making it squeak. "Something to do with her parents. Has to be. Or the fire. Hey, maybe he's the arsonist wanting to apologize."

"Yeah, about that fire." Dean reached for a file. "More than potential evidence was destroyed. The warehouse contained a shipment of hundreds of tropical birds en route to a breeding preserve. They all died."

SATURDAY MORNING AT six forty-five, June pulled Uncle Mike's gas-guzzling Cobra into the parking lot at Matheson Hammock and found ten birders with binoculars draped around their necks waiting for her. The regulars recognized the car and waved or, grinning, placed hands over their ears.

Relieved to see a good turnout, she shut down the engine and welcomed the quiet.

"Damn, Junie," Jared said when she exited the low-slung bucket seat. "We could hear you coming for ten minutes."

"Oh, you haven't been here ten minutes," she said, pleased to see tall, redheaded Jared Bennett, her staunchest supporter in the fight against the sale of captured birds. He'd also published two books on birding and was considered the preeminent local expert. She was always glad to have him along for consultation in case she got stumped.

"Nice car," a man in his forties said, a newbie, someone she'd never seen before. "Is it a replica?"

"No, it's the real deal," she replied. "But it's my uncle's car. I just drive it for him every so often."

"Nice uncle."

Several of the waiting crowd gathered around the car to discuss its powerful engine. She sighed. The Cobra always gathered attention from any car nuts whenever she drove it, sometimes making her feel invisible.

June took a deep breath, inhaling the pungent, salty fragrance of the mangroves—an odor not to everyone's liking. But that ripe smell meant a healthy man-grove. Stretching her arms overhead, she looked up at the brightening blue sky. All around her birds were waking up, chirping, flitting from oak tree to oak tree in the hardwood section of the hammock. No rain in the weather forecast until this afternoon.

How could anyone care about a hunk of metal when they were in the middle of such a gorgeous natural area?

She dug her backpack out of the car, placed a sign-in sheet on a clipboard and handed it to the closest man, a regular whose name she couldn't remember.

"Please give me your name, address, phone num-ber and an email," she requested.

She noted two preteens this morning, a brother and a sister, and promised herself to encourage them along the way. She liked it when parents brought children because if they spotted a cool species along the trail, that youngster could be turned into a lifelong bird lover. Tropical Bird Society garnered tons of new members on these free birding expeditions.

"Do you think we'll see any redstarts?" a middle-aged lady asked.

"It might be too early," June said. "But you never know."

"Radar was lit up last night," Jared said.

"Radar?" the woman asked.

"Migrating birds show up on weather radar as ground clutter," June said, "so we know there are birds in the area. Whether they'll come down out of the sky to rest or eat is the question."

More birders arrived, and soon she had a group of twenty-one, an excellent number. She surveyed them, looking for bare skin that mosquitoes could feast on, pleased to see most wore lightweight, cotton clothing, some sort of hat and good hiking boots. June frowned at one young woman wearing shorts and a halter top.

"If you have bug spray, use it," she instructed. "I hope everyone has water to keep hydrated." Soon the chemical odor of insect repellant hung in the air.

"Let's begin in the hardwood section today," she said, turning in that direction just as a large white vehicle turned into the parking area. Deciding this was a latecomer, she waited for the occupant to join them—and froze.

Dean unfolded his tall frame from the car. As he shouldered on his own backpack, his intense gaze remained fixed on her from beneath a University of Florida baseball cap. He'd dressed appropriately for the walk with no bare skin and sturdy boots.

"Are you all right, Junie?" Jared asked beside her.

"What?" She gave herself a mental shake, realizing she was staring at Dean and ignoring her birders.

"Who is that?" Jared asked, following her gaze.

How the hell do I answer that question? "Oh, just a detective who thinks I know more about two murders than I'm saying"?

"His name is Dean Hammer," she said.

"Is this a new boyfriend?" he asked in what could only be a resentful tone.

June shot Jared a glance. *What's that about? Have I missed something?*

But before she could set him straight, Dean arrived at her side. She looked up into his grinning face and wondered what he was thinking. Why could she never tell?

"Good morning," he said, as if of course she'd expected his appearance.

"I thought this wasn't your kind of bird hunt," she said, trying to keep her voice neutral. His smile faded, a sign that she didn't succeed.

"Well, I thought the company might be pleasant," he said.

She thrust the sign-in sheet toward him. He raised his eyebrows, scribbled something and handed it back. She forced herself not to read what he wrote. *Am I actually going to get an address or a home phone number?*

"Thanks," she mumbled. While Dean introduced himself to the group, she tossed the clipboard into the Cobra and locked its doors, resisting the urge to read what he'd written.

"Okay," she announced loudly. "Let's get started."

Keenly aware of Dean's presence, she led the birders across Matheson Parkway into the oak grove. Speaking quietly and only occasionally, her group meandered through the trees, necks craned upward, searching for any movement in the branches.

"There," someone said. "Two o'clock on that dead branch."

June caught a flash of red.

"Cardinal," she reported. No one got excited. Cardinals and blue jays were abundant locally. Beautiful, yes, and a thrill for first-timers. But avid birders could see them most anywhere, probably at their own backyard feeders.

Today they were searching for visitors, migratory birds just passing through, dropping in for a bite on the way to their winter home in the tropics. Especially warblers, quick, colorful creatures, a real challenge because they never stayed in one place for very long.

After about ten minutes, June heard a single, sharp "dit" overhead and announced, "Black-throated blue."

Jared's binoculars were already focused on the warbler, and soon everyone in the group looked upward, searching for the elusive bird flitting in and out of branches.

"You can tell what it is from the noise it makes?" Dean asked beside her.

"After a while, you learn the calls," June said, refusing to look at him. Looking at him got her into trouble. "But Jared is the real expert. He can mimic songs to attract a bird in the area."

They watched until everyone had seen the pretty little bird with a white breast, black throat and dark blue upperparts, then moved on, remaining in the oak grove section about an hour, seeing a nice variety of species.

She noted that Dean often went ahead of everyone else or off to the side, constantly scanning the area with his binoculars. She didn't think he was looking for birds, but so far he hadn't behaved differently than anyone else. He struck up a friendship with Cheryl and Jim, the young brother and sister and, using his arm to point, helped them spot birds they couldn't locate.

Who'd have thought the sexy, bad-boy detective could be so patient when working with kids? Not her, that was for sure.

While the rest of the group focused on a plump ovenbird on the ground about fifty feet ahead, June paused and took a long draw from her stainless-steel water bottle. Sweat trailed down the side of her face, and she pulled her cotton blouse away from her sticky chest.

Productive morning, June decided, even if no one spotted a La Sagra's. They were about halfway through the walk. Maybe time to move to the mangroves, where they'd see herons and other water birds. That was the great thing about Matheson Hammock with its two distinct habitats.

"You're deep in thought." Dean materialized beside her, surprising her.

"Are you enjoying your first bird hunt without a gun?" she asked.

"What makes you think I don't have a gun?"

She scanned his body. No way was a holster hidden anywhere. "Where? In your pack?"

"That wouldn't be very convenient in an emergency," he said.

"But I don't see—"

"In my boot," he said.

Her gaze traveled to his feet. Had to be a small gun. Definitely not a rifle.

"Why did you bring a weapon?" she demanded.

"Because I'm a sworn law-enforcement officer."

"Well, I hope you're not planning to blast any birds out of the sky today."

His eyebrows drew together. "What are you talking about?"

She bit her lip, wanting to throw his bird-murdering tendencies in that too-handsome face, but embarrassed to admit she'd scoured the internet for information about him. Would he wonder why? Her outrage won.

"I looked you up on Google last night. Guess what I discovered?"

"That I've never been married?"

"No, that you—" She halted her tirade as his words sank in. "You've never been married?"

"Wouldn't want to make any woman a widow. So, what startling thing did you learn about me?"

She shook her head. Once again the man had thrown her off balance. How could he possibly know she'd tried to determine his marital status? "Forget it."

"Maybe I don't want to forget it. Whatever it was

sure ruffled your feathers." He grinned, obviously amused by his bird reference.

"Ha-ha," she said, not finding him funny.

"Hey. I seem to remember you inviting me on this little jaunt. Did I misunderstand?"

She sighed. "No. I thought you would enjoy yourself. That was before I knew you preferred to hunt birds with that high-powered rifle you're so damn good with."

"AH," DEAN SAID, noting June's face had flushed a delightful pink with her angry words, making her even more attractive. "Got it now."

She'd been prickly all morning. He'd known something bothered her, and should have realized what. He'd considered telling her about his bird hunting as a preemptive strike, but decided against that plan, hoping she wouldn't find out. No such luck.

"Yeah, 'ah,'" she muttered.

He nodded. "And that bothers you."

"Of course it bothers me."

"Then you understand why I never mentioned my hobby in our previous conversations."

"Yeah, I'd be ashamed of it, too."

"I'm not ashamed of shooting turkeys. I only hunt when and where it's legal. And there's thousands of them, so many they need to be thinned out."

Folding her arms across her chest, June stared at her boots and didn't reply. But he could tell that logic made sense to her. She just wasn't willing to admit it.

Not yet anyway. For some reason her opinion of him had become important.

"Hey," he said softly. "I promise not to shoot any of your warblers."

She looked up. "They're not mine. They belong to the world."

Cheryl and Jim raced away from the group over to their position. "There's a real cuckoo bird in that tree," Cheryl said excitedly, pointing back with her right arm. Dean followed the direction and noted Jared staring at them.

"Come see," Cheryl said.

"A cuckoo bird? Really?" Dean asked, giving Cheryl a smile. Cute kid. Her brother, too, although their timing wasn't so great right now. He wanted to finish this discussion with June.

"Are there cuckoos here?" he asked June.

"Yes," she said, also smiling at the kids. "Mangrove cuckoos."

"Well, you better show me, then," Dean said to Cheryl.

The kids scampered off, and he followed them, deciding to let June mull over what he'd told her. She was sensible, right?

Hell, maybe not when it came to birds. Best to leave her alone for a while. The knowledge that he killed birds, probably the worst thing imaginable to her, was out there now, and they had to deal with it. Could she get over it?

He felt a grin form. He'd gotten women to forgive him for far worse things.

When he realized the path his thoughts took, he gave himself a mental kick. Before he worried about securing her forgiveness, he needed to learn what her involvement had been with two murders. After the hike, he intended to show her the group photo and see if it sparked any memories. Would she recognize John Smith?

He should keep a professional distance from June, but damn, she was addictive. Being around her always made him want to get to know her better. Much better.

And the truth was, although he hadn't admitted it to her yet, so far he had enjoyed himself on this hike. He liked kids and found the experience of searching for tiny birds flitting from branch to branch much like a game. Ridiculous, really, how excited the birders got, but he found himself swept up in the silly thrill of each new sighting.

But his neck ached from looking upward. And if you asked him, those damn tiny warblers all looked pretty much alike.

Beside him, little Cheryl behaved like a bird herself, hopping from foot to foot. She was obviously delighted to be the one to help him spot a bird for a change. Dean exchanged a smile with her bored father, who'd earlier confided he was divorced from the mother and on a weekly outing with the kids. Life was tough on relationships. Cops for sure knew all about that, and he came from a family of cops. His mother had been widowed when he was ten, leaving her to raise three kids alone. His younger siblings were both divorced.

Dean raised his binoculars to look for the cuckoo.

Then, never forgetting why he'd come, he refocused and slowly swung his lenses in an arc, searching the immediate area for the barrel of a rifle. He'd thought John Smith might show for this birding trip, which had been promoted heavily on the bird society's Facebook page and website. Even if Smith didn't plan to kill June, this would be a perfect occasion to hook up with her.

Dean's analysis of the pet-shop video convinced him that Smith had wanted to talk to June. So why would he want to speak to a woman he supposedly didn't even know? Was she lying about knowing Smith? What Smith wanted to say to her was the key to this case. Dean didn't believe Smith was the shooter, but somebody else might be gunning for Smith, and that somebody might also be gunning for June.

He'd bet his badge that June was at the center of it all. He didn't know how or why yet, but he intended to figure it out.

Dean suspected if Smith hadn't shown by now, he likely wouldn't. Still, the mysterious man had surprised him more than once, and Dean didn't like surprises.

June led them into the mangroves, where the habitat altered into wetlands. Thick aerial roots emerged from brackish water on both sides of the trail. Startled by the appearance of humans, a great blue heron flapped its huge wings and flew away, the sight sending a couple from Nebraska into birder rapture.

As the group moved single file along the narrow path, he found himself directly behind Jared, the red-headed, lanky birder June called a local expert. In front of Jared, June hiked up ahead with long, easy steps. Dean scanned both sides of the trail, looking deep into the tangled branches for any signs of danger, but soon agreed with June that the mangrove wasn't a good location for an ambush or a sniper. Why rough it when there were lots of easier places to take her down?

Like walking along Brickell Avenue.

Jared swiveled his neck and shot Dean a glare. Dean met his gaze, and the man faced front again. What was that about? This wasn't the first time Jared had given him the evil eye. Sanchez's background check revealed nothing off about the guy, and Dean decided to dig a little deeper. Or maybe this so-called expert had feelings for June and noticed the tense chemistry between them.

Yeah, the woman was definitely addictive.

From the front of the line, the terrified shrieks of a little girl pierced the calm of the mangrove.

CHAPTER TEN

DEAN RACED TOWARD the child's screams. He passed June, and by the time he rounded a sharp turn and got to Cheryl's side, she'd stopped screeching. She stood in the center of the trail, hands on her cheeks, staring at the mangled carcass of a dead raccoon.

Her father and brother spoke to her soothingly, trying to comfort her. Dean met June's gaze and shrugged.

"Cheryl was in the lead," her father explained. "Jim and I were right behind her, but when we rounded this corner, we came upon a group of buzzards picking at the animal's remains."

As if embarrassed by all the attention, Cheryl buried her face in her father's legs.

"Of course the birds flew away immediately," the father continued, "but the noise and commotion startled her."

Pretty grisly find for a little girl. Dean looked up and saw turkey vultures circling overhead, waiting for the humans to move on so they could return to their meal.

"Vultures are the garbage men of nature," Jared proclaimed. "They actually perform an important task eating carrion."

"What's carrion?" Jim, Cheryl's younger brother, asked. Cheryl glanced up for the answer.

"Dead animals," the father said, with a quelling look at Jared.

"Yuck," Cheryl said.

"It's a natural part of life, sweetheart," her father said to her.

"Well, that dead animal really stinks," Jim said, wrinkling his nose.

Cheryl grinned at her brother. "That was cool how we scared the vultures away, wasn't it?"

"Awesome," Jim agreed.

Dean choked back a laugh. Only in a child's life could death and tragedy turn to "cool" and "awesome" so quickly.

June reached for Cheryl's hand. "Let's go back the way we came and take another branch of the trail."

Dean followed as the group retraced their steps. He doubted life had returned to normal that quickly for June after her own personal tragedy when her parents perished in an inferno.

JUNE WAS TIRED and hungry when the group returned to their cars just after 11:00 a.m. But it'd been a successful hike. By her count, they'd seen thirty-three species, although Jared insisted the number on his list was thirty-five. Whatever. Everyone had a good time, even little Cheryl, who got over her scare within minutes.

No one got lost or bitten by a snake. Dean didn't shoot any birds.

Best of all, no one had tried to kill her. Definitely a good day.

June removed her pack and tossed it in the Cobra, then rotated her shoulders to release tension created by the weight. Her shirt felt damp and cool from perspiration trapped beneath the pack.

"Bye, June. Thanks so much," said the couple from Nebraska.

"It was great. Will I see you next week at Barnes Park?" asked one of the regulars.

"Probably," June responded. She wasn't leading next week's trek, but frequently went along for the birding.

Soon most everyone had driven away, and she glanced over to Dean's vehicle, where he spoke on his cell phone looking serious. She knew he was waiting for her. He'd indicated they needed to have a conversation after the hike, and she suspected he had more questions. Maybe he wanted her to watch the video to see if it sparked a memory. She was pooped after the long hike, but why not? She could—

"Do you want to stop for a cup of coffee on the way home?" Jared asked, startling June out of her thoughts.

"Oh. Sorry, Jared, but I need to speak to Detective Hammer."

Jared's thick red eyebrows shot up. "*Detective* Hammer? That guy's a cop?"

"Yes."

"What's a damn cop doing here?"

"I guess he's looking for birds, just like everyone

else," June said, deciding not to tell Jared about her possible connection to two murders. For some reason he had a problem with Dean. That much had been obvious during the hike. And why was that? Did Jared have something to hide?

As Jared continued to glare at Dean, she took a long look at her colleague. Just how well did she know this man? Could he be involved in the— She stopped her racing thoughts with a shake of her head. What was wrong with her? She'd always known Jared to be a gentle soul. Dean's warning had made her paranoid, and now she was even doubting her friends.

"Maybe next time," she said to Jared, trying to take the sting out of her last statement, which hadn't been overly collegial.

"Sure," he said, refusing to meet her gaze. "Maybe next time. Okay. See ya, June."

When the last of the birding group had driven away, Dean approached the Cobra.

"Tell me this isn't your car," he said, gazing at the bright red car with worshipful approval.

June sighed. *Men and their expensive toys.* "You know it's not."

"Your uncle's?"

June nodded. "Want to drive it?"

A huge grin spread across the detective's face, crinkling his deep blue eyes. "I thought you'd never ask."

June expected Dean to respectfully motor the Cobra a mile or so down Old Cutler Road at a sedate pace, then circle back to his car. Instead he took full advantage of the powerful engine, expertly clutching and shifting through the gears like a seasoned NASCAR driver, roaring south toward some unknown destination.

She didn't object. It would have been hard to voice a protest anyway, since he couldn't hear her over the noisy engine. Besides, she enjoyed watching him concentrate as he listened to the workings of the motor and the transmission. He'd nod and smile as the car responded to the quick, athletic movements of his arms and legs.

Yep, she decided. This muscle car was definitely wasted on her.

After a long drive down a one-lane gravel road, on which he thankfully slowed his speed, Dean finally braked to a stop in front of a weather-beaten, one-story wooden cottage perched on the edge of Biscayne Bay. The parking lot contained mostly pickup trucks, and the side yards were filled with trailered boats of various sizes and conditions, as well as an assortment of rusted anchors, old marine equipment and crab traps. A wooden dock extended into the bay behind the house with another twenty or so boats tethered there.

He turned to her with an exhilarated grin. "That was fun, Ms. June. Thank you very much."

She couldn't help smiling back. "You're welcome. Now, where the hell are we?"

"Are you hungry?"

"Starved."

He nodded. "Me, too. Do you like fresh fish?"

Looking for signage, she glanced at the structure again. "You're telling me this is a restaurant?"

"Ruth's Fish Camp. The best-kept secret in South Florida. Bring your field glasses and let's go inside."

When they entered Ruth's, June discovered the place wasn't air-conditioned, but slowly rotating ceiling fans provided a pleasant breeze. Most of the ten or so tables were occupied by men and women with deep tans and sun-streaked hair, as if they spent most of their lives out on the water. Old nautical charts covered the walls.

Dean gestured her to a table in the corner where her view through the screening provided a panorama of a natural Biscayne Bay. A narrow sandy beach and dense mangroves full of herons and pelicans hugged the shoreline. She marveled at the sight, knowing this was how the entire bay had looked before development crowded out nature.

"Oh, look," June said, raising her binoculars to focus on a large brown bird with a white breast sitting atop a wooden dock piling staring out to sea. "An osprey."

"And with any luck, we might see a bald eagle."

She lowered her lenses so she could see his face. "Are you serious? The only place I've seen an eagle in South Florida is deep inside Everglades National Park."

He nodded. "That's why I brought you here. They're frequently spotted in this area."

"Thank you," she said meaningfully.

"You're welcome."

He caught her gaze and smiled. Warmed by his thoughtfulness, she couldn't look away, deciding his eyes reminded her of an eastern bluebird.

"See, I'm not all bad," he said in a soft voice.

"No one is," she said. She raised her binocs again to scour the area for any sign of the elusive raptor.

"No guarantees, though," he cautioned.

"Of course not." Oh, but how she'd love to sight a bald eagle. As she inspected the sky and surrounding landscape, she wondered if Jared knew about this particular spot and if he had birded the area. Should she tell him about it? No, she decided. Not until she spotted a baldie herself.

Convinced none were within range, she placed her binocs on the table and retrieved a menu from its holder.

"What's good?" she asked.

Dean shrugged. "I've never had anything bad, but the conch chowder is the best in Florida."

Her hunger mounted as she read the menu. Everything sounded delicious, but she decided on the conch chowder, plus a grilled mahimahi sandwich with french fries and coleslaw.

"And a glass of pinot grigio," she said to the waitress, whose name tag read "Ruth."

Dean ordered the same, except he requested a beer instead of wine.

With Dean watching her intently, June reached for

the ice water provided by Ruth and took a long drink. Unexpectedly nervous by his scrutiny, she wished it were the wine instead. *What is he thinking? And why is he being so nice?*

"Is our waitress the owner?" she asked, unable to think of anything else to say.

"No, her granddaughter."

Fortunately the wine appeared within two minutes, and June took a grateful sip. Dean took a long swallow of his beer and met her gaze again. There it was again, that compelling, electric connection. But he wasn't smiling now.

"What's wrong?" she asked.

"Not a thing. I'm enjoying the surroundings and the company."

She nodded, but knew he was thinking about his case and deciding if he could trust her. And why should he, really? She hadn't been exactly welcoming when he showed up on the hike.

"This is a great place," she said. "I'm surprised the birding community doesn't know about it."

"Big Ruth wouldn't appreciate a horde of hikers tramping all over her private property."

June laughed at the image. "I guess not. Do you come here a lot?"

He shrugged. "When I can. It's a bit far from where I live."

She pounced on the opening. "Do you live on Miami Beach?"

"Can't afford the taxes," he said with a lazy smile.

"Oh." Disappointed, she glanced back to the bay. The osprey remained on the piling, still searching the choppy water for signs of food.

"Cops don't usually live in the area they police," Dean said. "It can be awkward if you have to arrest your neighbor."

"I never thought about that," June said. She took a quick swallow of wine. "Listen, if I was rude to you earlier—"

"If?" He eyed her steadily.

"If. When. Whatever. It's just that when I—"

"Is this an apology?" Dean interrupted.

"Not if you don't let me finish."

He shook his head. "You don't need to."

She sighed. "It was going to be more of an explanation than an apology."

He laughed, a deep belly laugh that made her narrow her eyes at him.

"What's so funny?"

"Considering the way we met, do you think you really need to explain why you were upset that I occasionally hunt birds?"

She nodded. "I guess not."

"What if I told you this birding trip with you has shown me the error of my ways?"

Now it was her turn to laugh. "I wouldn't believe you."

"I'm wounded, June," he said.

She caught her breath at his soft, quiet tone and searched his face for intent. He couldn't be serious.

He produced that killer smile again. "I promised to be honest with you."

"What I remember is you said you'd try." She stared at his mouth, suddenly thrust back to the night in her condo when he had almost kissed her. And she'd wanted him to, had been sorry when he didn't.

"Here you go," Ruth said. She placed steaming cups of chowder on their table, along with a basket of warm corn bread and a bottle of sherry. "Be back with your sandwiches in a jiff."

June exhaled on a quick rush, glad for the interruption. The spicy fragrance from the soup reminded her she was ravenous. Plus, she needed to eat. She needed energy to keep up with Dean's quick mind.

Damn, but the man excited all her senses, drained her and thrilled her at the same time.

DEAN ALWAYS BELIEVED it was a testament to the food at Ruth's that no one spoke much the first ten minutes after a meal was delivered. This afternoon was no exception. He was pleased to note that June was no picky eater. She liberally doused her chowder with the sherry and then proceeded to thoroughly enjoy her food—with regular glances toward the bay in hopes of spotting an eagle.

He wasn't sure if he enjoyed watching her or eating his own food more. She was a delight in every way.

He chomped down on a crisp french fry. Well, maybe not in every way. She loved to give him shit and could definitely hold her own in any verbal sparring match.

She pushed her empty plate away with a contented sigh. "That was delicious."

He nodded agreement and took the last swallow of his beer. Damn good meal all around.

She relaxed back in her seat and raised her binoculars for a long look at the bay. He scanned the water himself. Still no eagles. Maybe they were all too far out hunting.

She lowered the glasses and said, "I'm assuming you brought me here because you have more questions."

Dean leaned forward. Time to do his own version of hunting. Hunting for the truth. For the first time in his career, he didn't know where to start an interrogation. He didn't want to believe June had anything to do with the shootings, but he couldn't ignore the facts. He'd deliberately left the photographs in his vehicle, wanting to have a peaceful interlude with her before hitting her with suspicion, knowing she'd react as if he'd tossed a bucket of cold water over her head. Afterward he'd get nothing out of her.

So he'd start with the easy questions.

"Do you know a Donald Gillis?"

"Agent Gillis?" She smiled uncertainly. "Sure. He's my contact with Fish and Wildlife. I give him my proof of smuggled birds."

"Is that the only way you know him?"

"No. My parents considered him and his wife their best friends. Why?"

"I've been looking into the circumstances of your parents' death, and his name is all over the files." He watched her carefully for a reaction, but detected only puzzlement.

"But why would you look at the circumstances of the fire?"

"Because, darling, I'm looking for a reason someone would want to kill you, and you've come up squeaky clean."

Her lips quirked, and he knew she fought a smile. "I'm not sure if I like being thought of as squeaky clean."

"Well, I can tell you it sure makes my job difficult," he drawled.

She produced a huge grin, which made her even more lovely. "Well, I am so very sorry."

I'll bet you are. "So you've stayed in touch with Gillis?"

"Yeah, he's been a friend. He tried desperately to prove my parents were innocent, but the evidence against them was so overwhelming even he became convinced of their guilt."

She all but spat out the last word, and Dean again noted June's bitterness over her parents' criminal activity. He resisted pulling a napkin toward him to make notes, not wanting to make the interview appear too formal. Maybe his notebook had turned into a crutch.

"You know, I've always thought that's what killed Janice, Agent Gillis's wife," June said in a softer voice.

"Explain."

"She and my mom were like sisters. I even called her Aunt Janice, and she was devastated by the thought that her 'sister'—" June raised her hands to create faux quotation marks around the word "—had been smuggling. A year later Aunt Janice had a heart attack. I think it was the stress."

"Yeah, stress is a killer," Dean agreed. "So, why don't you call Agent Gillis Uncle Don?"

June lifted her eyebrows in surprise. "I don't know. Just never did."

"Maybe because you already had an uncle," Dean suggested.

"Agent Gillis isn't the friendly uncle type."

"But Michael Latham is?" He'd been wondering about the uncle, even though the background check from New York came back spotless. June had been a beautiful, vulnerable child when her parents died. He hated the direction of his thoughts, but what if the uncle was a perverted predator? He'd be in a perfect position to take advantage of a lonely, frightened niece.

She shrugged. "He's my father's brother."

"And that's it?" Dean asked the question casually, running a finger down the cool, moist water glass on the table. He lifted his gaze and scanned her face for any tells, any sign that her relationship with her uncle wasn't a normal family one.

She leaned toward him. "Exactly what are you asking me, Detective Hammer?"

She was close enough that Dean felt her soft breath against his arm. "I'm inquiring into the nature of your relationship with your uncle," he said.

"I think you're asking if there's something improper going on between us." She lifted her hand and stroked his arm with a light touch. "Something…sexual," she said in an intimate tone.

Fascinated by her unexpected response, sensing she was toying with him, he suddenly had to know the answer. His flesh burned where she touched him. She was deliberately driving him nuts. "Is there?" he asked, his voice hoarse.

CHAPTER ELEVEN

JUNE STARED AT where her hand remained in contact with Dean's muscled forearm, his flesh warm and alive beneath her fingers. Ever since they'd escaped the bugs on the hike and he'd rolled up his sleeves, she'd wanted to touch him right here.

This was so unlike her. She could hardly believe she was stroking Dean, teasing him, deliberately making him wonder about just how "close" she and Uncle Mike really were. She met his gaze, pleased to note his confused reaction, the first time she'd been able to plainly read him. Served him right. First he thought she was a hooker, and now he thought she was a mistress being kept in style by a rich uncle.

Of course he wasn't the first person to harbor such suspicions about her and Uncle Mike. The innuendo usually insulted her, but not today. She sensed Dean's interest stemmed from true concern, and she wasn't sure how she felt about that. She wasn't used to anyone actually caring about her. She was used to taking care of herself.

He placed his hand over hers. "June?"

She considered dragging this out. She could look away with a sad expression and ask if he would hate her if it was true, but decided to put him out of his misery.

"Sorry to disappoint you," she said. "But Uncle Mike is gay."

After a pause, he choked out, "Gay?"

She nodded. "And, regardless, he's not that kind of man."

June watched Dean's thoughts zoom off on a new path. She had no clue what he was thinking, but she knew he'd left her and traveled somewhere else, sifting the new information against what he already knew about his case.

His case. Always his case. But of course that's the only reason we're here.

"Is the fact that my uncle doesn't date women important?" she asked, unable to imagine how it would be.

Dean refocused on her. "No. I'm just glad that in addition to everything else you went through after your parents' deaths, you weren't a victim of child abuse."

She swallowed and looked out to the glittering bay. Dean was the first person to acknowledge that she'd gone through pure hell because of her greedy father and mother. Ten years ago, all the adults told her to be strong, be brave, she was a big girl, that nothing was her fault. Her friends didn't know what to say or do.

How could a man she barely knew understand how she'd felt?

"So, what's your relationship with that Jared character?" Dean asked.

She swung her gaze back to him. "Jared? He's a colleague."

"If he thought he could get away with it, he'd have

pushed me into a gator hole this morning. Should I be jealous?"

"Why would you be jealous?" she challenged.

He took her hand in both of his and squeezed. "Because you have the most curious effect on me, June."

She blinked. "And what effect is that?" Now he was serious again? Hard to keep up with his quick changes.

Holding her gaze, he raised her hand to his lips and kissed her palm.

His warm breath felt delicious, his lips impossibly sensual. She closed her eyes as a reckless, languorous sensation took hold of her. *Oh, that effect. Does he know he has the same effect on me? Of course he does.*

"Are you two all done here?" Ruth asked in a booming voice.

June opened her eyes and found Dean watching her with a knowing expression.

He released her hand and sat back. "Yes, ma'am. Delicious as ever."

"Glad you enjoyed it," the waitress responded. "You all want any key-lime pie?"

"Would you like something sweet, June?" Dean asked, holding her gaze again, smiling his dangerous bad-boy smile.

Yes, sir, I believe I would. She shivered.

But she said, "I couldn't eat another thing right now."

"Just the check," Dean said to Ruth.

On their walk to the Cobra, June noted threatening

clouds in the western sky, the typical weather pattern for South Florida in mid-September.

As they put on the Cobra's custom-made hardtop, Dean said, "I have some photographs I'd like you to look at."

"Photographs?" *Oh, right. Back to his case.* "Of what?"

"I'd rather you see them without knowing the subject ahead of time. But they're back in my vehicle. I got so excited about driving with a beautiful woman in an honest-to-God real 1965 Shelby Cobra that I forgot to bring them."

"Yeah, right," she said, suspecting he never forgot a thing. "You are so full of it, Detective Hammer."

A HALF MILE from Matheson Hammock, the dark skies released their burden and wind-driven sheets of rain made it hard for Dean to see the road. He downshifted to slow the Cobra, noting with approval the quick response of the fifty-year-old car.

The rain was a godsend, he decided. He'd been second-guessing his decision not to show June the photos at lunch, now thinking the process would be awkward in his vehicle. He'd rather she be relaxed and comfortable.

So this nasty weather provided the perfect excuse for his new plan.

Would she agree? He smiled, liking the fact that he wasn't certain how much urging she would need. June was definitely a challenge. He liked a challenge.

He stopped next to the Crown Vic. Rain beat loud enough against the Cobra that he had to raise his voice to be heard.

"Hell of a storm," he said.

A flash of lightning was followed almost immediately by a booming clap of thunder. June jumped, then laughed at her reaction.

"Wow. Look how dark it's gotten," she said peering outside.

Dean watched water sluice down the windshield, enjoying the intimacy of this moment, how close they were, dry and warm inside her uncle's car.

Her gay uncle. When June had dropped that bombshell of info, his mind snapped to his partner's initial theory that Rocky and John Smith had enjoyed a romantic evening before the homeless man's murder. Had he missed something? Could there be a homosexual component here? But after exploring any possibility of a connection, he decided that was a dead end.

Yeah, and this case was full of dead ends. Unfortunately, every time he crashed into one, he had to turn around and head back to June.

He glanced at her. Much as he liked being with her, they couldn't sit here the rest of the day.

"Listen," he said. "Would you mind following me somewhere dry? We definitely need more light, and I don't want you or my evidence to get wet."

She shrugged. "That's probably a good idea."

"Thanks," he said, then hauled his butt out of the Cobra before she could change her mind. Cold rain plastered his shirt to his skin by the time he slid behind the wheel of his car, but he didn't give a damn.

His home was thirty minutes away and he was taking her there.

Dean hoped the storm would clear before they arrived at his duplex, but no such luck. The rain had slowed to a drizzle when they pulled into his driveway, but they both ran for the front porch to escape a drenching.

"Sorry," he said as he inserted his key into the lock. "I guess you got wet anyway."

"Not as wet as you," June said, eyeing his chest. "You must be freezing."

She pushed damp hair away from her forehead and laughed as if she didn't care in the least. She was a good sport. He liked that about her.

"Is this where you live?" she asked with bright, curious eyes.

"Guilty as charged," he responded, pushing open the front door.

"Then I'll bet you have a dry towel somewhere."

Dean quickly surveyed his living room, but knew it would be presentable. His furniture was fairly new, purchased from a retailer that sold entire rooms to make decorating easy. He rented out the other side of the duplex and spent more time working than here. This was more of an investment than a home. It'd do for now.

He grabbed a towel from the linen closet and tossed it to June.

"Thanks," she said, swiping the terry cloth across her face. Eyes wide, she openly checked out the room, seemingly pleased to be inside his home.

Why was that? He'd violated one of his cardinal rules by bringing her here. Had he made a mistake?

Pushing away his suspicions, he said, "Have a seat. I'm going to put on some dry clothes."

TOWEL DRYING HER HAIR, June stepped over to a bookcase full of books, plaques and photographs. A group of photos featuring parents and young children surrounded some sort of memorial to a man in police uniform who'd been killed in the line of duty. The man looked very much like Dean. Another photo contained two men in uniform. One was Dean. Who was the other?

Once again it struck her that Dean knew her complete life history, yet she knew next to nothing about him.

Her attention shifted to the numerous framed awards, which were mostly police commendations, containing the phrase "Above and beyond the call of duty" over and over. Oh, and here were sharpshooting medals. She narrowed her eyes, thankful he didn't proudly display proof of his dead prey. The books all focused on police procedure, forensics or something to do with various weapons.

"Find anything interesting?" Dean asked. He stepped beside her, smelling great, wearing a fresh cotton shirt and shorts. She'd never seen him in anything but slacks and was pleased to finally get a look at some bare skin other than his arm. Nice legs. He'd combed his damp hair away from his face, which accentuated his cheekbones.

She indicated the memorial. "Was your father killed on the job?"

"Yes."

"I'm sorry."

"Thanks. I was just a kid."

She picked up the photo of two men in uniform. "Your brother?"

"Yeah," Dean said with obvious affection. "My younger bro."

"Different uniforms, so a different department?"

"Don works for Miami-Dade County. So did my dad."

"So, why do you work for the city of Miami Beach?"

He placed the photo back on the shelf. "Do you want the truth?"

She met his gaze. "Of course."

He grinned. "I like South Beach."

"And here I thought you were going to tell me something like you wanted to be your own man."

"That's what I tell most people. Can I get you something to drink?"

"No, I'm fine. I'm assuming these aren't the photographs you want me to look at."

"You're right." He gestured to the sofa. "Let's sit."

June sat on a comfy-looking cloth sofa while Dean

retrieved a folder from the briefcase he'd left by the front door.

"Is this something to do with a crime scene?" she asked, worried about the determined set to his jaw. *Is this going to be gory? Like the photos of the turkeys?*

"No, nothing like that." He sat beside her, so close that their thighs touched, and handed her an eight-and-a-half-by-eleven color photograph. "Do you recognize anyone?"

June accepted the picture. When she glanced down, she tensed. "Oh, my God."

"What?"

"My parents."

"Your parents are among the group?" He didn't sound surprised.

June ran a finger over the image of her mom and then her dad. She'd forgotten her mom used to wear her hair in that poufy style. And look how long Dad's hair was. "I remember this," she said.

"You would have been very young."

"But it was an exciting day. There was cake and balloons." Suddenly she was transported back almost twenty years to the grand opening of Latham Import. Yeah, she remembered all the worry and the preparation leading up to that day, but mostly she remembered the party. She didn't understand everything, but had sensed how thrilled her parents had been that their dream had finally come true. She stared at all the beaming faces in the photograph.

"How could they have let all that joy just slip away?" she wondered aloud.

"Latham Import?" Dean asked.

"That's what I never understood," she said. "I reviewed the financials later. The business was doing fine. They didn't need to—"

"It probably started small," Dean said. "Someone, probably a customer, likely made a suggestion, said they'd handle everything. It worked the first time, they made a lot of money and it escalated from there."

"But they didn't need the money. They were greedy."

"Criminals usually are."

She raised her face to his. "You obviously loved your father."

"Yes," Dean said quietly.

"You haven't mentioned your mother."

"But I love her, too. June—"

"Well, I hate my parents," she said bitterly, looking away from the kindness, the sympathy in Dean's eyes.

"Hey."

"It's true. Everyone, including shrinks, told me to forgive them, but I can't."

He placed a warm hand on her thigh. "They didn't mean to die."

"Oh, I'm sure they didn't," she said with a harsh laugh. "They had way too much fun partying at the Turf Club."

She stopped speaking and sucked in a breath, refusing to give in to useless emotion. Dean remained quiet, and she felt the weight of his hand on her leg.

"Sorry," she murmured.

"You don't need to apologize."

"I believed them," she said, staring at the photo. "We had a big family conference when they were out on bail. God, I remember how relieved I was that they were home. They sat me down in our beautiful house—a house later confiscated by the government—and swore to me that it was all a mistake, that they could prove it, that I wasn't to worry." She met Dean's gaze again. "And I believed them."

"Of course you believed them," Dean said. "They were your parents."

"They made me think everything was going to be all right, that our lives would return to normal, and it was all a big fat lie."

She heaved a sigh, knowing she needed to get a grip. What was she doing, telling Dean she hated her mom and dad? She'd never even told Sandy how she felt. Certainly not Uncle Mike, who still mourned his older brother all these years later. In fact, she'd never talked to anyone about her parents, even those damn head doctors. All they'd wanted to do was make her cry.

She lifted her chin. She hadn't cried then, and she damn well wouldn't cry now.

And what did a murder investigation have to do with her long-dead parents anyway?

"Why did you want me to see this?" she asked.

CURSING HIMSELF AS the biggest fool in the county, Dean wanted to pull June into his arms even though he knew she'd resist any attempt to comfort her. She'd somehow shut down about her parents after their deaths, talked herself into believing she hated them. Likely a form of self-preservation.

He'd assumed at least one of her parents was in the photo, but never dreamed she'd react this way. He thought he knew her, but there were layers to June Latham he didn't get.

Or maybe this was a well-rehearsed act.

Reluctantly he removed his hand from her leg. He needed to keep his mind on business and ask his questions. No matter what horrible memories surfaced, he needed to know if she recognized anyone else in the picture. He had two murders to solve.

She smoothed hair away from her forehead with her palm, as if trying to clear her thoughts. "Did you really think I wouldn't know my own parents?"

"My interest isn't in your mom and dad," he said. "Does anyone else look familiar?"

"Oh. Of course." Shaking her head, she studied the image again. "This was so long ago."

"Just do your best."

"Hey." She used her index finger and tapped at the first row, right in the center of John Smith's grinning face.

Dean wasn't sure whether to be relieved or sorry she made the ID. It didn't mean she'd been lying before. She'd been six or seven years old at the time of this party. She might not remember her parents' employees.

"Is this the man who released the birds?" she asked. "John Smith?"

Dean nodded. "We think so."

"So he was an employee of Latham Import?"

"That's the theory."

"So, then, he did know me," she said wonderingly. Dean watched her carefully. If she was lying, she was the best he'd ever come up against. *Or do I just want to believe a beautiful woman?*

"But you don't remember him from before the bird release?" he asked.

"I probably met him." She shrugged. "I didn't visit the warehouse too often, although I loved it there. My mom thought it was too dangerous with forklifts roaring around and being right on the Miami River." She looked up. "That's why I learned to swim so young."

Dean nodded. Maybe her mom and dad were greedy, but they sounded like responsible parents.

"But why would—" June narrowed her eyes, as if recalling something. "Wait a minute."

Dean continued to study her, convinced she was genuinely reaching for an elusive memory.

"I vaguely recall my uncle telling me there were a couple of employees who were steadfast in their defense of my parents even after Agent Gillis discovered the proof. Maybe this John Smith was one of them."

"What proof was that?" Dean asked.

June gave a wobbly laugh. "You're really making me work hard here, Detective. Believe me, I've tried not to think about these details for a long time."

"This is important."

"The drugs were with a shipment of blue-and-gold macaws," June said. "Imagine that. Signatures on something proved my mom was in on it. Agent Gillis found a witness in Peru who completed an affidavit. He later told me the case was solid and there was nothing he could do." She smiled faintly. "Poor Aunt Janice. She begged her husband to bury the evidence to protect my parents. It nearly killed him, but he couldn't do it."

"Because he'd have been arrested, too," Dean said, making a mental note to contact Agent Donald Gillis at Fish and Wildlife for more details. "Do you know where the records of Latham Import are kept?"

"There aren't any. Everything burned. That was the point of the fire."

"Did your parents have an accountant who prepared their taxes, payroll?"

"I don't know. Probably. Why?"

"That CPA might still have copies."

"Not after ten years. What about IRS?"

Dean ran a hand through his still-damp hair, wondering how the hell long it would take to get ten-year-old tax returns from Internal Revenue, if they were even available. And would there be supporting schedules with names of employees?

"I can try," he said. "Damn, but I need to know John Smith's real name. Any chance your uncle would remember the names of these loyal employees?"

She made a face. "I guess I can ask."

"What's wrong?"

"He doesn't like thinking about the fire any more than I do. That fire—well, it was bad. Uncle Mike worshipped his older brother. He still misses him." She glanced down to the photo again and touched her father's face; then her finger slid over to her mother.

Dean considered himself a hardened police officer. He'd dealt with plenty of unbelievable, heartbreaking tragedies during his career. But the mournful expression on June's face right now made his gut clench. He felt the heat of her thigh pressing into his.

She's convinced herself she hates her mom because that's easier than remembering her love.

He was torturing June with all these damn questions. He was forcing her to remember events best forgotten.

By now he'd read the case files so many times he'd memorized most of the info. Her parents' charred bodies had been discovered by a locked exit, clutching each other, knowing they were finished. *Does June know the grisly details? Is she thinking about them now?*

Hating himself for putting her through this, he placed his arm around her shoulders. "June?"

She closed her eyes and rested her cheek on his shoulder. "Sorry," she murmured.

He wrapped his other arm around her and pulled them both back against the sofa. "It's okay," he said.

He half expected her to start sobbing, something she probably needed to do, but she surprised him again by placing her cheek against his chest and pressing deeper into his embrace.

He gave her a gentle squeeze and said, "I think that's all the questions for today."

She placed her arm around his waist and hugged him back.

He continued to hold her, breathing in her sweet fragrance, lightly stroking her back. He closed his eyes. This felt nice. He could stay here all day.

They remained that way for a moment or two, until she lifted her face to his and tried to smile. He wondered how much the effort cost her.

He cupped her cheek and smiled back. "Hey."

"Thanks for being so nice," she whispered.

"Oh, I'm a real prince," he murmured and lowered his mouth to hers.

CHAPTER TWELVE

JUNE MET HIS kiss eagerly, thankful Dean had known exactly what she needed.

She was tired of thinking about a painful past, done with answering questions. She wanted to lose herself in the inviting warmth of this man and forget about everything that had happened before this moment.

She parted her lips, and he made a rumbling sound deep in his throat. When he slid his velvet tongue inside her mouth, she raised her hands to his neck, moved her fingers into his wet hair and pulled him closer.

There would be time for regrets later. She knew all about regrets, knew there'd be plenty of opportunities for wishing things had been different. It was what she did best.

Right now she only wanted to get closer to Dean. It seemed as if she'd spent her entire life aching to feel his mouth somewhere on her body. She arched her pelvis against his, felt him harden and realized she was stretched out on his sofa. Dean was on top of her, making love to her with his mouth.

She wasn't sure how that had happened and didn't care. Oblivious of anything but their connection, she rotated her hips again to let him know she was okay with this, but instead he pulled away.

"Mmm," she managed in protest, the best she could do with her senses spinning out of control. She didn't want him to stop. *Isn't this why he brought me here? Why I willingly followed him home?*

She opened her eyes reluctantly. Unsmiling, his gorgeous mouth hovered just above her face. His intense blue eyes stared down at her. He didn't speak.

"What's wrong?" she whispered.

He shook his head. "Nothing. Everything."

She searched his eyes. She knew he wanted her. The evidence was clear, pressing into her belly. He held himself above her with forearms resting on either side of her head, his impressive arms easily handling the weight, his fingers absently combing through her hair. But he wasn't kissing her anymore.

"Do you know how beautiful you are?" he murmured.

She didn't, but slid her hands through his dark hair to bring him down to her again.

He resisted. "We can't do this," he said in a voice so hoarse it didn't sound like him.

"Yes, we can."

He grinned, that cocky bad-boy smile that shouldn't melt her defenses but always did. "Yes, we definitely could, and it would be great."

She nodded in agreement and smiled back to encourage him.

"But we shouldn't," he continued, and she knew the moment had passed. Painful memories had already begun flooding into her brain—Sandy's murder, the fire. The regrets would soon follow.

"Because I'm a suspect?" she asked.

He pushed himself away from her. "You're not a suspect."

June remained with her back on his sofa, watching as he placed his forearms on his knees and glared at his carpet.

"But you don't trust me," she said.

He rose and walked across the room. That was all the answer she needed.

She sat up, trying to organize her tumbling thoughts, wishing she didn't care what he thought. Why should she? Because he had a killer smile and an amazing body?

No, because he's a police detective investigating two murders he thinks I know more about than I'm saying. I need to convince him I don't so he can find the real killers.

Hands on his hips, Dean stared out his front window. She couldn't see his face. *What is he thinking?*

"Do you really think I should have remembered John Smith worked for my parents?"

"No."

"But you think I've been lying to you?"

He turned to face her. "I believe you, June. That's not why I..." He trailed off, shaking his head. "You know, there are some people in this county who would laugh themselves silly to think I developed a conscience."

"Old girlfriends, you mean?"

He nodded. "Maybe a few husbands, too."

"Why would you develop a conscience about me?"

She raised her chin. "I've been taking care of myself for a long time. Give me some credit for knowing what I'm doing."

He walked back toward her. "Maybe I don't know what *I'm* doing. I have a rule about getting involved with…" He paused, searching for a word.

"Persons of interest?" she finished for him.

He sat beside her again. This time their thighs didn't touch. "You're connected to two murders. I believe it's unknowingly, but if we get involved, it complicates things. I'm crossing a line I shouldn't."

"I won't tell if you don't," she said, unsure why she didn't let it go. Maybe because she was miffed he'd been able to put on the brakes when she wanted nothing more than to rip his clothes off.

"You say that now, but if it ends badly it could get messy."

"Do your love affairs always end badly?"

"Not always badly, but they always end. Being a cop is tough on romance."

She raised her eyebrows. "What makes you think I'm looking for romance?"

His lips compressed into a thin line, but otherwise he carefully controlled his features so she couldn't tell what he was thinking.

"Whatever," he said.

She looked away. *Yeah, whatever.*

"June, please understand I need to maintain some distance. Solving this case will get me out of my lieutenant's shit can, and you—" he shook his head

"—you seriously interfere with my focus. Two people are dead, and you could be next."

"So you keep saying. I still don't understand why."

"That's what I'm trying to figure out, why I need to keep a clear head. Why I showed you the photo when I know how difficult it is for you."

"So now you think the murders lead back to my parents?"

"I do. Sandy and Paul Taylor have no skeletons in their closet. The dead homeless guy is a down-on-his-luck construction worker from Maine with no priors. I need to find out what John Smith's real name is and why he was trying to contact you."

"Then I guess I'd better go and let you get to work."

DEAN DIDN'T WANT to let her go. Not like this, not with her thinking that he didn't want her when nothing could be further from the truth.

When had he become such an effing hero? He couldn't ever remember wanting a woman as badly as he wanted June Latham and not acting on the desire. But once again she'd been vulnerable, scraped raw because he'd forced her to think about her parents. Maybe she pretended not to care, but he knew better.

She walked toward the door, where she'd dropped her purse beside his briefcase.

"June."

She turned back. "What?"

What should he say? *I'll call you after the case is*

*over and make love to you until we're both slick with
sweat and unable to move?*

He swallowed away that image. "I want you to do
me a favor," he said.

She picked up her bag, refusing to meet his gaze.
"What's that?"

"Don't walk home from work until I solve this
case."

That got her attention. She narrowed her eyes at
him. "You think someone is going to take a shot at
me along Brickell Avenue? Seriously?"

"Take the bus. I saw a stop right outside the animal hospital."

"I could be shot while I'm standing there waiting."

"Hang back under a tree until the bus comes. Or
even better," he said, moving closer, wanting to pull
her into his arms again, knowing if he did he wouldn't
be able to stop himself this time. "Don't go to work.
Why take chances?"

"Oh, please. You cannot expect me to hide inside
my apartment."

But that was exactly what he wanted her to do,
which was ridiculous. So maybe it was too late.
Maybe his head was already muddled when it came
to June. He'd allowed himself to get too close, to care
too much about what happened to her, and it was af-
fecting his judgment.

"You could spend some quality time with Lazarus,"
he said softly, hoping to make her smile.

She didn't. "I have to work, but I'll make a deal with you."

"What's that?"

She glanced back to the sofa. "If you let me have the photograph of Latham Import, I promise to be careful."

"You want that old grainy photo?" Once again she'd surprised him, but of course she didn't truly hate her parents.

She nodded. "It looks like a copy. Can't you make another?"

"Sure." He grabbed the image from the sofa and handed it to her. "So you'll take the bus?"

"You got it, Detective."

And with that she disappeared out his front door clutching the photograph to her chest. Feeling a strange emptiness inside him, Dean watched her drive away in the Cobra, already plotting another excuse to see her. She still hadn't seen the video, although he no longer believed that would lead anywhere.

What he believed was that she wouldn't be careful, no matter what she said. He'd like to put her in a safe house, but there was no concrete evidence to support that kind of budgetary drain. Only his gut feeling that she was a killer's target. His lieutenant would bust him back to patrol just for the suggestion.

Not that she'd go into protective custody anyway. He smiled. Although she might agree to move in here. Maybe she wasn't looking for romance, but she'd wanted him as much as he'd wanted her.

Yeah, and living in the same house, they wouldn't be able to keep their hands off each other. And if they made love, he wouldn't be able to keep a clear head where she was concerned, which could be deadly for them both.

Shaking his head, cursing himself for his weakness when it came to June, he grabbed his briefcase and spread files out on his dining room table. He'd work the case, see what new links he could find.

The case against June's parents had ended with their deaths. There was no one to prosecute, so why bother to tie up loose ends? But there had to be something here, some detail that had caused John Smith to come looking for June ten years later. What if the Lathams *had* been framed?

Just who the hell was John Smith? Dean added contacting IRS to his growing list.

But first thing Monday he'd contact this Agent Don Gillis from Fish and Wildlife to get more details about the evidence he'd developed. Would he even remember a case this old? June said her parents and Gillis were friendly, so the details were probably etched in his brain.

Dean nodded to himself. The sooner he solved the case, the sooner he could rip June's clothes off and bang her silly. She wasn't looking for romance? Fine. He wasn't, either.

JUNE WAS STILL fuming when she pulled into the parking garage at the Enclave. Although she realized *fum-*

ing might not be the best word to describe her feelings. Yeah, she could picture steam coming out her ears, but still...

Smarting was a better word. Her feelings were hurt. She'd obsessed about Dean's rejection all the way home, wondering what was wrong with her.

Why didn't he want her?

And why did she care?

She was pathetic. That was all there was to it.

And now, driving through the tombs, she had to slow down and pay attention on the sharp curves down to the bottom level or risk dinging this damn car all men seemed to love. Dean had certainly enjoyed driving it. Apparently more than he enjoyed her.

The heavy, weighted feeling she always got in the parking levels pressed her into the seat. She turned on the headlights so she could better see the concrete walls on the turns.

Dean thought being a cop was tough on romance? Ha! Try being screwed up about your parents and life in general. She couldn't even get a man to make love to her.

The photograph on the seat next to her loomed like another person in the vehicle. She'd studied the image at every stoplight, getting more than one impatient honk from the driver behind her, another reason why she seldom drove. Everyone was always in such a hurry.

Like the hurry she was in right now. She wanted out of this mausoleum.

She carefully rounded the last turn and pulled onto the bottom level as a sense of urgency to get the hell back into daylight settled over her. She'd ask Uncle Mike again about letting the valets park his precious car. He was due for a visit anyway.

As she maneuvered the Cobra toward its assigned slot, her memory flashed to how skillfully Dean had driven, urging amazing performance out of this powerful engine. Just as his kisses had urged more passion than she'd ever imagined possible out of her. Just kisses.

What the hell?

She slammed on the brakes so hard the rear end fishtailed. She stared in horror at three small gray lumps evenly spaced in Mike's designated spot, creating a triangle.

She shut down the engine, the sudden quiet a balm to her ears and nerves. Taking a deep breath, she stepped from the car and walked toward the lumps, her steps echoing off the walls.

Three dead doves, their vacant eyes staring at her in mute reproach, lay where the Cobra needed to go.

DEAN ARRIVED IN far less time than it had taken June to make the same drive. She had never been so glad to see anyone in her life.

He'd assessed the situation with a quick glance, comforted her with a hug and just like that switched into police mode. He called the crime-scene people and walked her up to her apartment.

They'd barely spoken on the elevator ride. He'd eyed the only other resident they'd encountered as if he were a serial killer. Poor old Mr. Jacobson had actually fidgeted under Dean's intense scrutiny. Otherwise he'd been lost in his detective-work musings.

Before he went back down to the garage, he made sure she locked her doors, including the door to the aviary. But really, unless an intruder were Spider-Man, he'd have to drop from a plane with a parachute to gain access through the balcony.

Dean's last words had been *Stay away from the windows*. Not exactly comforting.

So she'd curled up on her couch to wait, nursing a glass of red wine, wishing he'd come talk to her, tell her what he thought. It'd been two hours and light was fading as the sun sank lower toward the horizon. She didn't get up to turn on any lights.

She tried not to think about those poor dead doves, obviously killed as some sort of— What? Warning? How ironic that doves were symbols of peace.

Whoever had done it had known using birds would rattle her. The act had been deliberate and personal. And cruel. Really cruel.

So of course this hateful person knew where she lived. Even where she parked her car. Well, Uncle Mike's car, which she drove on such rare occasions it made this whole terrifying situation even scarier. Did they follow her every move?

What was going on?

Was it John Smith? If so, why did he hate her? How

could he know her so well when she didn't know him? June thought hard, but had no memory of anyone from the company except a nice Spanish-speaking secretary who always kept a jar of Hershey's Kisses on her desk.

And what had her parents done that would make an ex-employee want to kill her ten years later? The more she thought about it, the less it made sense.

She stared at Uncle Mike's phone and knew she should call to ask if he remembered any of Mom and Dad's workers. Would he know if any of Latham Import's personnel records still existed? How else could Dean figure out who this John Smith person really was?

But maybe John Smith wasn't responsible for today's nightmare. If not, who else?

She jumped when the concierge desk rang, almost spilling her wine. When she picked up the security phone, Magda informed her Detective Hammer was on his way up. June waited by the front door. She told herself to calm down, that he couldn't possibly know anything yet.

He knocked, and she threw open the door to find Dean frowning at her.

"Did you check to confirm it was me?"

"Magda called. I knew it was you because she released the elevator for you."

He stalked into her apartment as if pissed off. "You should have checked. What if someone had been holding a gun to her head?"

She hugged herself, wishing Dean would hug her instead. "Wow. You're really scaring me here."

He slammed her car keys on the dining room table. When he turned back to her, his expression softened. "You promised to be careful, remember?"

June swallowed and looked away from him. She'd waited for him to return to her as if he were the oracle from above, and he was treating her like a stupid child. When would she ever learn?

"Hey," he said in a quieter voice.

She refused to look at him. She didn't want him to read her feelings.

He stepped back and gathered her into his arms. She went willingly, pressed herself closer to his strong, steady warmth. Feeling safe, she placed her cheek against his chest.

"You've had one hell of a day, haven't you?" he said.

"Parts of it were nice," she said.

"Yeah," he agreed. "Parts of it were very nice."

They stayed like that another breath or two, and then she pulled away. He cupped her cheek and smiled down at her.

"Sorry I barked at you," he said. "Not a good excuse, but it's because I'm worried."

Loving the warmth of his hand against her face, she whispered, "I know." Whatever the complicated nature of their relationship, she believed he cared about what happened to her. What bothered her was he thought that meant he could tell her what to do.

Considering what was going on, how fast this crazy

situation was escalating, maybe his instinct to keep her at a distance was a good one. She appreciated his help, but didn't like being ordered around.

She retrieved her wine and took a swallow. Aware that he watched her, she said, "Would you like some wine? Or are you on duty?"

He hesitated, then nodded. "Thanks."

She moved to the bar and poured a glass. "It's one of Uncle Mike's nicest cabs," she told Dean as she handed it to him. "I decided I deserved it tonight."

Dean accepted the wine, eyeing her steadily. "I'm sorry you had to go through that."

"Poor little mourning doves. At least they're common." She sat on the sofa, but Dean remained standing, still watching her. He hadn't tasted the wine yet. She placed her glass on a side table.

"It was some sort of a warning, wasn't it?" she asked.

"Maybe."

"A warning about what, though? I still don't know what I've done or I'm not supposed to do."

He took a swallow of the wine. "This *is* nice," he said.

"Uncle Mike has good taste. I was planning on calling him tonight to ask him if he remembers anything," she said, hoping to prime the pump of information.

"Good," Dean said.

June heaved a sigh. This was like trying to get a sick dog to tell her what his symptoms were. Dean should be able to verbalize a little better. "Are you going to tell me what you've learned?"

He shook his head. "Police work isn't like on TV. There isn't always a magic breakthrough in the first hour."

"So no clues as to who was responsible?"

"A few."

But he wasn't going to tell her, obviously. "Do you think it was John Smith?"

Lost in thought, Dean took a sip of wine.

"Could it be related to my attempts to stop pet stores from selling captured birds?"

He finally sat beside her. "I've investigated the illegal bird trade in South Florida looking for a link to the murders, especially the pet stores you've raided. You're right, there's some pretty nasty stuff going on and something should be done."

"Well, thank you," she said.

"But I don't think what happened today is related to your commando raids at all."

His tone told her he'd developed some sort of theory. "Did the same weapon that killed Sandy kill the birds?"

"No. The birds died because someone broke their necks."

June shook her head. "What's this about, then?"

He remained silent, staring into the deep red liquid.

"Why won't you tell me?"

He looked up. "Because I don't know yet. This is just another piece of a very complicated puzzle."

"Please be honest with me."

"I will when I have something to tell you."

Was he lying to her? She looked down at her slacks, realized she'd had on the same clothes since early this morning and needed a shower. Using her index finger, she traced the pattern of a grass stain from the hammock. "Does this have something to do with my parents?"

He placed his wine on the table beside hers, and she knew he was going to leave before he told her anything important. She was pushing him away with incessant questions, but didn't she have a right to know what was going on? Apparently Dean didn't think so and, as usual, wanted to control the flow of information. She really hated that.

"I need more time before I can give you solid answers, but I'll tell you this much."

She looked up when he paused. "What?"

He gave her a half smile, and she realized he was relenting a little, telling her something he didn't want to. "I can almost guarantee that those dead birds in the garage had nothing to do with your parents."

"But—"

Before she could finish, his mouth was on hers, cutting off her words. She wanted to lose herself in the sensation of his soft warm lips, but it was a quick kiss. A goodbye kiss. Damn him.

"That's all I can tell you tonight," he murmured, his breath gentle and warm against her cheek, whispering the faint fragrance of wine.

She knew he was leaving. She wanted to ask him

to stay, but her pride wouldn't let her. He'd already turned her down once today.

"I need to go," he said.

She sat back with a sigh. The reluctance in his voice made her feel a little better, but not much.

"Will I be safe here?" she asked.

CHAPTER THIRTEEN

DEAN TOOK A deep breath. She'd asked the question he'd been struggling with since he'd arrived at the Enclave. But his instincts told him if the shooter had wanted June dead, had known she'd left in the Cobra this morning, she'd be dead.

And she wasn't. She was very much alive, and every enticing breath she took tested his control. Tempted him to cross a line he'd established at the beginning of his career.

He never got intimate with women associated with his cases.

June wasn't just associated; she *was* the case.

He didn't have many rules when it came to women, but this was one he'd never broken. But damn. Just looking at her created an ache. He longed to touch her, kiss her, taste her. He wanted to take her into the bedroom for hours of hot, sweet, satisfying sex.

But if he wanted her to keep heaving those gorgeous breaths, he needed to remain objective.

Hell, who was he kidding? Way too late for that. He'd lost all objectivity where June was concerned. What was it about her? Couldn't be her beauty. He'd known plenty of women more beautiful. Her vulnerability?

What did his sister always tell him? He needed to think with the head above his waist, not below. He needed to get the hell out of here before he forgot he'd even made a rule.

He smiled down at her troubled expression, wishing he could smooth away her worry. She had a reason to be worried, but not why she thought.

"Are you frightened?" he asked.

"I wasn't until you said that about a gun to Magda's head."

"Yeah, well, I wanted to make you think. The security in this building is already damn good, since no one can even get on an elevator or enter the stairwell without knowing the code. I've spoken to the building manager and he's hiring on an extra guard for the lobby. He also says each unit has a panic room."

Her blue eyes widened. "Oh, that's right. Uncle Mike says his safe room is impossible to breach, so I can lock myself in there and send out an SOS."

"Good. So as long as you confirm that whoever is on the other side of your *locked* front door is who it's supposed to be—"

"And if it's not, I'll run into the safe room."

Dean nodded approvingly. "Then you're safer here than almost anywhere."

And he didn't believe the shooter would try to get at June inside the Enclave. If the sniper was responsible for the dead birds—and that really wasn't his pattern to issue a warning—he'd know how tight security was and wouldn't take the risk.

He'd go after her outside. Fast, deadly and without a heads-up. That was the way this shooter worked.

She was far safer here than at his house. Safer from a lot of things.

"I've got some more work to do tonight," he said. "As soon as I'm sure what's going on, I'll let you know."

"Are the doves—gone from the garage?"

"Of course. I parked the Cobra where it belonged, locked it and put the tarp back on."

"Thanks," she said, hugging her chest. She nibbled at her bottom lip, a troubled expression still in her eyes.

Hating that she was obsessing about the dead birds again, Dean moved toward the door. He didn't want to leave her like this. Hell, he never wanted to leave her. For the thousandth time he considering staying, rejecting lame reason after lame reason about why it would be okay if he did.

Maybe he'd invite her to accompany him tomorrow. Why not? He could ensure her safety at least for the day, and as long as he wasn't alone with her, he wouldn't be tempted to peel off her clothing. Well, he would, but in a crowd he couldn't act on the impulse.

When had he ever thought up excuses to see a woman with other people around? Damn, what had happened to him?

He turned back. "Are you busy tomorrow?"

She shrugged, looking interested. "Nothing special."

"Want to come to a barbecue with me?"

She grinned. "That sounds delicious. Where?"

"At my sister's house."

He was tempted to laugh at the dumbstruck expression on her face. She definitely wasn't worrying about the dead birds anymore.

"You want me to meet your family?"

"You saw the photographs, June," he said in his most wounded tone. "You know I wasn't raised by wolves."

She laughed softly. "I'd love to meet them."

"I'll pick you up at noon."

THE NEXT MORNING, Magda buzzed June before eleven to tell her that her friend Dean had arrived at the Enclave. Why so early? June wondered, dripping water on the white marble floor, clutching a damp towel draped around her hips. She'd just completed her morning swim. If she'd indulged in a few more laps, she would have missed this call.

"Well, send him up," she said. *No help for it.*

"No, no," Magda said in a theatrical whisper, as if she didn't want anyone to overhear. "He and other policemen from the city of Miami went up to Mr. Di-Novio's unit on the twelfth floor."

"What? Why?"

"I'm good, Junie," Magda said, "but not telepathic. They did not share their purpose with me, only insisted I let them go up."

"Okay, thanks. Keep me posted." *Wow. What the hell is going on?*

June resisted the urge to call Dean to find out. She

always avoided Alfonso DiNovio, the most vocal of the residents who wanted her to remove the aviary. Unfortunately they used the same elevator. More than once she'd refused to get on with him so she wouldn't have to listen to his vitriol. What had he done that would cause the police to visit him on a Sunday morning? And why would Dean be with cops from the city of Miami? He worked for Miami Beach.

June hurried into the bathroom. She needed to shower and get ready. Dean could arrive any minute, and she'd been looking forward to his arrival since last night. She figured today was almost like a date. No, not almost. It was a date. She was going to meet his family. When was the last time she'd met a boyfriend's family? Not since high school.

Not that Dean was a boyfriend. He'd only asked her to his sister's so he could keep an eye on her, another example of how controlling he could be. She knew that, and so what? She hadn't anticipated an outing this much since the fire.

She also knew her overwhelming attraction to Detective Dean Hammer made zero sense. But she'd quit worrying about it because she'd decided the pull was purely physical. How could she help herself? He was gorgeous, incredibly sexy and had a sweet side to him hidden beneath his dictatorial police exterior.

The problem was her emotions were scrambled by Sandy's death and all mixed up with the fact that he was a cop trying to protect her.

As soon as the case was solved, it would all be over. Or at least he'd given her no reason to believe otherwise.

But what was Dean doing with Mr. DiNovio?

June clicked off her blow dryer and stared into the mirror. Horrified blue eyes reflected back at her. Was this about her? About Sandy's murder?

Had Mr. DiNovio left the dead doves in Uncle Mike's parking space? No way.

DiNovio hated her, sure, but killing birds was over-the-top. The man owned five or six restaurants and was well-known within the community. Why would he do such a thing? He wouldn't.

Fine. So why was Dean paying DiNovio one of his little "visits"? Probably for one of his special "conversations." For sure DiNovio was not the mysterious John Smith. They looked nothing alike. For one thing, Smith appeared anorexic, while DiNovio obviously enjoyed the food at his Italian bistros.

Last night she'd called her uncle to find out about Latham Import employees, but Mike had been out and hadn't yet returned her call. She slammed her brush down on the bathroom counter.

She wasn't good at waiting, and now she had to wait on both her uncle and Dean.

She dressed in khaki shorts and a loose yellow cotton blouse. Afternoon barbecues in South Florida could be hot, and she wanted to be comfortable. Would Dean and his brother watch football? Dr. Trujillo had mentioned the University of Miami and the Dolphins were playing this weekend.

The security phone rang, and June dashed to answer.

"Oh, my God, Junie," Magda whispered, her Russian accent making her hard to understand. "They just took Mr. DiNovio away in the police car. He was in handcuffs."

"They arrested him?"

"Acht. Here comes your friend." Magda disconnected.

June left her hand on the phone and sure enough in less than a minute it rang again. "Ms. Latham, you have a visitor," Magda announced, all cool and collected concierge.

"Thank you, Magda," June said, matching her tone, although of course she didn't need to. "Please send him up."

Pacing by the front door, June heard the elevator doors open into her vestibule. She peered through the tiny security window to confirm the arrival was indeed Dean, also wearing shorts and a short-sleeved shirt, and threw open the door before he could knock.

"I checked to make sure it was you," she said before he could open his mouth and chastise her.

He lowered his arm. "Good morning, June." He smiled, looking more relaxed and pleased than she could ever remember. Of course he did. Putting people in jail probably cheered him up.

"Why did you arrest Alfonso DiNovio?" June demanded.

He didn't appear surprised that she knew. "May I come in?"

"Yes, yes. Sorry."

"Your Magda works better than the police dispatchers," he said as he stepped inside.

June closed the door. Dean looked back at her and raised his eyebrows.

She sighed, clicked the lock and punched buttons to engage the alarm.

"Satisfied?" she asked.

He nodded. "DiNovio left the dead birds to scare you. I guess you know he doesn't like your little rescue operation on the balcony."

"Oh, my God," she said. "That's crazy. Why would—"

Dean shrugged. "The man is under a lot of stress because business is down. He apparently decided torturing you would be his outlet."

"Did he confess?" Her knees as shaky as if she'd completed a thousand laps, June plopped onto her sofa.

"He was one of those perps who couldn't wait to admit he'd done the deed." Dean shook his head and grinned, obviously remembering the interview. "The guilt ate at him. Unburdening was a relief."

"How did you figure it out?"

"It wasn't difficult. The guy was an amateur."

June nodded, realizing Dean had solved the mystery in less than twenty-four hours. Not bad. "What will happen to DiNovio?"

"The crime is barely a felony, so he'll bond out

by tomorrow morning. He'll likely get probation and some community service. This building is out of my jurisdiction, so Miami PD took over."

"God, he must really hate me."

"He's not too happy with anyone right now."

"And I'll still see him around."

Dean sat beside her and took her hand. "You don't have to ever worry about that wing nut again. He's quite clear about the fact that he's to leave you alone."

June stared at Dean's grim face, wondering what he had said to her neighbor. "Then this had nothing to do with Sandy's murder?"

"Nothing. Feel better?"

Dean studied her so carefully she had to avert her gaze. He'd worked hard, probably all night, to solve this latest disaster. She suspected—no, she knew he had only done so because of her, that such a minor crime wouldn't usually warrant so much police attention. Yes, she did feel better. She didn't have to constantly wonder who had done such a horrible thing.

Still, she hated the idea that anyone could despise her enough to kill innocent creatures.

"Well, I'm glad the murderer hasn't been inside the Enclave," she said, "but it's all way too creepy."

He squeezed her hand. "So let's get out of here and go to a party."

"How long have you known Dean?"

The question from Dean's mother startled June enough to make her pause rinsing plates at the sink.

Steam from the hot water rose, obscuring her vision. How long had it been? Only two weeks? Impossible.

It felt as if she'd known him forever.

"Stop the inquisition, Mom," said Katrina, Dean's sister, who resembled her mom with similar light brown hair and eyes, while Dean had his dad's coloring. "June was nice enough to offer to help clean up, and she doesn't need you badgering her."

"Just a simple question," Mrs. Hammer said, using a dish towel with quick, efficient motions. "I'm not badgering."

"We met a few weeks ago," June said.

"See? June doesn't mind," Mrs. Hammer said.

Katrina threw June a look. "Don't indulge her. She won't stop until she knows everything about you."

June resumed her work with a sponge and soap, wondering if it was a common occurrence for Dean's mother to probe his guests. Did he bring a lot of women to meet his family? At the moment, he was relaxing in the living room with his brother and, as predicted, watching football. Noise from the TV, overlaid by frequent shouts of disappointment or encouragement, filtered into the kitchen where the three women worked.

The afternoon had been relaxed, the food delicious. Everyone, including Dean's mother and a friendly golden retriever, had made her feel welcome and comfortable, something she hadn't expected. But she had little experience interacting with a family, much less a large one. Most of her school friends had been only children like her, or at the most had one sibling. She'd never been in the midst of such a large, boisterous group. She found the experience exhausting yet exhilarating. She found herself a little envious.

Dean appeared to have a close, easy relationship with both of his siblings. His brother had ribbed him about being busted back to patrol. Dean took it good-naturedly, but she could tell he didn't want to talk about whatever had happened.

What would it have been like to have a sister? Or a brother? Or parents that cared about more than money?

The back door burst open, hitting the wall with a bang. Katrina's two sons, along with their two cousins, all four of them red-faced and out of breath, rushed into the kitchen from games out back.

"We're thirsty," Jeb, Katrina's oldest, announced.

"What do you say?" Katrina instructed her son.

"Please!" they all responded in unison.

Mrs. Hammer opened the refrigerator and handed each child a bottle of cold water. They thanked her and promptly headed back outside. Looking for trouble, June thought.

"Don't forget it's my turn," Cassie, the youngest and only girl, shouted at them from the rear.

As she watched them hurry away, June figured the kids ranged in age from five to ten. They'd drafted their uncle into the backyard to toss the football almost immediately after she and Dean arrived. He'd willingly participated, and June had gone outside to watch, eventually racing to catch the ball herself a couple of times, which had been fun. Even little Cassie took part, although Dean had thrown a smaller, softer ball to her with an easy underhanded throw.

It'd been obvious to June that the games were a regular thing and that Dean enjoyed interacting with his niece and nephews. He'd removed his shirt after a while, which June had thoroughly enjoyed. Unfortunately, after the game, he'd taken a shower and changed into slacks and a fresh shirt.

On the ride over, Dean had explained that both of his siblings were divorced, and the entire family got together every couple of weeks to catch up.

"We're close," he'd said. "I've taken care of them since my dad's death."

Did that explain why Dean had never married and had kids of his own?

"How did you meet?" Mrs. Hammer asked, breaking into June's thoughts.

"Either on a case or South Beach, right?" Katrina supplied, apparently having decided to join in the interview.

"Is Dean that predictable?" June asked.

"Never, but he does like to party." Katrina dried her hands as she faced June. "You're pretty enough to be one of those models he talks about."

June felt heat rush into her face, but who wouldn't like such a compliment?

"Word of warning," Katrina said with a glance

toward the living room. "Dean loves to tell the women in his life what to do."

June grinned, having already experienced Dean's orders firsthand. Maybe his family didn't always appreciate him "taking care" of them.

"He was right about your ex, wasn't he?" Mrs. Hammer asked Kat with lifted eyebrows.

Kat rolled her eyes. "Don't remind me."

"After my husband passed, Dean considered himself the man of the house," Mrs. Hammer told June as if to explain Kat's warning. "He takes that responsibility seriously."

"A little *too* seriously," Kat said. "When I was in high school, he wouldn't let me go out with a guy until he'd personally checked him out. He'd do the same now if he thought he could get away with it."

"Well, let's go see how the Dolphins are doing," Mrs. Hammer said, apparently having decided the interview was over.

June turned to exit the kitchen and found Dean and his brother, Don, entering.

"Game's over," Don announced. "Dolphins lost, but I won ten bucks off Hawk here."

"I'll subtract it from what you owe me," Dean said.

"Isn't there another game?" Kat asked.

"Of course," Don said, rubbing his stomach. "But I need another slice of Mom's key-lime pie to keep up my strength."

"Be careful, bro." Dean poked his brother's abdomen. "They'll throw you off SWAT if you get any more out of shape."

"Yeah?" Don said. "Well, I'll take you on anytime, hotshot."

"Oh, please," Mrs. Hammer interjected with a weary shake of her head. "You two are worse than the kids."

"But you love us." Don gave his mom a quick hug on his way to the refrigerator. He emerged with the pie and cut a large slice. "Anybody else? June? You should eat here 'cause my cheap brother sure won't feed you later."

"No, thanks," June said with a laugh. She glanced at Dean and found him eying her so intensely it took her breath away.

DEAN SEARCHED JUNE'S FACE. Had his mom and sister ferreted out her entire history? They were a good team, worked well together, often using a good cop–bad cop technique to find out what they wanted to know from guests. But why not? They'd both been married to cops, although Kat had divorced hers after five miserable years.

June looked a little lost. Maybe it was time to get the hell out of here. Too much family could be a bad thing. Especially considering her history.

His mom and sister exchanged knowing looks and left them alone in the kitchen, following Don back to the living room.

"How you doing?" he asked softly. Could be his

mom hadn't learned much about June's background after all. She knew how to keep secrets.

"I'm good," she said. She folded a dish towel and placed it on the counter. "Sorry your team lost."

The afternoon sun streamed through the window over the sink, highlighting her blond hair, making her look like some sort of lovely earthbound angel surrounded by a halo. He moved closer, needing to touch her. All afternoon as he'd observed her easily interacting with his family, he'd wanted to touch her.

He'd been worried how she'd react to his crazy family. Constant teasing was practically a Hammer tradition. To those who didn't know them, the sparring might appear like insults. She might not understand that the brother who mocked his temporary demotion would actually take a bullet for him. And vice versa.

June seemed so solitary, independent, always doing everything on her own. Strange. How could a woman appear vulnerable yet self-sufficient at the same time?

He reached out to feel her sleeve, a damp spot where water had splashed onto the cotton. He closed his hand around her shoulder and longed to pull her into his arms and thoroughly kiss her.

"Do you like football, June?"

She shrugged. "Don't really know that much about it."

His gaze moved to her face. She moistened her lips with a quick tongue. "I could teach you."

"I have a feeling you could probably teach me a lot," she said, her gaze locked on his, her voice breathy.

His own breath hitched as she stepped closer to him. He slid his hand down her arm, loving the warm feel of her, and intertwined their fingers.

Damn. He'd known this would happen. Since arriving at his sister's, he'd been careful not to allow himself to be alone with her. And now here they were—June making him ache, making him forget any stupid rule he'd ever made. He'd thought the commotion while hanging out with his family would distract him from the need she created inside him. Instead, watching her play with the kids had created a new desire, one that he'd never experienced before and didn't know what to do with.

He grinned at his thoughts. Well, technically that wasn't true. He knew precisely what would cure that particular itch. But kids of his own? God, what the hell had come over him?

June Latham had obviously made him lose his mind.

"What's so funny?" she asked.

He squeezed her hand. Who needed any damn rules?

"Let's get out of here," he said.

She remained quiet on the ride home. Dean allowed her time to think, to absorb the afternoon. She'd been through a lot the last couple of weeks.

She broke the silence with "We're going back a different way."

"Old habit," he said. "Just a precaution."

"You think someone might have followed us to your sister's?"

"No one did."

She lapsed back into her thoughts, which now might not be pleasant, so he said, "Did you have a good time today?"

"Yeah, I did," she said. "Your family is nice. Thanks for inviting me."

"We can be a little much."

"But you love each other. I definitely get that."

He shot her a glance, pleased that she understood. "Might not always seem that way."

"You're lucky," she said softly as he braked to a stop under the portico of the Enclave. The valet glared at him but didn't approach. By now they all knew the drill.

Dean turned to her. "June, I—"

She placed her fingers on his mouth, and he forgot whatever he'd been about to say.

"Shouldn't you make sure I get upstairs safely?"

CHAPTER FOURTEEN

JUNE INTERTWINED HER fingers with Dean's again as they entered the lobby and smiled at Julio behind the concierge desk. Magda was off duty. She noted Dean's hawk-eyed vigilance as they approached the elevators. He observed everything around them, peered into every corner, every shadow in the spacious lobby.

As they ascended in the elevator, tension hummed between them. She didn't look at him, didn't speak. She didn't want him to speak. She didn't want anything to change, to interrupt what had to happen between them.

Had to.

She felt it. She knew he felt it, too.

She unlocked her door, disengaged the alarm and immediately reset it.

When she turned, he pulled her into his arms. Her purse slid to the floor, and his lips were on hers, warm, insistent, soft. She slid her hands around his neck, felt his muscles tense, relax. She opened her mouth and pressed her body into his and felt his erection. She heard herself moan.

This wasn't about protection. This wasn't about him being a cop. This was about pure physical need. He wanted her, and he was exactly what she needed. Maybe what she'd always needed.

But she didn't want to think about any of that now. She only wanted to…

Somewhere in the deep recesses of her barely aware mind she heard a noise.

Someone cleared his throat. Loudly. Not Dean.

He pushed her behind him and whirled. In a blur of motion he reached for the gun strapped to his ankle beneath his pants and brought it up gripped in both hands.

"Good evening— Hey! Hold on there."

Her heart pounding, June gaped at her usually dignified uncle, who looked terrified as he backed away from Dean with both hands in the air.

"Dear God, man, don't shoot."

June tried to speak, but the words caught in her throat. "That's my uncle," she finally squeaked, her voice two octaves higher than usual.

"This is your uncle?" Dean demanded, not lowering his weapon.

June swallowed. "Yes. He has a key. It's his penthouse."

Dean nodded, aimed the pistol at the floor but didn't relax.

"What the hell is going on here?" Uncle Mike asked, returning his arms to his sides, his gaze darting from Dean to June. She noted her uncle's formerly thick, dark hair had receded and thinned a little more since his last visit. He wore dress slacks, although he'd removed his jacket and hung it over a chair along with his tie. Mike's resemblance to her father startled her every time he came.

She took a deep breath and released it slowly. "You surprised us. I didn't know you were coming."

"It was a last-minute decision to attend a meeting rather than teleconference. I didn't expect to be greeted by your gun-toting boyfriend."

"Detective Dean Hammer." Dean replaced his weapon in the holster by his ankle and stepped forward with his arm extended.

"Michael Latham." The men shook hands, sizing each other up. "You're a police detective?"

"City of Miami Beach," Dean said. "Sorry about the scare, sir, but we've had a bit of trouble."

"Trouble?" Mike looked at June. "What sort of trouble?"

With her pulse finally returning to normal, she moved to give her uncle a hug. As the only family she had left gathered her close, her gaze locked with Dean's. He looked worried, but shrugged and gave her a smile. She smiled back.

So much for the passionate night in his arms she so desperately needed.

"I got your message," Uncle Mike said, pulling back. "Something about employees of Latham Imports?"

"It's a long story," June said. "You'd better sit down."

Starting with the incident in the North Beach pet shop, June explained the situation to Uncle Mike. Dean filled in details where necessary. When she got to Sandy's murder, Mike paled and went to the bar to pour himself an inch of his expensive Scotch.

"Go on," he said after a healthy swallow.

At the conclusion, Mike stared into his drink. "So you believe this John Smith is at the root of the murders?"

"We're certain that's not his real name, but yes," Dean said. "Somehow he knows June, but she doesn't know him."

"And you think he's a former employee of Latham Import?"

"That's one theory," Dean said.

"Do you know where any of the old records are?" June asked.

"No," Mike said. "And I doubt if the old CPA firm still has any records after all this time." He rose and walked toward the aviary. Lazarus issued a quiet squawk.

Mike turned. "You know, I never believed my brother was involved in smuggling."

June stared at him. "I didn't know that."

"You were shell-shocked, Junie." Mike smiled gently at her. "There was never a good time to talk about your parents."

June looked away. Of course that was true. For years she hadn't wanted to even think about her mom and dad, much less talk about them. She'd change the subject if anyone dared bring them up.

"This may mean nothing," Mike continued, "but there was one employee who remained insistent that your parents would never have involved themselves in something illegal."

"Do you remember his name?" Dean asked.

"Al Kublin."

"Is there any way to locate him?"

"Oh, yeah," Mike said, swirling the amber liquid in his glass. "The murdering bastard is locked up in Raiford Prison. He got life for setting fire to the Latham Import warehouse, but never stopped swearing to anyone who would listen that he and June's parents were innocent."

"You're saying the man convicted of the arson and the Latham murders insisted his victims were innocent of smuggling?" Dean asked.

Mike nodded. "And himself of murder, of course, but the evidence was overwhelming."

"Why don't I recall any of this?" June said.

"I kept you in New York during the trial," Mike said. "The media were all over the story, and I wanted to protect you. You were only seventeen."

"And furious with my parents for their lies," June remembered. *And I still am.*

"We were both hurting," Mike said. "I wanted to be in that courtroom every day to watch Kublin get what he deserved, but knew I had to keep you away from more turmoil."

"Did you ever meet Kublin?" Dean asked.

"Many times."

"June, where's that photograph of the grand opening of Latham Imports?" Dean demanded.

"In my bedroom."

"Can you get it, please?"

Realizing where Dean's thought process had led, June hurried to retrieve the photo and handed it to her uncle. Dean stepped close and the three of them stared at the festive scene.

"Do you see Kublin?" Dean asked.

"Right there," Mike said and placed his finger beneath the beaming face of John Smith.

"Bingo," Dean said, meeting June's gaze. "There's our connection. But he's not in Raiford anymore."

THE NEXT DAY, after his shift, Dean went to the gun range. Target practice was good for more than brainstorming and clearing his head; it was also excellent for releasing frustration. And man, was his life full of that these days. Was it because he was getting old, losing his edge? Had he always felt this gnawing sense of unease when a case didn't go right? Or was it just this case because of the lovely June Latham? Maybe he needed a night out on Ocean Drive.

He put on ear and eye protection, sighted the target and released a round. Then another, and another. And another. Until the clip was empty. He lowered his weapon. He needed to empty his gun a few more times before he felt better.

As the silhouette returned to him to examine for placement, he wondered who he was shooting at. Al Kublin? The warden at Raiford Prison?

All of his shots had hit the bull's-eye, but the pattern was more random than Dean's usual. He replaced the target and activated the pulley system to return it to the range.

He decided the prison authorities in Starke, where Al Kublin should have been safely incarcerated in the state penitentiary known as Raiford, were the primary source of his ire.

Kublin hadn't been at Raiford for a long time. Dean emptied his weapon into the new target.

According to the warden, Kublin had demonstrated what the shrinks labeled aberrant behavior once incarcerated a few years. Dean slammed a new clip into his weapon—hell, what prisoner didn't exhibit crazy behavior behind bars? Being locked up changed a man. But some bleeding-heart judge had released Kublin to Sunrise, a state psychiatric hospital in Melbourne, for evaluation and treatment. The warden had agreed with the transfer. What a crock.

Dean emptied the new clip into the silhouette, lowered his weapon and took a deep breath.

Sunrise was what was known as a country-club facility. By faking a mental disorder, a smart man, a careful man, could enjoy privileges other prisoners didn't. Was Kublin that kind of man? Or had guilt legitimately made him crazy enough to be locked away from the regular prison population?

So there was the number-one question, and not knowing was making *him* nuts. Dean emptied his weapon into target after target until his muscles grew fatigued. Was Kublin still locked up? Dean hadn't heard back from the authorities at Sunrise to confirm Kublin was where he should be. But how could he be?

Maybe Mike Latham's ID was faulty. Hell, maybe Kublin had a twin. Yeah, right. He needed confirmation, but Dean suspected Kublin wasn't anywhere near Melbourne. He was somewhere in Miami Beach, where he'd caused at least two deaths. Junie had been the intended target for one of them.

And there was another source of his frustration. June Latham.

He wanted her with a hunger that ate at him to the point of distraction, interfering with his work, a situation he'd never before allowed to happen. He didn't understand it. His obsession with June made no sense. He'd been in lust plenty of times—hell, way too many times, if he were honest—so what made her different?

Sure, she was beautiful, intelligent, feisty. Committed to the things she loved. And that body. Man.

Was it because he'd paid attention to his stupid damn rules and resisted her so far? That resistance had come close to ending last night. More accurately, there'd been no resistance. If her uncle hadn't shown up— Dean allowed himself to imagine the bliss of undressing Junie, of making love to her, and felt himself harden. Shit. June made him as horny as a damn teenager.

"Detective Hammer?"

Dean turned and found a gray-haired man in his fifties holding his hand out to him. He'd seen the man around the range occasionally and had noted his skill in shooting.

"I'm Hammer," Dean confirmed, knowing the man had to be law enforcement of some kind to be granted privileges at the police gun range. They shook hands.

"I'm Don Gillis, a Fish and Wildlife officer. You phoned me a few days ago."

"Agent Gillis, yes. I've been trying to reach you." *So this is Junie's contact with Fish and Wildlife, the old friend of her parents'.*

"I was out of town and got your message this morning. When I saw your name on the sign-in sheet, I asked around if you were still here. Nice shooting, by the way," Gillis said with an appreciative nod.

"Thanks," Dean said.

"Your message said you need information about an old case?"

"Yes. Have you got a minute?"

Shooting on the range resumed, making it difficult to hear. Gillis nodded.

"Let's move," Dean yelled over the gunfire.

Dean packed up, and he and Gillis relocated inside the range's office, finding a quiet spot close to the coffee machine.

"I'm investigating the Latham Warehouse fire from ten years ago," Dean said.

The pleasant expression on Gillis's face sobered. "Bad business. Why would you be looking into that?"

"I believe the fire has a connection to two recent murders."

Gillis nodded, looking as if he finally understood something. "You're the detective working with June."

"That's right," Dean said. So June had mentioned him to her FWC contact. What had she said? "I understand you were friendly with her parents?"

Gillis's face tightened. "Their criminal activity and deaths were a huge blow to me and my wife. Sometimes I still can't believe it."

"It sucks when a case gets personal," Dean said. *And that's exactly what's happening to me with this case.*

"Amen, brother," Gillis said. "So I'm guessing you want any notes or files I have on the Latham case?"

"Anything at all. I know it's been a long time, but was hoping because of that personal connection, you might have kept a file."

"I haven't looked at it in years, but yeah, I still have something. Or should. I don't remember tossing those records. I'll make a copy and send it to your office."

"That'd be great." Dean handed him a card. "Thanks."

"You do know they convicted the arsonist," Gillis said after inserting the card in his wallet.

"Yeah. My cases have hit a roadblock, and I'm just following up loose ends, looking for anything."

Gillis nodded knowingly. "I've been there. Good luck."

"Thanks."

Gillis turned to go, but hesitated as if he had something else to say. Dean waited him out.

"June is a fine young woman," Gillis said, "but her parents' death changed her, made her a different

person. Stirring up that tragedy again will be difficult for her."

Dean nodded, knowing Gillis was right on. Reliv-
ing her painful past was torture for June. And in a
way she was stuck back there because she obviously
hadn't gotten over her parents' betrayal.

Gillis shrugged. "I'm not sure what I'm asking here,
but do me a return favor and just be—I don't know—
sensitive when dealing with her."

"You got it," Dean said. *Sensitive? No kidding.* He
shook his head, watching Gillis move back to the gun
range, thinking how very sensitive June's satiny skin
was, how she reacted every time he touched her.

Whoa, Hawk. Wrong kind of sensitive. Maybe
he should attend some sensitivity training with Sanchez. His phone buzzed, interrupting his thoughts.
He checked the readout. Finally. The call from North
Florida.

"Hammer," he answered. The smell of scorched
coffee seared his nostrils.

"Detective Hammer, this is Jeff Fisher, assistant
warden at Raiford. You inquired on the status of Al
Kublin, and Warden Moore asked me to follow up
with that information."

"Yeah?" *Damn chickenshit warden afraid to give
me the bad news so he had his lieutenant make the
call.*

Fisher cleared his throat. "I believe Warden Moore
informed you that Kublin had difficulty adjusting to
prison life, became a danger to himself and others

and was transferred to Sunrise, the state psychiatric hospital in Melbourne."

Fisher took a deep breath, and Dean wondered if the assistant was reading from a prepared script.

"I'm sorry to tell you this," Fisher continued, "but Kublin disappeared from the grounds of Sunrise three weeks ago."

JUNE RELAXED IN her macramé chair in Laz's aviary, listening to the muted sound of Uncle Mike arguing with someone on the phone in the living room. She couldn't understand the words, but sensed her uncle's growing anger. So did Laz, and the tension made him nervously shift on his perch.

She reached out and stroked his feathers. "It's okay, sweetie."

The macaw issued a guttural squawk in reply.

Mike had driven her to work today on his way to a business appointment. Four short blocks. How ridiculous. She missed her walk. But she had done what Dean requested and taken the bus home.

The thought of Dean caused a long, slow, pleasurable pull on her center. She loved her uncle—she really did—and normally enjoyed his visits. But Mike showing up last night had been the worst timing ever, because Dean was finally going to make love to her. The tug in her belly traveled south, and she felt herself grow moist.

God, but she wanted Dean. She enjoyed sex as much as anyone, although she'd never felt this wild impulse to rip off a man's clothes. She'd had sex occasionally with old what's his name—she really had to quit calling her ex Rick that—and the experience had been pretty ordinary. No fireworks. He'd enjoyed it a lot more than she had.

But just picturing Dean's body made her wet.

Still clutching the phone, Uncle Mike knocked on the glass door and pointed toward her cell phone inside next to the sofa. Junie raced inside and answered.

"It's me," Dean said.

"I was hoping it was," she replied, returning to her swing.

"How are you?" he asked.

"I'm good. You'll be pleased to know Uncle Mike drove me to work and I took the bus home."

He released a sigh. A little dramatic, she thought.

"Thanks for that," Dean said. "I've got some news."

She pushed against the wall to make the seat sway. "Bad news, I'm sure. That's the only kind I ever get."

"Our friend John Smith, also known as Al Kublin, went bonkers in Raiford and was transferred to a psychiatric hospital."

June planted a foot to stop the swing. "Oh, my God. Did they release the man who killed my parents as all cured?"

"He escaped three weeks ago."

It shouldn't make a difference, but she felt better her parents' murderer hadn't been deliberately set free. "Then Uncle Mike's identification is correct. John Smith is Al Kublin?"

"I never had much doubt but needed to confirm. Because of privilege, the hospital won't release information, but I'm getting a warrant and going up there as soon as I can. Probably Wednesday."

"How long will you be gone?" June asked, hating the idea he was leaving town.

"It's a long trip, but I'm hoping to do it in one day. I'll take my rookie to share the driving."

"Okay," she murmured. "Where is this hospital?"

"Sunrise in Melbourne."

"Sunrise?"

"Right. Why?" Dean's voice became alert, interested. "Does that ring a bell?"

"Maybe. How long ago was Kublin transferred to the mental hospital?"

"Five years."

"The timing works, then. About four years ago I received a phone call from someone in Sunrise wanting me to come visit. I didn't recognize the name and don't remember it, but it could have been Kublin. Someone from the facility called me back almost immediately to apologize. They said it was a mistake, promised it wouldn't happen again."

Dean was silent for several long moments. "Assuming the caller was Kublin, why would he contact you?"

"I don't know."

"You'll keep thinking about what Kublin wants with you, right?"

"That's mostly what I think about these days." After a pause she added softly, "That and you, Detective."

"God, June," he breathed, his voice husky.

"Yeah?"

"You're making me crazy."

"Am I?"

"You know you are. You're *all* I think about."

"Good. But I want you to solve Sandy's murder, too."

"That's a promise. When is your uncle leaving?"

"Tomorrow."

"I'll be in touch." He disconnected, and June stretched her arms overhead, feeling as if she'd just had phone sex. Unsatisfying phone sex. She wanted, no, needed the real thing. With Dean. She needed it badly.

Her uncle rapped on the door again, so June went inside.

"Who were you talking to?" she asked. "You sounded pissed."

"The president of Enclave's condo association," Mike answered, settling himself on the sofa.

"Uh-oh."

"She denied knowledge of DiNovio's dead-bird trick, but I wanted to make it very clear that you weren't to be hassled again or there would be legal consequences."

"Is the association going to take any action against my aviary?"

"No. Not unless something else happens."

June released a grateful sigh. "Thanks, Uncle Mike. I'm sorry for the trouble."

He waved away her apology. "It's not your fault. You're really having a rough time, aren't you?"

"Things have been a little crazy," she admitted.

"Do you want to come to New York?"

"No. My life is here, Mike. I'm not going to run away, take the easy way out. That's what my parents did."

He shook his head. "I wish you didn't feel that way."

"Me, too." She remained silent a moment, then asked, "Have you remembered anything else about Kublin?"

"Yeah, one thing, although I don't see how it could help find him. Kublin loved sailboats, even lived on one for a while. He invited your father to go sailing shortly after he'd purchased the boat. I was in town and went along for the ride."

Mike closed his eyes, and June wondered if he'd been transported back to that day with his older brother.

"That was a wonderful afternoon," Mike said. "Sunny, windy. We flew over the water. Your dad loved it."

"When was that?"

Mike shrugged and opened his eyes. "Maybe two years before the fire."

"I'll tell Dean. Maybe the police can check out marinas."

"I doubt they have the manpower for something so vague," Mike said, rising. "Well, I've got an early flight."

"Do you want me to fire up the Cobra and drive you to the airport?"

"Not necessary. I'll call a cab."

She nodded, having known he'd refuse. "By the way, Dean loves your car."

"I think he loves you more than my car," Mike said with a wink and disappeared into the guest room.

Love? June blinked and remained on the sofa. She hugged her knees into her chest. Whatever existed between her and Dean—powerful as it was—couldn't be love. Not this quick. She didn't believe in love at first sight. She'd been with Rick for two years before... before what? She'd never loved Rick. He was just... safe. Kept her life on an even plane: no ups, no downs.

She sighed. A waste of time.

Dean was the polar opposite of safe on a whole lot of levels. He made her feel deliciously tingly and alive. It might not be her definition of love, but it sure was something.

CHAPTER FIFTEEN

TUESDAY AFTERNOON DEAN waited for June near the bus stop by Brickell Animal Hospital. He kept the Crown Vic running and parked so he could see her exit the building. She didn't know he was coming, but he had poor impulse control when it came to June. For all he knew she could have other plans.

Maybe it would be better if she did.

Nope. Too late. He was past the point of no return with the lovely Miss June.

He felt himself relax when she appeared on the sidewalk with a purse slung over her shoulder, and edged the car forward. She'd changed from her vet assistant scrubs into a skirt and blouse, something he'd suggested to make her less obvious to a sniper. *Good girl.*

She hesitated by the bus bench, glanced toward the roofs of the high-rises and with a frown stepped back into the cover of a nearby tree.

He nodded in approval. *Excellent.*

When he'd gotten as close as he could, he rolled down the passenger window and beeped the horn. She grinned when she recognized him—that welcoming smile making him feel damn good—and scurried into the car.

As soon as she'd closed the door, he accelerated into light traffic.

"Are you my new chauffeur?" she asked.

"I am today."

"Well, thank you, kind sir," she said, buckling her seat belt.

"Is your uncle gone?"

"He flew to JFK this morning."

Dean nodded. *Thank God.* "Have you got any plans this evening?"

"Nothing important."

"How about dinner?"

When she didn't answer, he threw her a look and found her watching him with another smile and faint blush on her cheeks.

"What?" he demanded. "Not hungry? Too early?"

"Well, the thing is," she began, and he was convinced she was deliberately making her voice sultry, "I am hungry. Very hungry."

He swallowed hard. "Okay. Good. Me, too."

"But what I want can't be found in any restaurant."

"No?"

"No," she emphasized. "So why don't you come upstairs with me and see what we can find...to eat?"

Dean took the turn into the Enclave faster than he should have. Next to him, June laughed in what sounded like pure delight. He braked to a quick stop and raced to her side of the car to grab her hand. He tried not to pull her too fast, but she had to hurry to keep up.

He needed to get her somewhere private, and soon.

"Hi, Junie," Magda called.

"Hi, Maggie Mae," June responded breathlessly.

When the doors to her elevator opened, they all

but leaped inside. When the doors silently slid shut, he pushed her against the polished wall and lowered his lips to her open, welcoming mouth. So warm, so sweet, like honey. She pulled him closer. He growled as she rotated her hips against his, instantly making him hard, and he pressed into her soft middle.

She laughed, the sound soft as the wind, and pulled her delicious mouth back. "I hope Mr. DiNovio doesn't need the elevator," she murmured.

"The hell with DiNovio," Dean managed, placing his hands against the wall on either side of her head. He groaned when she began kissing his throat, sliding her lips upward, toward his mouth, nibbling on his chin. The woman made him lose any logic, any sense. "Just tell me no one is waiting inside your front door."

With her gorgeous lips hovering close to his, she whispered, "Only Lazarus." Then she kissed him, and he ground into her again. He wanted to devour her.

As if in a fog, he heard the elevator doors slide open. He pulled back and they moved into the foyer. Breathing hard, June had trouble with her keys, so he took over. Inside, she worked on disengaging the alarm with trembling fingers while he made a quick check of the unit.

When he got back to her, she clicked the dead bolt home and gazed up at him. "The alarm is on," she murmured.

He wished he understood the emotion burning in her eyes, but knew she wanted this as much as he did. Her purse slid off her arm. Leather met the hardwood floor with a soft thud.

They were close but not touching. Her chest rose as she took a deep breath. His hands twitched as he longed to feel her glorious breasts cupped within his palms. His erection hardened.

They stared at each other, neither speaking. For a fleeting moment he told himself to step back, do the right thing, not make June's already complicated life more difficult.

She shook her head. "Not this time, Detective," she said softly, as if reading his mind. She closed the tiny distance between them, reached for his hand and pressed it against her right breast.

All coherent thought fled. Watching June's face, he pulled her blouse from her skirt. He needed to feel bare skin, but met a lacy bra and slid his hand inside to delicious soft warmth. He teased her already taut nipple with his thumb, and she closed her eyes, arching into his strokes.

"Don't stop," she whispered, and he kissed her, taking her soft, warm words into his mouth.

They moved into her bedroom. He sat on the bed and positioned her between his legs. He wanted to take her now, quick and hard, needed it bad, but far better to take time with June. Undress her slowly. Reveal her secrets. Give her beautiful body the attention she deserved.

She smiled at him, a little uncertain, but letting him do what he wanted.

He began with her blouse, slipping each button loose, tracing his fingers over her soft skin—that oh-so-sensitive skin—with each release. He made quick work of the bra, a lacy, satiny wisp of a thing.

June noticed.

"Got some experience with that, don't you, Detective?" she wondered as her breasts finally sprang free.

He answered with a greedy mouth on her left nipple. As he suckled, she moaned and swayed slightly. She wanted to collapse, but he supported her with his arms.

"Not yet, sweetheart," he said, his mouth moving across her belly, licking, kissing, tasting. To steady herself, she placed her hands on his shoulders.

He unzipped her skirt, let it slide off her hips and pool on the tile around her feet. He stared at panties that matched the bra and breathed in her musky female fragrance.

She was more beautiful now than he'd imagined. He needed to bury himself in her. He moved his hands to the panties, intending to rip the lace away, but she placed her hands on his to stop him.

"My turn," she said and pulled him to his feet. He smiled down at her as she unbuttoned his shirt. Slowly. Or it seemed that way with bare breasts inches from his fingers, ripe, pebble-hard nipples beckoning his attention. He cupped one breast, loving the feel of its soft weight against his palm. She paused her movement and took a deep breath, which pushed her amazing flesh deeper into his hand. They were close enough that his erection jerked against her soft belly.

When his dress shirt finally fell away, moving

quicker now, she pulled his T-shirt overhead and flung it aside. Eyeing his chest with an appreciative smile, she placed a hand on each of his biceps as if judging their strength. After a gentle squeeze, she slid her hands to his shoulders and allowed them to glide over his pecs and down to his abdomen in one slow, languorous stroke.

"June," he breathed, closing his eyes against the intensity of his need, hardening almost to the point of pain.

Those talented fingers fell to his belt buckle, which she deftly released, swiftly took care of one last damn button on his pants and lowered his zipper. He sucked in a breath. Needing to feel her touch, he pushed into her hand as his pants dropped.

"Mmm," she murmured, stroking his erection through his briefs with one finger. Without warning, she stepped into him, sliding her hands beneath the briefs to cup his buttocks and pulling him against her soft center.

She raised her mouth, swollen lips begging for his, and said, "Now that we've unwrapped our presents—"

He crushed his mouth against hers and lifted her onto the bed. He stretched out beside her, pressing his body against hers. No more games. No more waiting.

He slid his hand beneath her panties and found her wet and more than ready. He pleasured her with a few slow, teasing strokes. She whispered his name, arching her hips against his questing fingers. Unable to wait any longer, he quickly removed the lacy barrier, hearing a tiny rip. June laughed, the sound strangely erotic, and moved a hand toward his briefs.

And then they were bare flesh to bare flesh, the way he'd wanted to be with June from the moment he'd laid eyes on her.

He sheathed himself and entered her, and suddenly everything in this upside down world righted itself. He began a slow, easy rhythm. With her eyes closed, she answered each thrust with her own. He watched her face as a wave of tension tightened, built, crescendoed. He became lost in June, her passion, his own, until he had to also close his eyes against the power of what was happening between them.

The wave crashed over them with a release that left him drained, yet somehow complete. And deliriously, ridiculously happy.

JUNE OPENED HER eyes when Dean pulled away, moved off of her and tossed the condom. She sighed, not yet ready to break their connection. She rolled onto her side and placed her cheek on his chest, breathing in the essence of him, of their sweat and sex. Delicious.

He wrapped an arm around her and pulled her closer, looping one of his legs over hers.

Dean's desire to maintain their intimacy warmed her, reassured her. Rick would leap out of bed after sex and pour a glass of wine. She'd hated that.

She sighed, not wanting to think about the past, much less the future, wishing she could stay right where she was for a long, long time, content in the bliss of the best sex she'd ever had, probably anyone ever had, snuggled up close to this amazingly talented man.

Hmm. Was it a talent? Or experience? She turned her head to plant a kiss on his damp chest. Whatever. Who cared? Dean had aroused her beyond anything she'd ever imagined, taking her to the brink of complete dissolution, to where she utterly lost herself in him. Remembering the power of her orgasm, the taste of him in her mouth, still feeling the sweet friction between her legs, she shivered.

"Are you okay?" he murmured, raising his head to look at her.

"Oh, yeah," she said meaningfully.

"Thank God," he muttered, plopping his head back down, tightening his arm around her to draw her closer. "Because I'd be no help right now. You've destroyed me, woman."

"I destroyed *you*?"

"Maybe *annihilated* is a better word." He laughed, his chest rumbling with the sound beneath her cheek. "You feeling the same way?"

"Pretty much," she murmured, thrilled with the idea that she'd affected him as strongly as he'd affected her. Annihilated? Yeah, that perfectly described the sensual experience they'd just shared.

"Pretty much?" Dean asked, his tone indignant as he lazily stroked a finger up and down her arm. "That's a *pretty* lukewarm response. Give me a minute—well, maybe five—to recover, and I'll try to do better."

Grinning, she propped herself on an arm to study

his face. He gazed at her, the intensity in his eyes belying the humorous tone of his words. She placed her lips against his to give him a light kiss. Pulling back, she said, "I don't see how you could top that."

He stroked her cheek, shaking his head as he stared into her eyes. Then he slid his hand behind her neck, pulled her to him and kissed her thoroughly, as if trying to convey some emotion neither of them could yet name.

She broke the kiss and again placed her cheek on his chest, relishing the warmth and weight of his hand against her head until he began to absently comb his fingers through her tangled hair. She closed her eyes. How could Dean know such sweet, intimate, sexy things to do? How could this dangerous bad boy, a man who hunted other men for a living, probably killing them when necessary, make her feel so whole, so content, so at peace with the world?

She'd felt the controlled power of his body, his ferocity as he'd made love to her. Fierce and controlling, yes, that described Dean perfectly. But yet he could also be gentle, caring, considerate of her feelings. She sensed he understood her, how she felt about her parents, better than anyone ever had. Maybe that explained why she was so drawn to him.

But she didn't understand him.

"Have you ever killed anybody?" she asked, surprising herself with the question. She stared across her bedroom, looking at nothing. "A human being, I mean."

His fingers stilled. "I'm a police officer, Junie."

"I know, but—"

"Yes, I killed a man once in the line of duty."

When she didn't respond, he said, "This is ugly, June. Do you really want to talk about it right now?"

His words frightened her. Maybe he was right. Maybe she didn't want to know him. This thing between them was temporary, purely sexual, the result of two strangers being thrown together under highly charged circumstances. When he solved the murders, he'd move on to his next exciting case, another set of witnesses. She should let it go.

But she said, "You know everything about me. I'd like to know you better."

"And even though I'm a cop it bothers you that I've killed?"

"Not if it was you or him."

"It was either him or two kids he was holding hostage. When I took the shot, he held a Glock against the skull of a terrified eight-year-old and announced he was going to show the cops he meant business. My only safe shot was a kill shot."

She sucked in a quick breath at the scene playing out in her head. "Were the kids okay?"

"Definitely traumatized, but both still breathing."

"Did you get a medal?"

Dean issued a sound that was half snort, half laugh. "Actually, I got busted back to patrol for acting before my superior gave the go-ahead."

"But if you hadn't acted…"

"At least one of the kids wouldn't have made it out alive." He fell silent, absently stroking her arm again.

She gave him a gentle squeeze, realizing she'd forced him to relive painful memories. Most times it was better not to think about ghosts from a haunting past. She of all people should have known better. Why had she done this to Dean? Sometimes she could be a real jerk.

"I'm sorry," she said. "I—"

In an unexpected, swift motion, he flipped them so that she was under him again. Her words got lost and she heard herself laugh breathlessly. His forearms rested on either side of her head as he stared down at her.

"Forget it," he said. "As it turns out I'm more than okay with my punishment."

"You are?"

"Damn right."

She nodded, loving the smoky expression that had crept into his eyes. "Because in your heart you know you did the right thing that day," she said.

"Well, there's that," Dean agreed, "but I just got it that being on patrol again is how I met you."

She grinned and lifted her hand to touch his cheek. "When you answered the call to the pet shop?"

"Carrying out my sworn duty to put down a bird riot stirred up by a gorgeous do-gooder."

"Activist," she corrected, noticing that his hips now moved rhythmically against her again, creating that sweet, sensual pull on her center, and she decided he'd forgiven her. She parted her legs and reached her hand between them to stroke a growing erection.

He sucked in a breath and positioned himself in just the right place. "Activist," he repeated. "You just love to stir things up, don't you, June?"

She wrapped her arms around his neck and pulled him to her. "Your five minutes are up."

WHEN JUNE AWOKE the next morning, Dean was gone. She sighed and stretched long on her bed, wrapped in delicious memories of the previous evening.

At some point in the night—maybe around nine when they realized they were ravenous and got their butts out of bed to eat something—she'd given him the code for her alarm so he could rearm the system when he left the next morning. She'd teased him about being overly protective, but he hadn't cracked a smile, so she gave it to him to avoid a lecture. Later, she vaguely remembered his wrist alarm beeping while it was still dark, him rolling out of bed, kissing her, telling her he had to go, he'd call her later.

She smoothed her hand down her belly to cup her center. A little tender and definitely sticky. They'd showered together around midnight—she closed her eyes, remembering how Dean had gently soaped and massaged her breasts—but afterward, well, there'd been more stirring up and definitely some activism, and now she needed another shower.

She placed her feet on the floor and shrugged on a robe. Should she feel guilty for spending most of the previous twelve hours playing naked games with Dean? Maybe she should, but she didn't. No way. Not when every cell in her body tingled with the joy of just being alive.

There'd be time for regrets later, but not yet.

Yawning, she padded into the kitchen to start coffee. She had to leave twenty minutes earlier for work because she couldn't depend on the bus being on time. She sighed. Walking was so much easier and quicker, but Dean insisted a sniper could be waiting for her at the top of a high-rise. And he ought to know.

He'd killed by sighting a man's beating heart down the scope of a rifle.

She paused in scooping grounds into her machine, remembering the story he'd told her last night. She shivered, wondering how he lived with an ever-present threat of violence. Perhaps Dean had more ghosts to live with than she did.

More alert after her first sip of caffeine, June found a note from him on the dining room table.

"Out of town today with Sanchez re Kublin at Sunrise Clinic. You can reach me on my cell." *Considerate.*

"Stay away from windows and doors." *Hardly romantic.*

"Take the bus to work." *Dictatorial.*

"I'll call you tonight." *Better.*

She folded the paper and tucked it into her purse. Damn. She was analyzing his note as if it were a coded message from the CIA. She regretted nothing they'd done, but did he? She couldn't help wondering what Dean was thinking today, how he felt about last night in the harsh light of day. She wished she could talk to him, judge his reaction.

Pitiful. She wouldn't call him for that.

Did all women obsess after making love with a man for the first time? Did men ever think about the repercussions of sex, how a little time together naked changed everything between two people?

Lazarus squawked, and she moved to the aviary. "I agree, big boy. Not likely."

In response, the macaw raised his giant claw and scratched his head.

Laz had been quiet last night, but she ought to give him some attention this morning. She glanced at her watch. She also needed to clean the aviary, so she should get her butt moving.

While she was working on the balcony, the phone rang. Thinking it was rather early for calls—but hoping it could be Dean—June hurried inside to answer.

"It's Jared. Did you see my email?"

June sat on the sofa. "No. I haven't been online in a while." *Too busy having wild sex to worry about bird society business.*

"You didn't answer the phone, either."

"Sorry," June said, remembering, yeah, the phone had rung and quite insistently, but they'd ignored it. Dean said if it was police business, they'd call his cell.

"I need your help," Jared said after a pause. "We have a situation in the Redlands with the buntings."

She stood. "You've found a trap?"

"Damn right. Didn't you tell me your office was closed today?"

"What? Oh, right." Perhaps that wild sex had destroyed her memory. Dr. Trujillo was attending a seminar in Boca Raton today, so they'd scheduled no appointments. Elaine was staying home. June had intended to go in to make follow-up phone calls and do some filing, but she didn't have to.

"I want to be there when the poacher shows up," Jared said. "Probably around nightfall."

"Did you release the birds?"

"Of course, but there may be more overnight. I left the trap in place to lure the poacher in."

"Were any buntings injured?" June closed her eyes against the image of a tiny, magnificently colored bird cowering in a wire cage while suffering with a broken wing.

"No."

She released a breath. "Thank goodness. I'll call Agent Gillis. Fish and Wildlife needs to be there."

"I already left him a message," Jared said.

"That's not good enough. I have his cell number. I won't go unless I reach him."

"What's got you so spooked?"

"Never mind. What time can you pick me up?"

"I'll be out front at noon."

CHAPTER SIXTEEN

DEAN ASSESSED THE dignified man sitting across the massive oak desk from him and Sanchez. Dr. Avery Harkness, medical director of Sunrise Rehabilitative Clinic, appeared to be in his sixties, graying, but otherwise aging well. Trim, very little paunch. Neatly manicured fingernails. He wore a white lab coat over a pale yellow dress shirt and blue tie. Professional, pleasant, yet on guard. Not panicked, but definitely concerned about the outcome of this interview.

As he effing well should be. Here was the man in charge, and he'd lost a murderer from the grounds of his facility.

Dr. Harkness folded his hands on the desk and leaned forward. "I'm confident you understand about patient confidentiality, Detectives."

Dean slammed the warrant on the desk.

Dr. Harkness sighed. "I understand you have a warrant, but—"

"And I understand you lost a homicidal maniac from this hospital," Dean interrupted. "A man who went on to murder two more citizens after your security failure."

The doctor paled at Dean's words. "There have been more deaths?"

"And we have no reason to believe the killing will stop."

Harkness shook his head. "I don't believe Al Kublin is a murderer. In fact, I don't believe he is capable of harming anyone."

Dean narrowed his eyes at the doctor. Now they were getting somewhere. "Why?"

"Al is a gentle soul," Harkness said, leaning back in his chair. "I've been treating him for years and am convinced he was wrongly convicted, which ruined his life. His wife divorced him and remarried."

"So he was framed?" Dean asked, trying not to sound sarcastic.

"Let's say I believe a mistake was made. Al worshipped the Lathams, felt he owed them everything and would never have harmed them."

"But this couple Kublin adored had been accused of smuggling. How did he justify his worship in light of that crime?"

The doctor picked up a pen and tapped it on his desk, obviously considering. "Look, I know this will sound like the ravings of a convicted lunatic, but Al maintained the Lathams were innocent, that they would never break the law."

"Okay. If Kublin is such a sane, stand-up guy, why did he bust out of here?"

"He didn't bust out. Because of excellent behavior, he'd been afforded certain privileges, and frankly never came back from a walk one morning."

"I don't care how. I want to know why," Dean said.

"To right the wrong."

"What do you mean?" Dean asked.

"He wants to prove the Lathams were innocent, that he was innocent."

"How is he going to do that?" Sanchez asked, speaking for the first time.

Good, Dean thought approvingly of his rookie. *Keep the subject off balance, come at him from a different direction.*

"That's an excellent question," the doctor replied. "I don't know. However, there was a daughter that—"

"You think he'll go after the Lathams' daughter?" Dean demanded.

"No, not go after her. I think it's more likely he'll seek her out, maybe try to protect her. In Al's mind, this daughter is another victim of a horrible injustice. It bothers him that she would never know what he sees as the truth."

Dean stared at the doctor. Actually, that theory went along the same path as his own thoughts. What if June's parents weren't criminals? What if there had been a frame and a fire to cover up any evidence? Not to mention the fact that Kublin had no history of skill as a sharpshooter. He could have hired a pro, but Kublin didn't make the actual kills. And where would he get the money for hits? Even if he'd stashed away cash before his conviction, it'd be hard to access.

"The only pathology I see in Al is he's fixated on a conspiracy theory," Harkness continued. "He believes whoever framed him will try to kill him to shut him up, and maybe go after the daughter, too."

"So why now?" Dean asked. "After all these years,

why would Kublin decide to go back out into the world and set the record straight?"

Harkness looked down at his hands, dropped the pen and shook his head again. "You're putting me in a difficult ethical position."

"Your escaped patient is connected to two brutal murders," Dean said.

"You're certain?"

"He's all over them," Dean said. "We're trying to prevent another death."

The doctor released a heavy sigh. "I guess Al won't be around to sue me anyway. He's got pancreatic cancer, a few months to live at most. I think he escaped to find the Lathams' daughter, to let her know her parents were innocent before the truth died with him."

"And you didn't think you needed to tell anyone about this theory?" Dean asked.

"But I did," Harkness insisted. "I reported everything to the county sheriff. And in my medical opinion, Al is not a danger to anyone except himself. Between his illness and the years of wrongful incarceration, the man is terrified of every noise."

"It meant that much to him for the girl to know the truth?" Sanchez asked.

The doctor nodded. "I believe it's the only thing keeping him alive."

"So, Hawk, what do you think?" Sanchez asked as they returned to the Crown Vic.

Dean tossed him the keys. "I think it's your turn to drive."

Sanchez grinned and slid behind the wheel. Dean climbed into the passenger seat and snapped the seat belt in place. Sanchez fiddled with the electric seat, finding just the right position, adjusted the rearview and side mirrors, tilted the angle of the computer to better suit him and then finally started the car.

Dean smothered a grin of his own. Damn rookie had been itching to drive since they partnered up.

"Let me hear your assessment of that interview," Dean asked when they'd accelerated onto I-95, headed back south.

Sanchez remained quiet a moment. Dean liked that. Showed the kid had a brain and wasn't afraid to use it.

"Harkness was nervous, edgy," Sanchez began, his eyes focused on the road. "He knew he'd royally screwed up by letting Kublin escape, but it's not his fault the sheriff buried the report."

Dean nodded. *Good start.*

"I sensed the doctor was telling us the truth. He's convinced Kublin wouldn't hurt anyone. I examined the credentials hanging in his office, and the doc is well qualified, someone who should be able to tell when a patient he's been treating for years is about to go postal."

"So, what does that mean?"

"Kublin isn't our shooter. It fits with what we saw on the surveillance video at the hotel on North Beach. If this loony tunes patient believed someone wanted to off him, he could have invited the homeless guy up for a shield, a decoy."

"What about the hit at the Turf Club?"

"We have no proof Kublin was even there. The shooter could have been after June Latham, tying up loose ends knowing Kublin was on the lam and maybe looking for him at the party since June was there. The shooter made another mistake."

"Two mistakes," Dean muttered. "Unlikely for someone as skilled as our sniper."

Sanchez nodded. "I thought about that. But if any of this is right on, then the shooter has been living with this shit for ten years. Guilt can eat at you, create errors."

"Did you learn that in your sensitivity training?"

"Nah," Sanchez said, "Psychology 101."

"Good job, Sanchez," Dean said. *This rookie just might make a good cop.*

"Then you agree?" Sanchez asked, shooting Dean a glance.

"I've been trying to talk myself out of it, but the theory the Lathams were framed and murdered just won't go away."

"Does June know you feel that way?" Sanchez asked, his tone hesitant for the first time.

"Let's leave June out of this," Dean said. Damn, had Sanchez picked up on his attraction to their witness? He'd have to be more careful. If his lieutenant learned he'd started something with June, he'd be slammed back to patrol.

Sanchez shrugged.

"So, assuming any of this is true," Dean continued, "which means an innocent man has been in prison for ten years, who is our shooter? Who would want June and Kublin dead?"

Sanchez drummed fingers on the steering wheel for several long seconds. "Whoever set the fire that killed two people."

"What does that say about the case against the Lathams?"

"That they were being framed by the real smuggler."

Dean rubbed his eyes. Damn. He hated to think law enforcement had screwed up a murder case this badly.

A woman began warbling "We've Only Just Begun" from the area of Sanchez's hip. By now, Dean recognized the ringtone for the rookie's new wife. She always called at least once during his shift, but they'd only been married three months.

"That's Tina," Sanchez said.

"I know. Can you drive and talk at the same time?"

Sanchez threw him a look. Dean grinned and pretended to read his notes so his partner wouldn't think he was listening to his marital conversation.

Must be nice, though, to have someone care about you so much that she couldn't stand not to hear your voice for ten hours. He knew June wouldn't call him unless there was an emergency. She wasn't the clingy type. He told himself he liked that.

He stared at his notes as he realized the path his thoughts had traveled. He was comparing June to Sanchez's wife. *Wife*. As in married, hooked up for life. He wasn't the type for that one-woman-for-all-time shit. His job was too dangerous. He didn't want to make any woman a widow or a single mom struggling to raise kids like his own mother.

But he conjured an image of the way June had looked this morning when he left her: warm, soft, sexy. He shifted in his seat. Be damn nice to wake up to that every morning.

He'd avoided thinking about last night by yacking with Sanchez for most of the trip, but now he couldn't get June out of his head. Last night changed everything. He'd known it would. He'd tried like hell to resist her. Even before they'd made love, she'd created a need to protect far beyond any normal police duty. He couldn't stay away from her. Now he didn't want to stay away from her.

What was she doing right now? She'd damn well better have taken the bus to and from work.

If this new theory was correct, then her friend Sandy *had* died in her place. With June's overdeveloped sense of responsibility, she'd torture herself if he confirmed that. He didn't want to start keeping secrets, but he couldn't tell her about his current thinking—at least not until certain. He needed to control the situation. No telling how she'd react to the idea the parents she thought she hated might be innocent. Better to keep her in the dark.

"So, what's our next step, Hawk?" Sanchez asked, hooking the cell phone back onto his belt. "We've got the country club vic's husband coming in for a second interview tomorrow at nine thirty a.m."

Dean forced his thoughts back to the case. First things first. He needed to solve the murders. He'd worry about June constantly until he did.

"I want to reach out to the lead investigator in the old case against the Lathams," Dean said, "and see what shakes loose."

DEEP IN THE heart of the Redlands, fifty miles south of Miami, June leaned against the trunk of a gumbo-limbo tree. Overhead, the thick canopy of a rockland hammock didn't permit much light, but she raised field glasses to focus on the wire trap suspended from a live oak tree fifty feet across a small clearing. She identified a male painted bunting frantically flitting around inside, struggling to escape. No other bird that size had a red breast and blue head. Their striking beauty was what made them desirable to the scum who trapped them.

She itched to release the tiny, frightened creature, but waited, hoping the poacher would show. They needed to catch him in the act. This clearing, situated deep in the hammock, was well-known to birders wanting to sight a bunting.

Beside her, Jared slapped his palm against a cheek.

"Shhh," she hissed. "Put on some more repellant." It was near dusk, the time mosquitoes came out to feed on human blood.

"I'm already drowning in chemicals," he whispered.

June lowered her binocs. They had been lurking behind trees for two hours. Agent Gillis was hidden out here somewhere, too, waiting on the poacher. He'd texted her when he arrived. She knew Gillis wasn't happy with her, but they needed FWC to make an arrest because otherwise the poacher would be free to leave. And she felt safe knowing law enforcement was close by. Dean should be pleased by her caution.

She bit her lip. No, the man was so controlling he'd likely be furious even with Agent Gillis along for protection. Dean wanted her cowering inside her apartment. *No way, Detective Hammer.*

She just wouldn't tell him about this field trip. No reason to worry him. Anyway, for sure the sniper couldn't track her out here. Jared's car had been hidden by the overhang at the Enclave when she jumped inside.

"Did you hear that?" Jared whispered.

"Yeah, someone's coming," June replied, raising her binocs again, startled to see a young dark-haired female emerge into the clearing off the trail she and Jared had hiked. The woman carried a transport cage, obviously intending to take any captured buntings with her.

Jared, also looking through binoculars, cursed softly. "That's Louise Pembroke."

"Oh, my God. You're right," June said. "Did you tell her about—"

"Yes," Louise shouted when she could see the trap,

raising a fisted hand triumphantly into the air. "I got you, my beauty. Come to mama and make me rich."

"Oh, no," June murmured, watching Louise, an active member of Tropical Bird Society, even a frequent tagalong on her bird walks, approach the trap with the second cage.

Louise was their poacher? Stunned, June lowered her field glasses.

"That bitch," Jared snarled. He leaped to his feet and ran into the clearing. "You stop right there, Louise."

Louise whirled, her mouth open in horror. She dropped the cage.

"Jared, wait," June shouted, running after him. What if Louise had a weapon? Poaching was seriously illegal shit. And seriously lucrative if you knew who wanted to possess wild birds. Where was Gillis?

"Benedict Arnold," Jared yelled when he reached Louise. He picked up the dropped cage and threw it across the clearing. The cage shattered into three pieces when it hit the ground. "Judas. Brutus."

Louise held up her arms and took a step back. "Calm down, Jared."

Out of breath, June reached Jared's side. "How could you, Louise? How could you?"

"Everyone freeze." The booming voice came from the west side of the hammock.

June turned, and sighed in relief as Agent Gillis, carrying a large rifle, stepped into the clearing.

Then everyone began shouting at the same time.

Red in the face, Jared gesticulated wildly. Louise sobbed. June demanded answers from Louise, a woman she considered, if not a friend, certainly a colleague in the war to save birds.

"Quiet," Gillis yelled, finally imposing order on chaos.

Except for Louise's sniffles, silence reigned in the clearing.

"Thank you," Gillis said. After leaning his weapon against the oak, he took several photographs of the captured bunting and then opened the trap.

June felt herself relax as the colorful bird flew away, disappearing safely into the hammock. She sent a prayer after him. *Be happy and free.*

Gillis turned to June with narrowed eyes. "We've talked about this sort of activity, how dangerous it is."

She looked away, not answering. What could she say? She'd made her choice, and she'd chosen on the side of the bunting.

Gillis shook his head. "I want the two of you to leave," he said, nodding to June and Jared.

"Aren't you going to arrest her?" Jared demanded. "She's a traitor. A hypocrite."

"I need the money," Louise said and began to cry again. "I lost my job."

"Your membership in Tropical Bird Society is hereby rescinded," Jared announced. "I'm president," he said to Gillis, as if in explanation.

Gillis sighed. "Fish and Wildlife will handle this from here. It's nothing for a private citizen to be concerned with."

"Come on, Jared," June said, hooking her arm in his. "Let's get out of here and let Agent Gillis do his job."

"Snake," Jared yelled at Louise, but let June lead him away.

A gnawing sense of betrayal ate at June as they hurried on the darkening path toward Jared's car. How could Louise of all people trap a precious bunting? Jared was right. She was a traitor, taking advantage of information provided by their society to trap a bunting for her own profit.

Did you ever really know anyone? Did everyone, like her parents, have a secret heart that you couldn't trust? Her thoughts wandered to Dean. Could she trust a man who wanted to control everyone and everything around him? Especially her?

"Want to grab some dinner?" Jared asked.

"Why not?" she answered. Dean wouldn't be home from Melbourne until very late. She wouldn't see him tonight. "We deserve to celebrate."

But she needed to explain things to Jared, let him know that they were just friends and always would be. She hadn't seen it before, but Dean's comments had made her notice Jared harbored romantic feelings toward her. She needed to let him down easy. She liked Jared.

But what she felt for Dean had morphed into something quite…different. Something she wasn't certain she could count on.

AT HIS DESK the next morning, Dean thumbed through the box on the Latham fire, searching for a report with the name of the lead investigator. He could almost recall it. Dan or Daniel? Ah, there it was. Betty Daniels. Was she still on the job? Where was his old directory? He shoved aside the box Agent Gillis had sent via courier.

"Hawk."

"Yeah?" Dean looked up to find Sanchez standing by his desk.

"Paul Taylor is waiting in Interview Room Two," Sanchez said.

"Excellent." Betty Daniels could wait an hour. Taylor was no longer on his radar as a suspect—the case had moved in a new direction—but best practice meant he'd conduct this final interview and eliminate the husband once and for all.

"He's drunk," Sanchez said.

"What?"

"Mr. Taylor has been drinking. I can smell booze on his breath."

"A bit early." Dean glanced at his watch. Ten-fifteen. Taylor was forty-five minutes late for the interview and impaired. Interesting.

Sanchez shrugged. "It's five o'clock somewhere."

"Let's let him stew for ten minutes and see what happens," Dean said.

He and Sanchez moved into the observation room to watch Taylor through the one-way mirror.

The vic's husband had altered significantly since

the country-club murder. He'd lost weight, and dark circles extended below puffy eyes. He wore a suit, but the jacket and pants needed pressing. White dress shirt featured a mysterious stain that looked like coffee. Loose tie. Dark hair needed a trim. The guy slouched in the chair as if he was too tired to sit up straight.

Was Taylor suffering from guilt or grief?

Beside him, Sanchez snickered when Taylor pulled a plastic flask from inside his jacket and took a healthy swallow.

"A little liquid courage," Dean muttered. "Let's go have a chat with our grieving husband."

Taylor stared at Dean through dull eyes when he and Sanchez sat across the interview table. Yeah, the guy reeked of booze.

"How are you doing, Mr. Taylor?" Dean asked respectfully.

"Not so great," Taylor said.

And not so drunk that his words were slurred, Dean noted.

Taylor's gaze shifted from Dean to Sanchez and back. "Have you arrested my wife's murderer?"

"Not yet, sir, but we have a number of new leads," Dean said.

Taylor scratched his head, and Dean noted dirty fingernails. This guy was really in trouble. Was he even going to his office?

"I was hoping that's why you asked me to come in again."

"We just have a few more questions."

Taylor nodded. "I know I'm a suspect. The husband always is." His voice broke. "I still can't believe she's gone. Sandy has been my best friend since high school."

"I'm sorry for your loss."

"Yeah, yeah." Taylor waved away the flimsy platitude. "I can't help thinking it *is* my fault."

"How is that, sir?"

"You likely already know this—" Taylor threw him a look "— but I'd been working a lot lately. Well, more than lately. Last couple of years. I neglected Sandy. So much that she thought I was cheating on her."

"Was there another woman?"

"Never. I swear."

Dean nodded. Their investigation hadn't turned up any lovers for the husband.

Taylor hung his head. "I loved my wife. I thought I was building our future, but if I'd been a better husband, maybe we wouldn't have been at that damn party and she'd still be alive."

Dean chose his next words carefully. "Is there any chance that your wife could have gotten so tired of your neglect that she began seeing someone else?"

"What?" Taylor stiffened. "You mean Sandy take a lover?"

"We have to consider the possibility of a boyfriend killing her in a fit of jealous rage."

"Oh, my God. Have you found evidence of a lover?" Taylor asked, his voice ragged with pain.

"No, sir. Rest assured we have not. And you didn't have any suspicions?"

Taylor released a breath and relaxed slightly. "Not a one. No, my Sandy wouldn't do that to me." He hung his head again. "She loved me. I know she did. She was my best friend."

"Yes, sir. I'm sure she was."

Dean glanced at Sanchez and raised his eyebrows to see if he had any questions. The rookie shook his head. They agreed Taylor's demeanor and actions were appropriate for his horrific loss.

"Your whole life can change in a heartbeat," Taylor said wonderingly. "You always hear that stupid saying, but you don't know how true it is until something really bad happens to you."

"May I give you some advice, Mr. Taylor?"

Taylor looked up, meeting Dean's gaze.

"You won't find your way out of this tragedy in a bottle. Don't dishonor your wife by becoming a drunk and destroying the rest of your life."

Taylor gave a sad smile. "But that's the problem, Detective. Without Sandy, I haven't got a life."

Dean stood. So did Sanchez, their chairs sliding across the concrete flooring. "It just seems that way right now. Good luck, sir," Dean said, offering his hand.

Taylor stood, a little unsteadily, and shook Dean's hand. "When can I have my wife's body?" he asked, his voice breaking again. "I'd like to have a funeral."

Dean nodded. A memorial service might provide

this guy a little closure—if such a thing actually existed. "The ME should release the body soon. I'll see what I can find out and let you know."

CHAPTER SEVENTEEN

AFTER A DIFFICULT SEARCH, Dean found a good phone number for Betty Daniels late Thursday afternoon. Betty had been the first female African-American detective in their department, a much-respected and decorated officer. She'd retired to Stuart, Florida, seven years ago to raise grandkids, fish and live the good life.

And apparently she was doing just that today, because she didn't answer repeated phone calls. Dean left several messages while he and Sanchez reviewed old case files.

He had better luck with the medical examiner's office. After a little prodding, he got the ME to agree to release Sandy Taylor's body.

He reached Paul Taylor at home around 5:00 p.m. to give him the message. The grieving husband's words were now definitely slurred, so obviously he'd kept drinking all day. Too bad. Would the information about his wife penetrate the thick fog of alcohol clouding Taylor's brain? Would he even remember their conversation? Dean felt for the guy. Maybe he'd suggest June reach out to her friend's widower to check on how he was doing. No question June would attend any services. Would she want him to accompany her? He would if she asked.

Dean sat back in his chair and relaxed, his mood drastically improved as he thought about calling June.

Sanchez had gone off shift an hour ago, and he was free to go, as well. June was expecting him after work, although it was too late now to pick her up at the animal clinic. He planned to grab some Chinese so they could eat in. He didn't want her out in the open until he found the shooter. They'd discuss his trip to Melbourne and hopefully—

His desk phone rang, and he grabbed it. "Hammer."

"Detective Hammer, this is Agent Don Gillis."

"Yes, Agent Gillis. Thank you for the files. I've spent the day reviewing them."

"I hope they were helpful."

"Somewhat," Dean said vaguely. Gillis hadn't provided anything new. "Every bit of information helps. It's just a matter of finding the right thread to pull."

"I hear you. By the way, you should probably know June is up to her old tricks."

"What are you talking about?"

"She and one of her colleagues, a man named Jared, confronted a poacher at a trap down in the Redlands last night."

"Poacher? Explain."

"Some jerks like to capture wild birds and sell them to collectors. The captive birds always die within weeks, if not days, but, hey, someone made a tidy profit, right? June's bird group tries to stop the trapping."

"And you're telling me June traveled to the Redlands to confront a criminal over a trapped bird?" Dean demanded, a slow burn of anger igniting in his gut.

"Yeah."

"I'm assuming this was out in the middle of the woods where wild birds hang out, somewhere isolated."

"You got it. I've warned her repeatedly about this sort of activity," Gillis said, "but she ignores me. I'm worried she's going to get hurt. Maybe you'll have better luck convincing her."

Dean closed his eyes. *Fat chance, since she obviously ignores me, too.* "Yeah, thanks, man."

Dean sat at his desk for five long minutes trying to wrestle his fury into a manageable, ordinary anger. Did the woman have a death wish? How could she take a chance like that with someone already gunning for her?

Yeah, he understood how she felt about the stupid birds. He even understood why she wanted to save them all. The pet-shop escapade had been dangerous, yes, but confronting a criminal in the middle of an isolated forest was reckless beyond any possible— He paused his careening thoughts and drummed his fingers across the metal desk.

Reckless. He was accusing June of behaving recklessly. How ironic that he was furious with her for the very thing he'd been busted back to patrol for not so very long ago.

He shook his head. But he was a trained officer, had never taken a risk that wasn't justified. How could he convince her to stop this shit until he identified the sniper?

JUNE EXITED THE bus at the Enclave's stop and hurried under the overhang to get out of view of anybody watching for her. Damn Dean. She hated having to live this way.

But a buzz of anticipation surged through her as she conjured an image of his penetrating blue eyes. She wanted to get upstairs and clean the aviary before he arrived. Entering the Enclave's lobby, she felt a smile form as she decided to take a quick shower herself. *A girl should always be prepared.*

"Hello, Junie," Magda called out.

"Hi, Maggie Mae. I'm expecting a visitor later."

Magda nodded. "I'll send him up."

Wondering how Magda knew her visitor would be a male, June punched the button to call the elevator. *Am I that obvious?*

When the elevator doors opened, June stiffened. Mr. DiNovio stood inside. As horrified recognition spread across his face, and his eyes widened in what June took for fear. His face flushed a deep red.

What a way to destroy a good mood. But she'd known this would happen sooner or later.

Very dramatically, she took a huge step to the side, gesturing for him to pass by.

Mr. DiNovio swallowed, his Adam's apple bobbing, and hurried away without saying a word. June glared after him. *What, no apology?* Realizing the elevator doors were closing, she jumped inside the car.

While cleaning the aerie, she refused to brood on her neighbor. She'd much rather think about more pleasant things—like Dean. How did his trip to Melbourne turn out? She wondered if the shrink gave him the information he wanted about Kublin or if that all-important patient confidentiality got in the way. As she changed Laz's water, she remembered Dean could be very persuasive. Likely he'd had at least some success.

Lazarus squawked when she returned with sliced banana and apple.

"Does that mean you agree with me about Detective Hammer, Laz?" she asked.

The macaw dipped his head, a sure sign that he wanted attention, and June stroked the silky soft feathers.

"You're getting better, aren't you, boy?" she murmured. Head still lowered, Laz pressed deeper into her touch, shifting his weight from claw to claw. "Feels good, doesn't it?"

She shivered, wished Dean would get his slow ass here and moved into the bathroom to prepare for his arrival.

Warm and relaxed from a shower, she found a bottle of Uncle Mike's favorite Napa Valley cabernet and pulled the cork to allow the wine to breathe. Next she arranged a wedge of smoked Gouda and pepper crackers on a plate. As she placed two crystal stem glasses beside the wine bottle, she frowned at her offering on the granite counter. *Is this an obvious seduction? What's come over me?*

She shrugged. So what? Dean wouldn't care.

She grabbed the phone when it rang.

"Detective Hammer is on his way," Magda announced.

"Thanks."

"Just a heads-up, Junie. He doesn't appear to be in as good a mood as you."

Worried that something had gone wrong in Melbourne, June waited by the front door. Had he learned something ominous about Kublin? She peeked through the security window as soon as the elevator pinged. When Dean appeared, she flung open the front door.

God, he looked good. How could she forget how tall he was, how muscular?

"I confirmed it was you," she said before he could complain about greeting him before the knock.

"How nice to know you are so very concerned about safety." Dean marched into the room, barely looking at her. He carried a bag emanating a delicious garlicky fragrance and plopped it on her dining room table.

She stared after him. This wasn't exactly how she'd envisioned their reunion. She locked the door and reset the alarm.

"What's wrong?" she asked.

He whirled. "Were you going to tell me about your bird-rescue adventure yesterday?"

"Oh. That." S*hit. How did he find out?*

"Yeah, that."

"I didn't go alone."

He advanced swiftly back in her direction, forcing her to retreat a step.

"That's right," he said, looming over her, hands on his hips. "You invited the intrepid Jared, a man who wants to jump your bones, out into the middle of a secluded forest."

"No," she said, lifting her chin. "He invited me."

"Oh, that makes it better. What were you thinking?" Dean demanded, breathing hot fury at her.

"I was thinking I could save beautiful buntings."

"Damn the buntings! What if the shooter followed you out there? Your body might not have been found for days. Maybe weeks. Maybe never."

She took a deep breath. "I called Agent Gillis. Plus, I made certain I wasn't followed."

He placed his large hands on her shoulders as if he was going to shake her. He didn't. He stared into her eyes, searching, as if trying to understand her, and merely gave a gentle squeeze. "June," he said softly, "how could you be certain?"

She stared up at him, opened her mouth to speak, but couldn't formulate a response.

And then she didn't have to because his mouth was on hers, hungry, greedy and, yes, more than a little angry as he pulled her toward him. Of course Dean was angry. She'd ignored his warnings. She flung her arms around his neck, combed her fingers into his thick ebony hair. *But he still wants me. Even if he can't control me.*

Still kissing her, he lowered his hand to her buttocks and pressed her hard against his erection. Helpless to resist him, not wanting to resist him, she moaned into his mouth. Without saying another word, he lifted her off her feet and carried her into the bedroom.

DEAN LAY BESIDE JUNE, lazily stroking her arm, still needing to find a way to convince her of the danger. Trouble was, after such explosive, satisfying sex, his brain wasn't quite ready to work again.

"How did you find out about the bunting trip?" June asked. Her cheek rested on his chest, so he felt the soft whisper of her breath as she spoke.

"Agent Gillis called me."

"You talked to Gillis?"

"I asked for his file on your parents' case."

"Oh," she said softly. "Of course."

"Were you going to tell me about your trip into the jungle?"

She rolled away, and he had his answer. So they'd already started keeping things from each other. Hell, this thing with June—whatever it was—had barely begun and was already about to crash and burn. Strange. He was the one who usually kept secrets.

Hadn't he decided not to tell her his new theory where her parents were innocent? Maybe he should rethink that.

"I knew you'd be angry that I went out into the hammock," she said in a quiet voice, staring at the ceiling. "I didn't want to fight with you."

"I can't protect you if I don't know what you're doing."

"I alerted Gillis. So did Jared. And the trapper was

a woman we knew, a member of our club even. We were never in any danger."

"But you didn't know that."

"No."

She rose from the bed. He watched her, enjoying the sight of her naked flesh, the strong, muscled lines of her lithe swimmer's body. She had a natural grace that made her impossible to resist. And God, those gorgeous breasts. Long, sexy legs. He wondered if he'd ever get enough of her.

She wrapped a light blue silky-looking robe around herself, cinching it at the waist, and moved into the outer room without speaking.

Dean closed his eyes. This was why he'd made the rule to never get involved with women on his cases. Look at this shitty mess. Worrying about her would interfere with his focus on the evidence, on how to proceed with the investigation.

But he'd worry whether he'd made love to her or not. No point in denying himself the perks.

She returned carrying a tray of cheese and two glasses of wine. She placed the tray on a side table, sat next to him on the bed and held up a bit of cheese. Smiling, she moved the morsel toward his face to tempt him. He opened his mouth and took the length of her fingers inside, sucking as she withdrew. She closed her eyes, obviously enjoying the sensation.

He swallowed the tangy cheese, watching her face, wondering what she was thinking.

When she opened her eyes, she smoothed the tips

of her fingers across his lips. Was this an apology? Not bad. But she wasn't getting off this easy.

"You need some sustenance," she said.

"You do wear me out, woman."

"Thanks for bringing dinner."

"Sure." So they weren't going to discuss the bunting trip anymore. Damn, but June was frustrating.

She handed him a glass of wine and raised hers in a toast. "I promise to tell you what I'm doing from now on." She clinked her glass against his.

"So you don't promise to behave. You just promise to tell me about reckless trips into the wild afterward?"

She raised her eyebrows. "Behave?"

"You know what I mean." He tasted the wine, keeping his gaze locked on hers.

She took a sip of her own, staring at him over the rim of the glass.

The phone rang before either of them could say anything else. Obviously relieved by the interruption, June snatched the phone off the side table.

Her face clouded after her hello.

"Paul. Hi. How are you?"

Dean took another sip of wine. The grieving husband. How drunk was he by now?

SHE WAS GLAD that Paul had finally returned her calls—in part because his timing broke the tension between her and Dean. Nevertheless, June met his gaze. *Paul Taylor*, she mouthed.

Dean nodded and sat higher in bed.

"I've been worried," she said into the phone. "I left several messages."

"Yeah, I know," Paul replied, with slurred words. "Sorry I haven't called you back. Been…I don't know. Not busy."

"Is everything okay?" June wanted to snatch the words back the minute she said them. What a stupid question.

"Okay?" He laughed without humor.

June's stomach clenched. She looked at Dean again and mouthed, *He's drunk.*

Dean frowned, his gaze intent on her.

"Nothing is okay, June," Paul said. "But you'd inquired about services, and I finally got Sandy's body. The funeral is tomorrow night at Plymouth Funeral Home."

"You chose the perfect place. Sandy loved the chapel there."

"I know," Paul said in a shaky voice. He sucked in a deep breath, then cleared his throat. "It'll be a closed casket," he said, his voice under control. "She doesn't look much like the woman we remember."

"Oh, Paul. Is there anything you need? Can I—"

"No. But thanks for the offer. Sandy's mom is helping."

June pictured her friend's slender, normally cheerful mother. They had spoken a few days ago, one of the hardest calls June had ever made. "How is she doing?"

"I don't know how to answer that. Listen, I've got to go. Got a lot of calls to make."

"I understand."

"See you tomorrow night. The visitation starts at five. Services are at seven. I'm inviting friends to the house after, but it'll be a private interment for family only on Saturday morning."

Paul disconnected without waiting for her goodbye. June held the receiver for a long moment before she replaced it on the side table. Paul's call brought everything that had happened back into focus with a harsh kick to her gut. She ought to be ashamed. She'd been worried about her sexy new lover being angry with her when one of her oldest friends had been murdered and the family was planning a funeral.

But she'd been miserable, hiding inside herself for so long. Too long. It felt great to feel alive again. And now she was being sucked back into the pain of a life ended too soon. *I'm so sorry, Sandy.*

"How is he?" Dean asked.

June shook her head and took a sip of wine. "Services are tomorrow night."

"That was quick. He just got the body today."

June swallowed. "Her mom told me they had everything in place waiting for the body to be released."

Dean squeezed her hand. "Once she's buried, he'll be able to move on."

"I suppose." Her gaze drifted outside to the view of Biscayne Bay. The sun had gone down and lights were blinking on. "I hate funerals."

"So you're definitely going?"

She swung her gaze back to Dean. "Of course."

"Do you want me to go with you?"

"You wouldn't mind?"

He smiled and stroked her cheek. "I'll be your backup."

"That would be great. Thanks." She placed her hand on his and smiled. His presence would be a comfort. Dean really could be a sweetheart when he wasn't telling her what to do.

"I'll probably sit in the back, though," he said, placing the wineglass on the side table. "I could be an irritant to Mr. Taylor."

"Poor Paul." She heaved a sigh. Paul had never been much of a drinker, but now because of Sandy's murder... She narrowed her eyes.

"Wait a minute. Backup? Oh, my God. Are you worried the sniper might come to the services?"

"There's that possibility. The shooter will know you'd attend your friend's funeral. Is there any way I can talk you out of going?"

"Not a chance." She studied Dean's serious face. "So you think the killer could be waiting to shoot me."

He took her wine, placed it on the table beside his and grasped both of her hands. "I'll make sure that doesn't happen. Don't worry. There'll be more officers around the area besides me."

"Because the police will be there searching for the murderer?"

"Right."

She shook her head. "This is crazy."

"We won't be obvious. I promise that."

She stood and moved restlessly to the sliding doors,

staring at the view again without seeing it. "You probably go to a lot of funerals," she said over her shoulder.

"They're a good place to look for suspects."

"That makes sense, I guess, in some convoluted way. Is Paul still a suspect?"

When Dean didn't answer, June turned back to him. His back was against her headboard, his muscled chest bare. Sheets covered the lower part of his anatomy. Suddenly, even with all the unsettling thoughts and memories swirling around inside her head, she wanted him again. She wanted to drop her robe, crawl under those cool sheets and press her naked flesh against his strong, warm body.

While making love with Dean, she was able to forget that anyone had been murdered. Or that someone was gunning for her.

She moved back to the bed. "If you could hear Paul, you'd know it's not an act. He's completely torn up over Sandy's death."

"I interviewed Mr. Taylor this morning," Dean said. "I know he's in bad shape. I was going to ask you to reach out to him."

"So then he isn't a suspect?"

"No." After a pause, Dean said, "The case has actually taken a new trajectory."

"Really? So you learned something useful in Melbourne?"

"We learned quite a bit in Melbourne."

Realizing they hadn't yet discussed his trip, she asked, "What? Tell me."

"Kublin is dying and his shrink doesn't believe he would ever shoot anyone."

She sat beside him again. "Dying? The man who killed my parents is dying?"

"Some kind of quick-acting cancer. He's pretty much a goner."

"That makes no sense. Why the hell would someone on death's door bust out of a hospital?"

DEAN REACHED FOR the wine again, remembering how he'd felt when June had kept a secret from him.

But this was different. Completely different. She didn't need to know his new theory that her parents were innocent until he'd confirmed it. The idea would rock her carefully created world, tear down that protective shell of hating her parents, leaving her raw and even more vulnerable. She'd beat herself up for doubting them.

Then, if the theory proved wrong, she'd be devastated all over again. He didn't want to hurt her like that. He took a long drink of expensive wine without tasting a thing and set the glass aside.

"What aren't you telling me?" she demanded.

"The psychiatrist confirmed that Kublin still believes your parents were innocent."

"Yeah, right. No doubt he swears he didn't set the fire, either."

"Kublin knows he doesn't have long to live. According to the shrink, he's looking for you because he doesn't want the truth to die with him."

"What truth?"

"That your parents were framed."

"That's old news," she scoffed. "What's your new—what did you call it? Trajectory? What's different?"

Dean met her questioning gaze and made his decision. Maybe it was the wrong one, but he was going to be honest with her. Shit. When had he ever been completely honest with a woman before? Never.

But he couldn't lie to June. He couldn't hide the truth or his feelings anymore. Not if they had any chance of a future. *A future? What future?*

Damn, no question this woman had made him lose his mind.

He reached forward and clasped both of her hands. "Listen to me carefully. I don't want you to overreact."

Eyes wide, June withdrew her hands from his and hugged herself. "You're scaring me, Dean."

He hesitated, but plunged ahead. "I'm sorry. I don't mean to, but I once promised to be honest with you, and I need you to be honest with me."

She nodded. "Go ahead. What's happened?"

"Nothing has necessarily happened. But what's changed is the investigation has led me to believe your parents *were* possibly framed."

CHAPTER EIGHTEEN

JUNE STARED AT Dean for several long moments as she absorbed his words. She shook her head, denying what he'd said. His theory didn't make sense. Of course her parents were guilty.

"After their deaths, there was no trial, so the state's evidence against them was never tested," Dean said.

He paused, watching her with a wary expression. June continued to stare at him, unable to respond.

"That theory has been on my radar for a long time, but no law-enforcement officer wants to second-guess their colleagues, so I resisted the idea," he continued. "Now I'm going to follow up that possibility until I disprove it. Or prove it."

"Why?" she asked, her voice as hoarse as if she hadn't spoken since the fire. "Why do you think my parents were framed?"

Dean methodically went through the sequence of events, what he'd learned so far, some details about the arson, his growing doubts about her parents' drug case. He was waiting to hear back from the primary investigator, a respected but now retired officer. The evidence against her mom and dad had been, in his opinion, weak.

"Weak?" she said. "The evidence against my parents was weak? I was told the case was airtight."

"Who told you that?"

"Everyone. The TV stations practically implied

there wasn't any need for a trial." She remembered how the nightly news reported the fire that killed her parents, calling it suspicious. "Even the *Miami Herald* said the evidence was overwhelming."

"Strange, but remember I'm looking at an old case file ten years later. Some reports could be missing. A decade is a long time."

"Does it appear that anything is missing?"

"Not really. I've got the interviews, the logs, daily reports. I just need to confirm a few things with Betty Daniels, the primary."

"What makes you think she'll remember something ten years later that isn't in the reports?"

"There's a cryptic note from Daniels that I don't understand, some sort of personal shorthand that I need her to explain. It could be nothing."

"So, what about the arson?"

Dean sighed. "Maybe whoever was using your parents' business to smuggle set the fire to destroy any evidence."

"So under your new theory my parents were murdered."

"The operative word is *theory.*"

"You said you'd been thinking about this so-called theory for a long time. How long?"

He shrugged. "A while."

"Why didn't you tell me?"

"I need to confirm everything with Daniels."

"You should have told me."

"This reaction is exactly what I was worried about, why I didn't."

"I want to see the records."

He shook his head. "I can't let you do that, June."

"Why not?"

"Those records are not open to the public."

"I'm not the public. I'm the—the victim in all this."

"Let me track all this evidence down, unravel what happened ten years ago. That's my job, and I'm good at it."

She leaped to her feet and moved to the sliding doors again, looking out into a vast dark void, seeing nothing. She placed her palms against her cheeks and realized her fingers were ice-cold. "Oh, my God. What if my parents were innocent after all?"

Dean rose and moved beside her.

"I need to know," she said. "I want to see the entire case file."

"Be reasonable, June. Even if I could let you see the files, what would you do with the information?"

"I could help you."

He wrapped his arms around her. "How could you help?"

"I don't know." She pushed him away. Why had she just accepted what everyone had told her before? Because she'd been a child. A frightened young girl terrified of a world without her parents.

She faced him again. "I might see something. More eyes on anything is always better," she said. "Like when looking for birds. And doesn't your rookie help you look at files?"

"He's a sworn police officer. And you wouldn't know what you were reading. You wouldn't understand the police procedures, the codes, acronyms."

She raised her chin. "You could explain it to me."

"No, June. I don't have time for that."

"That's bull. You have plenty of time for this." She flung her hand toward the rumpled bed.

His jaw set into a firm line. "You're right. The truth is I don't want you anywhere near this case. It's too dangerous."

"I've been careful. I've done everything you've asked me to do."

"Not everything." He moved toward the bed, grabbed his slacks from the floor and stepped into them. "Look at you. You're a mess. I shouldn't have told you. I knew better."

"I wanted to know every detail. I *need* to see those files."

He pulled up his zipper. "You need to let me handle this."

"They were my parents. I have a right to know what the evidence was against them."

"No, you don't." He shook his head. "That information would only torture you. There are photos in the file that you should never see."

"Damn it, Dean. Stop trying to control me."

"I need to control the flow of this case." He jerked on his shirt and moved farther away from her.

"Look," she said after a deep breath. "I get why you want me to take the bus and why you were upset about my trip to the Redlands, but this is different. There's no reason I can't see your evidence. You're just being a bully."

"It's for your own good whether you believe it or not."

"Where are you going?" she demanded.

"Home."

"We're not finished."

He paused at the bedroom door and glared at her with dangerous eyes. "Yes, we are. This conversation is pointless."

"I can get a court order."

"Good luck with that."

"My uncle knows people." She flung her words at him. "He's influential."

"I'll have the case solved long before you're even in front of a judge. Where you will most certainly lose." He stepped out of the door.

"You can't control me," she yelled after him.

He stepped back into the bedroom and pointed a finger at her. "Set the alarm. And take the bus to work."

"Quit telling me what to do. I'm not your sister."

He narrowed his eyes. "What the hell is that supposed to mean?"

"You know exactly what I mean." She raised her chin. "You try to manage everyone."

"Yeah? Well, it's for damn good reasons."

And then he was gone. When she heard the front door slam, she ran to it and threw it back open in time to see the elevator close and begin its descent with a quiet hum. She was too late to get in one last word. Damn him.

How dare he drop that bombshell about her parents and then walk away? He made love to her and then left as if she were just so much police business for him to organize? *By the way, Ms. Person of Interest, don't forget to set the alarm.*

She reentered her apartment, locked the door and armed the security system, her thoughts swirling with sickening regret.

She moved into the aviary, where Lazarus eyed her suspiciously until she sat in the cloth chair, head in her hands, barely noticing the gentle sway.

What if her parents had truly been innocent all those years ago?

They had sworn to her the charges were false. She remembered their earnest faces at the family conference as they begged her to believe them. And of course she did. At first. But then came the fire, their deaths and all the nasty news stories afterward. The sidelong glances in the halls at school from fellow students, even her friends. The whispers, the giggles. The pity from her teachers, extensions on the work she couldn't concentrate on enough to complete. She'd been glad when Uncle Mike whisked her away to New York for a few months.

So she came to accept the awful fact that her mom

and dad had lied to her. She was a big girl, old enough to understand that her parents weren't perfect. Nobody was.

But she couldn't forgive the lie. That was what she hadn't been able to forget, what she'd resented for ten years. They should have been honest with her. They should have told her the truth.

And if Dean was right, they had. What kind of a daughter, a person, was she? She hadn't loved her parents enough to trust them.

What had really happened ten years ago? She needed to know.

AN HOUR LATER, Dean slid onto a bar stool at the outdoor Akroner Bar, the deep throb of a bass from the house band resonating from the padded seat into his bones. He took a deep breath, inhaling the salty breeze off the nearby Atlantic Ocean, mingled with the smell of spilled beer. Nestled between the bar and the surf, Ocean Drive was a parking lot full of barely moving vehicles, their drivers cruising, looking for someone to hook up with or some kind of trouble.

A young male bartender approached. Good-looking guy, if a little effeminate. Dean remembered he was trying to catch gigs as a male model.

"Hey, Dean. Been a while."

"Yeah." What was this guy's damn name? Dean focused on a name tag.

"Been working hard or hardly working?" Roy asked, having to raise his voice over the music from inside.

"You know me, Roy."

The barkeep grinned. "Good man. Want the usual?"

"Fine," Dean said.

When Roy moved away, Dean swiveled to look out over the swarms of people crowding the outdoor lounge and spilling onto the sidewalk. It was early, before 10:00 p.m., and the summer season even, yet South Beach was jammed with tourists. The outdoor tables at restaurants lining Ocean Drive—at least the ones he could see—were mostly full. The Chamber of Commerce should be very happy. Whatever. At least someone was.

He let his gaze roam over the groups of females in the vicinity, sizing up what was available. His habit was to look for two women engaged in conversation but casually evaluating the male pool themselves. That was where he had the most luck. A larger group was harder to break into and likely more interested in a ladies' night out.

That was why he'd come here, right? To see if he could hook up? That was what he always did when a woman gave him grief. He knew just the cure to get June out of his head.

"Here you go, buddy." Roy returned with a shot of Jack Black and a large draft beer.

"Thanks," Dean said and quickly downed the shot. Roy moved away, and Dean picked up the beer, swiveling back to the crowd. He needed to return to his old habits. He'd made a mistake with June. Broken his rules even getting involved with her. And then he was effing stupid enough to be honest with her—and what did that get him? An argument about how to do his job. Rules were made for a reason. Because they worked.

His life flowed smoothly when he focused on his cases and followed his normal dating pattern, keeping himself free of commitments. What the hell had he been thinking falling into bed with June? And why couldn't he get her out of his mind? He was surrounded by women. Some of them more beautiful than her.

"Hey." A brunette in her late twenties with a killer smile moved between him and the old dude at the bar stool next to him. She allowed her gaze to travel his body and then back to his face.

"Hey," Dean said, checking her out just as openly. Her body was as good as her smile.

"You look lonely," she said.

"Do I?"

She nodded, motioned for Roy and focused on him again. "I'm Noelle."

"Hi, Noelle. I'm Dean."

"Are you on vacation, Dean?"

Before he could answer, Roy arrived. Noelle ordered a frozen margarita with salt. Definitely a tourist. Dean nodded at Roy, an indication he should put Noelle's drink on his tab.

"Where are you from?" Dean asked.

"Indiana. You?"

"Right here."

"You're a local?"

"Born and raised." Damn, and now he was talking in clichés. Did he always do that when on the hunt? Surely he could be a little wittier. Either he was out of practice or—or what? Shit.

"What do you do, Dean?" Noelle asked.

He grinned, an easy answer popping into his head about the things that he could "do." And do well. Instead he said, "I'm a cop."

Her eyes widened. Her grin broadened. So she liked the idea of a little danger. Some women did. He'd known plenty of police groupies. He waited for the next question, knowing what it would be.

"Do you have a gun?" she asked, her eyes shifting to his waist, then his legs.

He leaned closer and lowered his voice. "It's required," he said. Her smile grew even larger.

Roy returned with her drink, and Noelle reached for her purse.

"I got that," Dean said, touching her arm.

"Thanks," she said. "Good-looking *and* a gentleman. I'm liking Miami a lot." She took a quick sip and rolled her eyes in obvious pleasure. "Delicious."

Dean held up his mug and clinked against her 'rita. "To a good time," he said.

She laughed, took another sip and then openly met his gaze. "So, Dean," she said in a silky voice, "what do you say we move to a table where we can, you know, talk a little easier?"

Dean took a long swallow of his beer. Noelle was

one fine-looking woman. She was available and more than willing to get to know him better. She was exactly what he'd come here to find. Things were proceeding precisely as they should, as they always did. This was why a guy like him loved South Beach.

So what the hell was wrong with him?

June Latham.

He rose, took a couple of bills from his wallet and dropped them on the bar. "Sorry," he said to Noelle, with a shake of his head. "I've got to go."

THE NEXT AFTERNOON June stared into her closet, looking for the right dress to wear to Sandy's funeral. She owned only one black dress, the one she'd worn to her parents' funeral.

Every time she bought something in black, thinking this time she could manage it—even those short, sexy cocktail numbers that looked great with her fair coloring—she ended up giving or throwing the damn thing away.

She hated wearing black, and she hated the idea of putting on that depressing outfit even more. She knew what would happen. She'd be flung back to the most miserable day of her life. But she'd always kept what she considered her funeral uniform.

Reaching to the very back of the closet, she searched for and found a hanger with the long black shapeless shift and pulled it out. Nothing else would work. Of course she had to wear black. With a sigh, she untied her robe and stepped into the ankle-length linen dress, which would also be miserably hot in the sticky September humidity. Oh, well. She couldn't get much more depressed than she was already.

Dean hadn't called. She hadn't called him, either.

He'd sent her a text that he would pick her up for the viewing at five thirty—fifteen minutes from now. She didn't know whether she was relieved or angry at his presumptive belief that she still wanted to go anywhere with him. But she couldn't decide about anything anymore. Not even what to wear to a memorial service when, hell, there was really only one choice.

June dropped her purse over her arm and picked up a sweater. Funeral homes were always freezing. She locked the door, set the alarm and stepped into the elevator.

She'd taken the bus home from work, half expecting Dean to show up at the bus stop outside the clinic. He hadn't. At least he'd sent the text. And yes, she *was* glad he'd sent the text.

She wouldn't apologize to him, though. He thought she was being unreasonable, but she was tired of being kept in the dark about her parents' case. Why hadn't she been more proactive over the years? She should have believed in her mom and dad, demanded the authorities seek the truth about the fire, continue to investigate and learn who had been the real smuggler.

But no, spoiled little brat that she was, she'd felt too sorry for herself, for all that *she'd* lost. Imagine. Having to attend public school. Such a tragedy. Boohoo.

With a wave at Magda, June waited inside the air-conditioned lobby, safely out of view of any mad snipers. At exactly five thirty she spotted Dean's white police Crown Victoria arrive at the guard gate. As the car slowly approached on the long driveway, she realized he wasn't driving. Sanchez, his trainee, was at the wheel. Dean sat in the passenger seat.

She stepped outside into a blanket of heat and humidity and decided Sanchez's presence was a blessing. She didn't have a damn thing to say to Dean. Not until he shared the entire police investigation with her, and she knew that wasn't likely to happen any time soon. Dean wanted to handle her like another piece of evidence and keep her away from his case. The man was stubborn and fixated on obeying departmental rules.

Well, she could be stubborn, too.

Looking impossibly handsome, if grim, in a black jacket and slacks, Dean stepped out of the vehicle and opened the back door for her. His gaze swept her appearance. She shivered slightly under his scrutiny, feeling, as always, that he noticed everything about her. Too bad she looked like a lump of coal.

"June," he said politely, nodding at her.

"Dean," she responded just as formally and climbed into the backseat with as much grace as possible.

"Good evening, Ms. Latham," Sanchez said. "In case you don't remember me, I'm Ruben Sanchez."

"Of course I remember you, Officer Sanchez." June noted Sanchez wasn't in uniform. Considering the nature of today's mission, that concession was of course considerate. How awkward, even distracting it would have been for Paul to have armed, uniformed police officers swarming what should be a dignified, spiritual farewell to his beloved wife.

Dean returned to the front seat and slammed the door. "Go," he ordered Sanchez, who accelerated away from the overhang.

"Thank you for the ride," June said. "I appreciate it."

"No problem, ma'am," Sanchez replied.

Dean punched a button on his cell phone and began barking orders about surveillance at the funeral home.

"Where's Acevedo?" Dean demanded. "Yeah. Okay. No. I want someone on the ground with high-powered binocs in that location. Right. What about Baker? Is he in position? Good. Okay."

June listened to every word, trying to process and understand what the police were planning. Sounded as if an army would be in attendance. Apparently Dean had positioned law-enforcement personnel somewhere high on every building in the vicinity in case a sniper lurked to take a shot.

Dean terminated call after call only to immediately initiate another. "Give me your status," he demanded each time, seeming mostly pleased by what he heard. Sanchez remained silent, and June knew he also listened to the one-sided communication. At least she didn't have to make meaningless conversation on the ride. She marveled at what a carefully coordinated police operation Sandy's funeral had become.

Sanchez made the turn into Plymouth Funeral Home as Dean told someone, "Until nine at least. The service is scheduled for seven and there'll be lingerers. No. I hope to have our target out of there by eight."

Target. June sucked in a huge breath, suddenly queasy. This whole complicated tactical surveillance business was to protect her.

She was the shooter's target.

CHAPTER NINETEEN

"GET AS CLOSE to the building as you can," Dean instructed Sanchez as they approached the mortuary's entrance. "I don't want her in the open for more than a second."

"Got it," Sanchez replied.

Dean turned to look at June for the first time since they left the Enclave. Damn, but she was pale. Maybe it was just the color of the dress. No, she looked terrified. Well, good. Yeah, he could comfort her, reassure her that she'd be perfectly fine, but he didn't want to. He wasn't in the mood for hand-holding. June needed to take her situation a hell of a lot more seriously. For sure she needed to get over the idea that she could help the police investigate.

And he needed to keep his distance from her before she screwed his concentration totally.

"You okay?" he asked, his voice gruffer than he intended.

She moistened her lips and nodded.

"When Sanchez comes to a stop, I'm going to open your door. Get out quickly. I want you to stay in front of me and haul butt into that building. There'll be an officer holding the door open. It'll be no more than four steps. Can you do that?"

"Yes," she said. "What about you? If the sniper takes a shot—"

"I have on protective gear," Dean said. "Don't worry about me. Are you with me on this, June?"

She nodded. "I guess I didn't realize it would be so scary."

"I know," Dean said meaningfully. He faced front again, wanting to say a hell of a lot more to her, but knowing now wasn't the time. Not on the day she was saying goodbye to one of her oldest friends. And whoever had murdered that beautiful young woman was trying like hell to stick June in a casket, too.

Not on his watch.

Sanchez maneuvered the Interceptor within four feet of the door, crushing a hibiscus hedge in the process. No doubt the department would receive a huge bill for collateral damage.

"Good job," Dean said to the rookie. "Meet me after you park."

Inside, an officer pulled the door open and gave a curt nod.

Dean turned back to June. "You ready?"

"Yes," she said, her voice firm, chin high. "I'm ready."

Dean smiled at her for the first time, pleased she'd gotten control of her nerves.

With Dean shielding her body with his, they dashed four steps to the entrance, and then June was safely inside, where she disappeared into a group of friends. He lingered a moment, listening, making certain she would be okay.

"June, thank goodness you're here."

"It's a closed casket. Can you believe it?"

"Paul is a wreck."

Everyone was in tears or sniffling. Tissue and hugs all around. June was in the bosom of her old cronies. She'd be fine. Needing to hook up with Sanchez, he took a step just as she turned back to him and gave him a shaky smile. A peace offering? Not good enough.

Thanks, she mouthed.

Dean nodded and went in search of Sanchez, dismissing June from his thoughts. She was secure, and he had a job to do.

Would the sniper be here looking for an opportunity to take a shot? Dean figured the chances were fifty-fifty at best. This shooter was good, but had already made two mistakes. He had to know the police would be all over this somber gathering. Or did he? Maybe he was arrogant enough to believe law enforcement hadn't figured out who his real target was.

Stepping out the back door of the mortuary, Dean raised his binoculars and scanned the roof of every building in the area for any sign of a human or the tip of a rifle. It would help if he could figure out why the shooter wanted June dead. Damn, but he needed the motivation. Did June know something? Or did the shooter believe she did? In his gut, Dean believed it all went back to the fire. She'd been a teenager at that time. What could she possibly know or remember?

And what about Al Kublin? He had to know June would attend her friend's funeral. All officers had a recent photograph of the escaped whack job and were looking for the guy. Showing up here tonight would be a hell of a risky maneuver on Kublin's part, since he was also a target. But the man was dying, running out of time. Maybe he'd take the chance. Maybe show up in disguise. That was what Dean hoped for, anyway.

And he'd be waiting. He had a lot of questions for Mr. Kublin.

AT SEVEN O'CLOCK, June took a seat in the second row of the chapel, directly behind the seats reserved for Paul and Sandy's parents, between Carole and Donna. Sad, haunting organ music floated through the room, barely audible over the hushed whispers of the mourners. If the number of people at a funeral was indicative of how loved the deceased was, Sandy had been adored.

June took a deep breath and inhaled the fragrance of the floral arrangements that surrounded the polished wooden coffin, which was blanketed by a huge spray of perfect red roses. Sandy had loved red roses. June looked for the bouquet she had sent, but couldn't find her crimson blooms among so many.

She fisted her hands, fingernails digging into her palms, and noted her hands were numb. Truthfully, she was numb everywhere, even her brain. The temperature in this room felt like a meat locker. A chill traced her spine, and she realized that was precisely what this room was today. She glanced at the coffin again, noticing brass trim, hating that Sandy was inside.

The music stopped, and the voices quieted. Paul entered the chapel, followed by Sandy's parents. They seated themselves in the front row. Carole reached forward and squeezed Paul's shoulder. He didn't react.

A minister in a black suit approached the front of the room and began to speak about love and loss.

June's thoughts wandered. She didn't want to listen to clichés and platitudes about how Sandy was in a better place and how there was a reason for everything. Maybe that was true—she hoped it was—but how could there be a reason for Sandy to die the way she did?

June bit her bottom lip. If Dean was right, she was meant to be the body in that casket. Nobody else knew that, of course. But she did, and the idea ate at her like acid.

All she wanted was to get this ordeal over with.

She supposed Dean would coordinate her exit as painstakingly as he'd arranged her arrival. Nothing but cool, polite distance between them now, but she accepted that was the way it had to be. Their affair would go down as something brief and explosive. Incredibly pleasurable and exciting as it developed, and miserably depressing at the end. This funeral was a fitting goodbye to more than Sandy.

She'd known better, had understood from the first tingle of awareness that getting involved with Dean was a mistake. He was a control freak, a womanizer and even killed birds. She'd seen all the warning signs of disaster but couldn't stop herself. She just let it happen.

Let it happen? She'd encouraged the passion that flared between them, had welcomed that heat and intensity. Dean made her feel alive, made her care about something besides birds for the first time in a long while.

The tone of the minister's voice changed, and June realized he'd asked everyone to bow their heads and pray. June closed her eyes.

She'd even thought she was falling in love with Dean, that something real and special was blossoming between them. Foolish, foolish Junie. Oh, no doubt he'd continue to protect her. That was his job. But something had changed because of her demands. She tried to take a tiny bit of control, so he'd keep his distance from now on.

When the mourners all murmured "Amen" in unison, June opened her eyes. The minister invited anyone who wanted to speak to come forward. Sandy's father rose and choked out words about his lovely daughter gone too soon. Paul lowered his head, his shoulders shaking. He was on the verge of breaking down. She prayed Paul wouldn't attempt to deliver a eulogy to his wife. He'd never get through it.

About half of those in attendance had been invited back to Sandy's home for a final catered farewell. June had intended to go. She'd been looking forward to reminiscing about Sandy with old friends, remembering the good times. She needed to talk to Paul, give him a big hug and a pep talk. She better than anyone understood all of the old gang needed to rally around him to help him through this difficult time.

But she now realized her attendance was a lousy idea. It'd be difficult for Dean to protect her, awkward for Paul to have cops lurking everywhere on his property. Her friends would wonder what the hell was going on. She couldn't bear for them to know Sandy's death had been a tragic mistake.

No, she'd just go home. That would be easier on everyone.

What would she do tonight instead? Sit by herself in the dark?

Once before her life had been totaled by death in a cruel, swift fashion, and she'd been isolated. And now, because of Dean's overbearing caution, it was happening all over again.

A LITTLE AFTER 9:00 P.M., Dean sat at his desk and stared at the paperwork before him. He had reports to complete, explaining the necessity for such tight security at Plymouth Mortuary. He could justify the manpower and expense. He wasn't worried about that. But damn, all that effort and neither Kublin nor the shooter had shown. Was he sorry? Hell, yes. Not that he'd wanted the somber and strangely beautiful memorial disrupted by violence. He just needed something to pop, and he'd settle for anything at this point. He desperately needed a break in the case. Betty Daniels still hadn't called him back, and he'd left two more messages.

He and Sanchez had delivered June safely back to the Enclave by eight thirty. She'd remained silent during the ride, but she'd just been through a heartbreaking experience. No one liked funerals—or no sane person anyway. And this one had been wrenching for June because she felt guilty about her friend's death.

He'd thought she'd go to Taylor's for the wake—or whatever you called the little cocktail party scheduled after the funeral.

"No," she'd said softly. "It's better if I just go home." The only thing she'd said on the entire trip.

So he'd taken her home and hadn't walked her up. The building was secure, and he'd have been tempted, even with Sanchez waiting in the car. That was why he kept the rookie by his side constantly, so he couldn't get sucked off track by June.

Although now Sanchez was at home with his new bride while Dean had to wade through the monotony of time-and-use reports.

He'd rather be with June. He ached to touch her, to make love to her. To make her feel better. He glanced at the cell phone on his desk. Should he call her? No. He needed to keep his distance.

Needing a moment before beginning the tedious paperwork, Dean pushed back in his chair and propped his feet on the desk. He'd sent Officer Baker in a marked car to monitor the gathering at Taylor's home, but he doubted Kublin or the shooter would show there. That gesture was more of a courtesy than anything, intended to reassure Taylor. Baker would stay in the background, probably wouldn't get out of the vehicle. It'd be a hot, boring, miserable couple of hours for the officer.

Dean pulled a bottle of water out of his bottom drawer and took a couple of swallows. It'd already been a long day for him, too. And for June.

So what did June know that the shooter-cum-arsonist wanted her dead for? Maybe he should call in a hypnotist. Leads could develop while a witness was under. Would his lieutenant authorize it? Would June agree?

He knew she was hurting, that she hadn't gone to the wake because she thought her presence and all the cops would be a disruption. And she was most likely correct about that. What was she doing? Yeah, he should call, make sure she wasn't beating herself up too badly.

Before he could talk himself out of it, he punched in her number. June answered with a soft, hopeful "Hello."

"It's me," he said.

"Hi."

Thinking she sounded weird, wondering if she was glad he'd called, he said, "I just wanted to make sure you were okay."

"Oh, I'm just awesome," she said and began to make sounds that sounded alarmingly like a woman crying.

Dean sat up, placing his feet on the floor. He'd never seen her cry. Not once in all their contact. Not even when talking about her parents' death. Or Sandy's.

"What's wrong?" he demanded. "Has something happened?"

He listened to a few garbled words and could tell she was trying to regain control of her voice. "I'm sorry," she said between sobs. "I don't know what's wrong with me."

"You're crying," he said. *God, that sounded like an accusation.*

"I never cry," she said and began to weep again.

"I'm on my way."

When June opened the door to her apartment, the penthouse was totally dark behind her. But light from the foyer showed Dean the moisture on puffy cheeks and swollen eyes. She still wore the black dress from the funeral.

"Come here," he said, pulling her into a tight hug. He should have stayed with her tonight. He never should have left her alone. Damn, she'd been sitting all alone in the dark weeping.

He locked the door and set the alarm, then led her to the sofa and gently pulled her down with him, placing her head on his shoulder. "I'm right here," he said. "Let it all out."

Shoulders shaking, she wrapped her arms around his neck and crawled into his lap. He held her, murmuring soothingly, telling her it was okay over and over. She needed this, had probably needed a good cry for ten years. Haunted by her parents' betrayal, she'd been holding in all her emotion, afraid to live her life.

She finally stopped trembling and sucked in a deep breath.

"I don't know what happened," she said, her words muffled into his shirt. "Once I started, I couldn't stop."

"You'd been saving up those tears for a long time," he said.

"How do you know that?"

"I've never seen you cry, June. Not once. Considering what's going on, I expected a few tears."

"You're right," she said after a sigh. "I think I even prided myself on never breaking down."

"You needed to cry. Everyone does. It's a normal release and helps process grief."

She lifted her head and looked at him. Her hair was a tangled mess, dangling into her face. He smiled and smoothed a lock behind her ear.

"Do you ever cry?" she asked.

"Sure. Sometimes."

She laid her cheek against his shoulder again. "I can't imagine you giving in to tears."

"Yeah, I'm a real badass," he murmured. More like a wuss. He'd promised himself he wouldn't see June alone until after he'd closed this case, but here he was, less than twenty-four hours later, holding her, wondering if it would help her or hurt her if he started peeling off her clothing. He ran a hand down her arm, wanting to get her out of this depressing black dress. He'd bet that alone would improve her mood.

"Thanks for coming," she said. "I didn't want to be alone tonight."

"You didn't go to Taylor's because of the protection, right? You were afraid the police presence would spoil the mood of the gathering?"

June nodded. "And I felt like I didn't have a right to go. No one else knows that Sandy died instead of me."

"June…"

"How can I look Paul in the eye when I should be dead, not his wife?"

Dean stroked her arm again. "Honey, your friend's murder isn't your fault. You know that."

"Maybe." She remained silent for a moment, then whispered, "But it is my fault that I didn't believe in my parents."

Dean closed his eyes. Damn. And that shitload of guilt was on him. He never should have told her until he'd confirmed that theory. "Ten years ago nobody believed in your parents," he said. "The evidence was stacked against them, and the fire ended the investigation."

"But I'm their daughter. What kind of daughter believes the talking heads on TV over her mom and dad? I should have trusted them, defended them to the rest of the world. I should have worked to clear their name."

Dean hugged her close, thinking her life had all but stopped with that damn arson. He needed to close this case, learn the truth with absolute certainty and put her mind at ease. Then she could move on. He hoped to move on with her, but right now he needed something to say, some useless cliché, anything to make her feel better. Unfortunately comforting weeping women had never been one of his strengths. When the waterworks started, he was usually out the door.

"Make love to me, Dean."

His thoughts stilled with her soft words. "Are you sure?" Would that be another misstep?

She pulled away from him and came to her feet. Dry-eyed, she extended an arm toward him. "Are you going to make me beg?"

Rising swiftly, Dean stepped behind her and lowered the zipper of the ugly black sack that hid her gorgeous body. He slid the fabric off her arms and down her hips. She leaned against his chest, now wearing a black slip and lacy black bra that made him hard.

"Thank you," she whispered. "I think I'm going to burn that dress."

"Please allow me to strike the match."

Praying this wasn't a fatal error, Dean raised June in his arms and carried her into the bedroom.

KNOWING NOTHING WAS settled between them, June rested her cheek on Dean's naked chest and allowed herself to enjoy the sweet intimacy that came after sex with Dean. Maybe they had a lot to hash out, but this was enough for right now. He wrapped an arm around her shoulders and pulled her closer, making her feel wanted. She needed to feel wanted.

No, she'd needed Dean tonight, and he'd been there for her. There for her in a whole lot of delicious ways.

No matter what happened between them from now on, she'd always be grateful for the past hour.

She released a sigh. Oh, just great. How pitiful was she to be grateful to a man for making love to her.

"What's wrong?" Dean murmured, lightly stroking her arm.

"Nothing to do with you," she said.

He sucked in a breath, making his chest expand beneath her cheek. "That's a stretch, considering what just happened between us."

"My every thought doesn't revolve around you." Which was a bit of a lie.

"Thanks for setting me straight," he said in a flat tone she couldn't decipher. Could she have hurt his feelings?

"Sorry. I didn't mean that the way it sounded."

"So, what are you thinking?"

"That I'm totally screwed up."

His chest rumbled, and she raised her head to look at Dean's face. "Are you laughing at me?"

He placed her head back against him. "Hell, everyone is screwed up."

"Not like me."

"Honey, you've been through enough in the last couple of weeks to be treated by the good shrinks at Sunrise." After a moment he said, "I shouldn't have told you I questioned the case against your parents. Not until I knew for sure what their involvement was. I hate what that's done to you."

"I asked you to be honest with me," she said. "It's my own fault."

"You need to stop thinking everything is your fault."

"I don't think everything—"

"Yeah, you know, June, you really do. Think about it."

She pushed herself up and sat cross-legged to stare at him. "What are you talking about?"

He reached for her hand. "Why is it you always want to talk about serious shit after we've just enjoyed fabulous sex?"

She jerked away, not certain why she was suddenly so angry. "You brought it up."

He regarded her steadily. "I knew this was a mistake."

"Don't try to change the subject."

"I'm not—"

"And it sure seemed like you enjoyed this. You didn't want to make love?"

"You know I did."

"And I want to know what you meant by that comment. You think I've got some sort of guilt complex?" Even as she said the words, June realized with a jolt that it might be true.

"Okay. If you want to do this, let's do it." Dean pushed himself up in the bed and leaned against the headboard. "I'm not sure I'd call it a complex exactly, but I think you're on a mission to save every bird you can because of the ones that died in your parents' warehouse fire."

"You know about the bird shipment?"

"Of course. And yeah, you feel guilty about those dead birds. You've been feeling so responsible for your parents' crimes, maybe even their deaths, you're afraid to truly enjoy life."

"That's crazy," she said.

"Is it? Tonight I found you sitting alone in the dark punishing yourself because some murdering psychopath shot your friend. You're furious with yourself for not believing in your parents, and now you even want to help investigate to prove them innocent. Misplaced guilt is eating you alive and putting your life in danger."

"I just want to know the truth."

"The truth is none of this is your fault, June."

She stared at him. "I know that. Of course I know that."

"Do you really?" he asked.

God, he sees right through me. Feeling naked and exposed, to Dean, to the world, she came to her feet and reached for her robe. Tying the belt around her waist, she said, "You interviewed some shrink and now you think you can psychoanalyze me."

"Yeah, that's it," Dean said. "That's it exactly."

"So you see me as some pathetic creature who takes on all the weight of the world?"

"You're not pathetic. But look how angry you are.

I've hit too close to the truth, and it's making you uncomfortable."

"Gee, thanks for the diagnosis, Dr. Hammer," she muttered. "You can try to sidetrack me all you want, but I still want to see all the records about my parents' case."

"You're back to that?"

She raised her chin. "Yes."

"I'm still not going to show them to you."

"Damn you."

After a long moment, he said, "Do you want me to leave?"

She didn't want him to go. She looked away, actually nauseated. Why did she need to see exactly what the evidence had been against her parents? What did it matter? Was he right? Did everyone see her as a guilt-ridden recluse?

God, she needed to figure out this unholy mess that was her life. "Maybe you should."

Sick at heart and weary through to her bones, June watched him jerk on his slacks and grab his shirt. She longed to go to him, to stop him from leaving, but didn't. Couldn't.

Dean didn't speak again, although she could see the thoughts churning in his head. He had a lot more to say to her but was resisting the urge. She was grateful for that. She was beyond confused and had no more defenses to mount. No more arguments to make.

Head down, she followed him to the front door.

With his shirt still unbuttoned, he paused, gave her a hard look and ground out, "Set the alarm."

Those three sharp words pierced her as cleanly as a knife. Of course his parting comment had to be one last order, one last attempt to control her.

CHAPTER TWENTY

JUNE BROODED FOR twenty miserable minutes after Dean left before deciding what to do. She reached her uncle in Manhattan around midnight. Yeah, it was late, but she knew his habits. He'd be awake.

In all the years since Mike had been her guardian, she hadn't asked much of him. She hadn't needed to. Mike had been extraordinarily generous, providing most anything the daughter of his beloved brother could possibly want.

Would he grant this request, one he'd no doubt think strange?

"What's up, Junie?" he asked. "Has your boyfriend arrested the sniper yet?"

"No, and he's not my boyfriend."

"Oh? Did you guys have a fight?"

"Never mind," June said, not wanting to discuss Dean. She needed to avoid thinking about him, occupy her mind with something else. "Don't you have some superprivate security team that you use?"

"I do," Mike said. "When I need that sort of service."

"Can you get me a bodyguard for a day?"

Mike was quiet for a long moment. "What's going on?"

"It's not what you think. I'm not in any new danger, but I want to go to Key Largo and check out the marina where Al Kublin used to live, and I want to have some protection just in case I'm followed."

"What does Detective Hammer say about that plan?"

"Detective Hammer insists I stay locked up in this penthouse, but I'm going crazy."

"What will you do if you find Kublin?"

"Tell the police where he is."

"You won't approach him?"

She didn't answer right away. "I don't know. Probably," she admitted. "I'd like to talk to him."

"About what?"

"Mom and Dad."

"Oh, Junie. I don't know about this."

Should she tell her uncle about the latest theory? Yes. He deserved to know. Especially since he'd never believed his brother was a criminal.

"The police now believe Mom and Dad were framed."

"Are you serious?"

"Dean is working off that theory, but he can't locate Kublin to learn what he knows."

"Finally," Mike muttered. "Finally. I'd given up hope."

"The police don't have the manpower to check out all of Kublin's old hangouts, so I want to go to Key Largo myself. I want to help clear Mom and Dad."

"Just how do you plan to find this guy?"

"I have a photo left at Sandy's funeral by the police. I'll show it around the marina, maybe a few bars."

June sucked in a breath when her uncle didn't respond.

"Look, Uncle Mike, I'm aware I'm not likely to learn anything, but I need to do something, and this is the only thing I can think of. Truth is, I need to get out of town even if it's just for a few hours. I'm hoping the change of scenery will clear my head. I'm going nuts."

"I don't know, June. This plan sounds a bit risky. Maybe you should let the police handle—"

"I'm going, Uncle Mike. I would be safer with a bodyguard."

"I see."

"Will you help me?"

"When do you want to leave?"

"Tomorrow morning."

"I'll see what I can arrange and call you back."

DEAN DROVE BACK to the precinct after the ugly scene with June, which he'd handled all wrong. He'd wanted to comfort her and ended up making her feel worse by forcing her to look at her behavior. She'd rejected everything he'd said.

No way would he be able to sleep, and he still needed to complete the reports. Might as well use the time being productive rather than obsessing about how stubborn the woman could be. Did she really not see how guilt weighed her down—like a dead bird hung around her neck?

The office was quiet when he arrived, but at this hour officers were in the field. With the shift change in thirty minutes, the place would start hopping.

He was ten minutes into the work when his desk phone rang. Thinking it was late, but hoping June had seen the light, Dean reached for the receiver. "Hammer."

"Detective Hammer?" said a tentative male voice.

"You got him."

Whoever was on the other end released a long, very audible breath but didn't speak. Dean frowned. What the hell? Was this a perv calling to get his jollies off?

"Who is this?" Dean demanded.

"My name is Al Kublin. I really need to speak to you."

Dean sat up. "I'd like to speak to you, too, Mr. Kublin. Where can we meet?"

"Not a good idea."

"Why not?" Dean grabbed his notebook and a pen to write every word Kublin uttered.

"I think you know I'm a hunted man. I need to keep a low profile."

Dean glanced at the timer on his phone. He needed to keep Kublin on the line for five minutes so the department techs could get a trace. Unless the guy was on a cell. Maybe less then.

"Who is hunting you?" Dean asked.

"Whoever set the fire at Latham Import."

Dean nodded. This jibed with what the shrink had said. "And who set that fire?"

"I swear it wasn't me," Kublin said. "I think it was a rogue cop."

Dean's gut squeezed. *Holy shit. A crooked cop?* "Why do you say that?"

"I've thought about it for ten years, and it's the only answer, the only way this deal went down. Everyone thinks I'm nuts, that I see conspiracy everywhere, but my mind is totally clear on this. Carl and Eileen Latham would never smuggle anything, certainly not cocaine. Junie needs to know that."

Kublin took a deep breath, as if that long speech had worn him out. Dean heard muffled coughing. Jeez, the guy sounded bad.

"Sorry," Kublin murmured so softly Dean could barely hear him.

"You tried to contact June Latham at the North Beach Pet Shop, right?"

"Right. But that awful man hurt her. I did what I could and left."

"Tell me what happened at the Sea Wave Hotel on North Beach."

Kublin remained silent for a few heartbeats.

"Mr. Kublin?" Dean prompted. "Are you there?"

"How did you figure out that was me?"

"You were on surveillance video. I recognized you from the pet shop."

"Things sure have changed since I went away,"

Kublin said in a wondering tone. "Technology everywhere."

"Yes, sir," Dean said with an unexpected spurt of sympathy. If the man had been wrongly convicted, he'd missed a lot of changes while locked up. The internet, social media, texting, half of the nonsense that drove modern life and communication. So Kublin definitely hadn't tracked June via her cell phone, although the sniper certainly could have.

"I'm sorry about that homeless man," Kublin said. "But I was being followed. Doctors tried to tell me I was paranoid, but I knew better."

"So you used him as a decoy?"

"Because I need to get to June before I die, and that's proving harder than I imagined. I don't want June in danger, but someone is after me. Two people are dead." Kublin coughed again, and Dean waited him out.

Two minutes and counting.

"That's why I called you. I want you to tell her the truth. She deserves to know her parents were not guilty."

"Why don't you call her? Tell her yourself?"

"Won't work. That kind of information shouldn't happen in a phone call from a stranger. Either she won't believe it or I'll frighten her. Maybe she'll believe you. You're with her a lot."

Dean paused his scribbling. "You're watching her?"

"Looking for another opportunity to safely approach her, but—well, I guess it's obvious I've totally bungled this. Now she'll be terrified, and frankly I'm not doing so good myself. I don't have much time left."

"Meet me, Mr. Kublin. Let the police protect you. I can arrange for medical care."

"It's too late for me."

"You don't know that."

The man sighed softly. "Yes, I do. Is June in any trouble with the police?"

"Someone is trying to kill her."

Kublin released a long, shaky breath. "And that's because of me. No question."

"Why does this sniper want her dead?"

"I'm not sure. I think to tie up loose ends. Whoever set the fire, whoever used Latham Imports, felt safe as long as I was locked away. When I busted out, he got worried. I misjudged what I could do, but I had to try. I thought it was the right thing."

"I think it was the right thing, too, Mr. Kublin," Dean said. "Your actions are going to finally right a very old wrong."

"Thank you for that," Kublin said in a tired voice. "It's up to you now to prove the Lathams were innocent. I'm not going to be able to do it."

"Help me. What proof do you have?"

"Proof?" Kublin's coughing began again. Dean frowned at the hacking. This guy probably didn't have long to live.

"Mr. Kublin?"

"I wish I had evidence, but all I can tell you is I'm

certain there's a crooked cop. I've been through it in my head a million times, and no one else would have the ability to manipulate the records." Kublin sucked in a ragged breath. "Please, Detective Hammer. I'm begging you. Please prove to June her parents were not guilty of anything but loving her."

"Meet me," Dean urged again. "I can make sure you're protected. You can tell June yourself."

"I would like to talk with Junie," he said in a wistful tone.

"The truth would mean more to her if it came from you."

"Yeah, maybe. Let me think about that."

The phone went dead.

Early the next morning, waiting for Sanchez to arrive for his shift, Dean listened at his desk as Officer Baker reported nothing had popped at the Taylor home following the memorial for Sandy Taylor the night before.

"No strange cars drove by. No one stayed too late. No one got too drunk. Pretty depressed group from what I could see," Baker said.

Sanchez joined them. "Well, it was a funeral."

"Thanks," Dean said to Baker. "Good work."

When Baker moved away, Sanchez asked, "What's next, Hawk?"

"I got a phone call from Al Kublin last night," Dean said.

The rookie's eyes widened. "Kublin? No shit."

Dean relayed the content of the phone call.

"So we should be looking for a crooked cop," Sanchez stated. "Could that be why Betty Daniels hasn't called back? Is she hiding something?"

"I don't think so. This stink had to start long before Daniels got involved with her investigation. No telling how long the Lathams' company was being used to transport contraband."

"What if the Lathams had a client who was also involved in law enforcement?" Sanchez suggested. "Maybe that's our rogue cop."

"And all the records were destroyed in the fire," Dean said.

"The perfect crime," Sanchez said.

Dean shook his head as his cell phone chirped. "There's no such thing. We just need to find the right angle."

"Hammer," he barked into his phone.

"Detective Hammer, this is Betty Daniels. You've been trying to reach me?"

Finally. Dean mouthed *Betty* to Sanchez. "Yes, Mrs. Davis. I need to ask you a few questions about an old case."

"The Latham case, I know. I just listened to your messages. I've been on a cruise with my family."

"Where are you now?"

"I'm waiting in the customs line at the Port of Miami. We're driving back to Stuart as soon as we're through here."

"Can you take time to meet with me before you go home?"

There was a long sigh from the retired officer. "I guess. I wouldn't do it if it were any other case. But you owe me, Hammer. My husband is in a fine mood from our vacation and you're fixing to spoil it."

They made plans to meet at the food court at Bayside Marketplace, a food and entertainment complex adjacent to the port, at ten o'clock.

"Get ready to roll," he told Sanchez when he ended the call. "We're meeting her at Bayside."

AT 9:00 A.M. June exited the lobby of the Enclave and stepped toward a long black limousine. The windows were so heavily tinted that she couldn't see anything inside the vehicle. A tall, serious-faced man in his thirties, whom she assumed was one of her bodyguards for the day, opened the rear door and said "Bluebird," the prearranged password Uncle Mike had given her when he told her two operatives from the Protection Alliance would pick her up this morning.

She started to speak, but the man said "Get inside first, Ms. Latham" in a low, urgent voice. His hair was light brown, but she couldn't see his eyes, as they were covered by reflective sunglasses.

June entered the limo and settled into leather seats as soft and smooth as butter. A second darker-haired man sat behind the wheel. This one's eyes were also shielded.

The first man slid into the passenger seat and turned

to face her. "I'm Brad from the Protection Alliance." He opened his wallet to show her an official-looking license featuring the familiar seal of the state of Florida. "This is Tony," Brad said with a nod at the driver. "Just so you know, this vehicle is bulletproof. That's why I asked you to get in first."

"Okay," June said with a glance at Tony, the driver, who hadn't yet spoken.

"Your uncle hired us to escort you wherever you want to go today and make sure you stay alive. It's our understanding a sniper is hunting you," Brad said.

"That's what the police believe."

"Do you have doubts?"

She shrugged. "Not really."

Brad nodded. "So I'm assuming the authorities don't want you to go anywhere."

"Right."

Brad and Tony exchanged glances.

"Okay. For us to do our job," Brad said, "we're going to need you to follow a few simple rules. Number one is to listen to us. Don't do anything unless we tell you it's safe."

"I'll do whatever you tell me," June said.

"Good," Brad said with a nod. "I'd like you to give me your cell phone, which can be a huge distraction at the worst time, something a shooter can take advantage of. Also, while unlikely, you could be tracked with the GPS. I'm going to put the device inside a box that blocks the signal."

When June hesitated, Brad said, "It's just for one

day, Ms. Latham. We need you to stay focused on your surroundings, not on a conversation with your friends or a game."

June reached inside her purse. No one was likely to call her. Her friends were all confused or annoyed that she'd skipped the gathering after Sandy's memorial service last night. Uncle Mike knew what she was doing. Dean didn't, but she didn't care if he did. He wasn't speaking to her anyway.

"Here," she said, handing him her phone.

"Thank you," Brad said. "There's a protective vest on the seat beside you. You don't have to put it on now, but don't get out of this vehicle without it."

June glanced at the bulky garment and nodded. Dean had worn one yesterday at the funeral. "Okay."

"The entrance of this building blocks a scope, so it will be almost impossible to pick up a tail. However, Tony will make sure we aren't followed when we leave, so don't worry about the circuitous route we take."

"Makes sense," she said. Sounded as though these guys knew what they were doing. "Anything else?"

"Probably. We'll play the day as it comes," Brad said. "So, what's your plan?"

She leaned forward. "I don't really have a plan exactly. I'm looking for a man and there's a chance he's in Key Largo at the Windjammer Marina. At least that's what I'm hoping."

"A marina?" Tony said, speaking for the first time. "Out in the open. You're making it easy for a sniper."

"But I can talk to management first," June protested. "Find out if he's there. I've got a photo."

"We'll do the legwork," Brad said. "Please don't get out of the vehicle until one of us gives the all clear. Agreed?"

"Agreed," June said, feeling like a kid watched over by two strict babysitters. Maybe this bodyguard idea hadn't been such a great plan after all.

"Why are you looking for this guy?" Tony asked.

June sat back with a sigh. Where to start? Should she tell her babysitters the whole story? Why not? They had a long ride south, and that information might help protect her.

"Do the police consider him a threat?" Brad prompted.

"He's an escaped mental patient," June said.

"A whack job," Brad said with a nod. "At least that's better than armed and dangerous."

"He was sent away for murdering my parents," June added, taking grim satisfaction from the way Tony's jaw tightened.

"Why would you want to find a murdering psychopath?" Brad demanded.

"Because he might be innocent. I need to talk to him, find out what he knows."

CHAPTER TWENTY-ONE

INSIDE THE NOISY, crowded food court at Bayside, balancing three cups of coffee, Dean approached the table where Sanchez sat across from Betty Daniels. Betty was in her midsixties, an attractive African-American woman of average weight. She had sent her husband and grandkids off on a shopping expedition to gain some privacy while answering questions. If looks could kill, Dean suspected he'd be mortally wounded by the glare her husband had sliced his way.

Dean slid a foam cup across the table toward Betty. "Cream and no sugar," he reported.

"Thanks," she said and pried off the lid. Steam billowed into the air, releasing a strong aroma.

"Are you sure you don't want something to eat?" Sanchez asked as he opened his own coffee.

"Oh, God, no," Betty said, with a grimace. "All I did for the last week was eat. Just ask me your questions and let me go home and start my diet."

"I'm sorry we interrupted your vacation," Dean said.

"No, you're not," Betty said. "I know that look in your eye, Hammer. You've got the scent of a killer and you won't let anything stand in your way until you bring him down."

Sanchez snickered.

"Yes, ma'am," Dean replied.

"So, why are you taking another look at the case

against the Lathams?" Betty demanded. "My investigation ended when they died in the fire at their warehouse."

Dean explained about Al Kublin and how the Lathams' daughter, June, was connected to two recent murders.

Betty listened intently, nodding when he'd finished. "So your theory is the Lathams were set up and murdered before they went to trial—not by Kublin—and that perp is now after the daughter. The country club hit was an error."

"Right," Dean said.

"You're operating on the idea that the arsonist is your current shooter."

"And he wants June dead to tie up loose ends. He thinks either that she knows something or that she could force the police to reopen the old investigation at some point."

Betty sat back, thinking.

"How solid was your case against the Lathams ten years ago?" Dean asked.

"I had my doubts about some of the evidence," she said. "Some of it seemed to fall into my lap too easy."

"I've read your reports." Dean shoved a slip of paper across the table. "I need you to explain this note."

"What? You can't read my writing, Hammer?" Smiling, Betty retrieved the report, but grimaced as she read it. "Shit."

"You drew a bent arrow pointing to a stick-figure cat. The cat was for *LEO*, law enforcement officer, right?"

She swallowed and murmured, "Yeah."

"You suspected a crooked cop, didn't you?" Dean demanded.

Betty shook her head. "Man, oh, man. I don't want to ruin anybody's career without proof, but this case has bothered me since the fire."

"How did it go down?" Dean asked. He didn't want to push Betty too hard. She had to give up the name on her own. "Who gave the order to pull the plug?"

"With the Lathams toast and no one to put in jail, of course the state's attorney dropped the prosecution against them. Why go to the expense? That part of the case, the smuggling, ended. Al Kublin was arrested and convicted of the arson. I wasn't the primary, but the evidence against him was strong, although yeah, I do remember him yelling long and loud about his innocence and that of the Lathams."

"Go on. Your note predated the fire."

"By a day or two," Betty agreed. "My doubts centered on an affidavit signed by a witness in Peru. The signature didn't match previous receipts signed by the same witness. Close examination of one document made me think it had been altered. I was thinking, *Betty, what's going on here?*"

"What were the receipts for?"

"Supposed to be shipments of artisanal handcrafts

made by Quechua Indians, baskets, pottery, shawls. But the shipments actually contained a certain white powder and illegally trapped birds. Before I could follow up, the warehouse burned to the ground and none of it mattered anymore."

"I can tell that bothered you."

"A lot." She shrugged. "But I had no case. The defendants were killed in the fire and the arsonist was apprehended. My lieutenant told me to concentrate on investigations where I could actually take a bad guy off the streets."

"Why did it bother you so much?"

Betty hesitated and took a sip of her coffee. Dean knew he was getting close to something important. He took a swallow of his own to give her time to think it through.

"Did you look at the case against Kublin for the arson?" Betty asked.

"Of course, since even Kublin's shrink thinks he's innocent. But that evidence looked righteous to me."

Betty nodded. "It was a solid case. But did you notice who the primary witness was against Kublin?"

"No. I didn't see a trial transcript in the file box."

"Too bad. The same witness who testified to seeing Kublin set the fire allegedly made the trip to Peru to obtain what I thought was a forged affidavit. Did I want to check all that out? You bet I did, but I received firm instructions from my lieutenant to spend my time on cases that weren't already solved."

Dean nodded. Betty was telling him where to look,

but didn't want to give him the name. Maybe that had to be good enough. "It had to be one of the investigating officers."

"That was a huge case," Sanchez said. "There are a lot of cops mentioned in the files."

Wearing a sad expression, Betty looked out the windows. Dean followed her gaze to the masts of hundreds of sailboats bobbing at anchor in the marina.

"I was a good cop," she said, "but learned the hard way you have to make choices. I'm making one right now. I've been out of the game for a while, and maybe I was wrong about that evidence."

"Considering your record, Betty, I doubt it," Dean said.

That made her smile. "You follow it up, Hammer. You're working an active investigation. Find out what really happened in that fire and then let me know."

IN THE BACKSEAT of the limo, June reached for one of the plastic bottles of chilled water courteously provided by her security team. She needed to hydrate, moisten her mouth. She'd just talked nonstop for an hour telling two complete strangers the sad story of her life and why she was on a journey to Key Largo.

"So your theory is this Kublin, the arsonist who killed your parents, is holed up at a marina he lived in a decade ago?" Tony asked.

Noting the skepticism in the driver's voice, June took a long swallow of cool water. He obviously didn't think much of her theory. She gazed outside. An endless expanse of calm water, partially blocked by low-lying mangroves next to the shore, streamed by the car windows as they drove south.

"People frequently return to old habits," June said. "My uncle didn't know Kublin well, but said he loved his sailboat, loved living on the water. That nautical connection is all I've got to work with."

"Sounds like you're itching to do something to clear your parents," Brad stated. "Even if your search leads nowhere, you want to do something."

"Exactly," June murmured. Why couldn't Dean understand that need?

Tony shook his head. "You realize the chance of finding him today is practically nonexistent, right?"

"Yes," June said. "But at least I'm trying."

"Well, you can relax, Ms. Latham," Tony said. "We definitely were not followed. I'm expecting this expedition to go off without a problem."

"How much farther to Key Largo?" she asked.

"Twenty minutes," Brad said.

"Better check in with Lola," Tony said to Brad.

While Brad made a call to their office, June settled into the seat and closed her eyes. Unfolding the long narrative for her guards with all its many twists and turns had exhausted her but somehow organized her thoughts and put her convoluted problems into perspective. The telling had been good for her.

She saw even more clearly that she should have believed in her parents. Yeah, she'd been young, frightened and insecure after the fire, but they had deserved her trust. Maybe Tony was right and this trip was a giant waste of time, but she owed it to them to make the attempt, and she was glad she'd come no matter what Dean thought.

And so her thoughts had circled back to Dean. What was he doing this morning? Probably something about the case. She missed talking to him, telling him what was going on in her life, hearing about his. He'd become like a touchstone that kept her grounded. Thinking of him first thing when she woke up each morning made her look forward to the day. She hated that she'd never again experience that flicker of anticipation.

What would Dean say about this trip? She smiled to herself, hearing him go ballistic in her head. But come on. She was well protected. He couldn't be angry with her about security.

Oh, hell, yes, he could. He'd find something to pick on about her bodyguards. He had this compulsion to run everything, likely a result of the void created by his father's early death. *But why is he so worried about my safety? Has he developed feelings for me— or am I just the latest in a long string of persons of interest he plays with on his cases?*

She sighed, pushing away that idea. No, she believed Dean when he said he didn't get involved with women connected to his work, but he'd admitted there'd been plenty of failed romances in his past. Even his sister had made comments.

How many women had there been? She doubted if any others went through life pulling a load of guilt behind them while demanding access to police files. Of course he'd stormed out last night.

So that behavior answered her question. He didn't really care about her. He wanted to keep distance between them, always maintaining control over the relationship. Like a big bully, he didn't like it when she tried to take any power. How could she be with a man like that?

Still, Dean had been kind to her, understood her complicated feelings about her parents when no one else did. Remembering their delicious lovemaking, picturing his gorgeous body as he lavished attention on hers, she felt herself grow moist. God, but Dean was a fabulous lover. He'd made her feel things she'd never known were possible.

Why was she beating herself up over Dean anyway? It wasn't as though she was in love with the guy.

June opened her eyes and stared at the passing landscape. Sun glinted off the calm water, creating a glare even through the tinted windows, and she accepted that she was again lying to herself. Even though they were all wrong for each other, even while conjuring every excuse in the world not to, she had fallen in love with Detective Dean Hammer anyway.

Now, wasn't that just about the stupidest thing anyone had ever done?

INSIDE ONE OF the interview rooms at the station, Dean used the table to spread out the contents of all the case files, both the smuggling case and the arson. He and

Sanchez were looking for trial transcripts. Bound transcripts were usually easy to spot.

"You were right," Sanchez said. "They're not in here. Why not?"

"Court proceedings aren't transcribed unless one of the parties files an appeal," Dean said. "Maybe Kublin didn't file an appeal."

"Seems like he would have," Sanchez said.

"Agreed, but transcripts aren't cheap, so the department doesn't get a copy unless there's a good reason." Dean stared at the mess before him, thinking. Who could he call on a Saturday that could access that information? He couldn't wait until Monday. He sighed and unsnapped his phone. No choice but to call Sheila Marks, an assistant state attorney he'd dated. Things hadn't ended too badly with her. Would she do him this favor? "Let me make a call."

He reached Sheila at home. After some banter— definitely some flirting—she agreed to see if she could locate the transcript and call him back. Of course he now owed her a drink during which he had to explain why he wanted the witness list on a ten-year-old case.

"Any luck?" Sanchez asked when Dean terminated the call.

"Maybe. Sheila remembers the arson because it happened when she'd just started her career. Turns out a few years ago, old transcripts and case files were all scanned into a database and the paper copies destroyed."

Sanchez glanced at the heaps of paper on the table. "Damn. That's what we ought to do."

"All it takes is money," Dean said. "My friend is going to try to find what we need, but I'm not holding my breath."

"Your friend?" Sanchez grinned. "Sounded like more than a friend."

"She's married now," Dean said. "Let's go at this a different way."

He rummaged through the paper trail and found the expense reports on the smuggling case covering the relevant time periods. He handed Sanchez half the stack. "Look for a request for reimbursement for a trip to Peru. That should give us the name."

Sanchez nodded and began leafing through the logs. Dean did the same, but doubted he'd find what he was looking for, finding it highly unlikely his hyper-frugal department would fund expensive airfare to South America. Still, he had to be thorough.

When he'd gone through every record twice, he looked up. "Anything?" he asked Sanchez.

"Nothing."

"Shit," Dean muttered. "So no one from our department made a trip to Peru."

"Then who was the witness?"

The name slammed into Dean like a shotgun blast. He cursed harshly, his thoughts spinning. Damn, it couldn't be. But as the pieces tumbled together in his head, it fit. It even made convoluted sense. Why hadn't he seen it before?

Lieutenant Marshall approached holding a slip of paper, his reading glasses perched low on his nose. The grim set of his jaw told Dean his lieutenant was more than a little pissed.

Dean held up both hands in mock surrender. "The time and use reports will be on your desk by five."

"No, they won't," Marshall said, his voice hard. "We've got another body. Another sniper kill."

Sanchez issued a long, shrill whistle. The sound sliced clean through to Dean's gut. *Another sniper victim. Shit. Where is June?*

"Indian Creek," Marshall added. "Inside one of those derelict houseboats around Fiftieth and Collins."

Dean came to his feet. *This vic couldn't be June. Not a pet shop within ten miles.*

"Male or female?" he demanded.

"Unknown," Marshall replied. "Get out there, Hammer. I need answers."

JUNE WAITED IN the limo with Tony while Brad went inside the office of the Windjammer Marina with Kublin's photo. She'd asked to go with him, but Tony couldn't position the vehicle close enough to the entrance for them to consider it safe even if she wore the Kevlar jacket.

So Tony repositioned the limo beside an outbuilding that provided cover from any rifle scope. Her guards didn't want her exposed or in the open for any time at all, even though they remained certain no one had followed them.

Itching to do something, she stared out the tinted windows at hundreds of boats, some with masts, some huge motor yachts, peacefully floating in Florida Bay. The docks seemed a long way away, maybe because the film on the window acted like a filter, muting the image of the scene before her.

Was this how she'd lived since the fire, with a protective barrier between her and the rest of the world? Even now, when actually trying to be proactive, she was being shielded by trained bodyguards and a bulletproof limo.

According to Dean, she'd been feeling so guilty over her parents' crimes that she'd been hiding from life. Was he right that the reason she saved birds was to make up for the ones killed in the fire? Now that she was over her initial knee-jerk reaction—hell, no one wanted to be told they'd been afraid to fully live— she saw the truth in his words. Not wanting anyone to know her secrets, afraid of being judged, she hadn't allowed herself to become close to anyone in a long time. Not until Dean.

How could a man she'd known for mere weeks know her better than she knew herself?

She shifted in the seat. All this damn time riding in a limo with nothing to do but think was making her screwier than she already was.

"Are you okay?" Tony asked.

He was watching her in the rearview mirror, his eyes still protected by dark lenses.

"Just impatient," she muttered.

"Yes, ma'am. Investigative work is tedious and often boring. Not at all like television."

"Were you a cop before this job?" she asked.

"Military police," Tony answered.

Before she could ask anything else, Tony accelerated the limo. She glanced toward the marina office and saw Brad emerge. Tony was moving to intercept him.

"Has Kublin been here?" she demanded when Brad slid into the passenger seat. Tony motored back to their cover.

"Yes." Brad shook his head, as if in disbelief. "You were right, June. The dockmaster—" Brad looked at his notes "—Bruce Martin, recognized the photo right away."

"Seriously?" June said. Could she really have found Kublin? Oh, did she look forward to giving Dean the news! "Is Kublin here now?"

"No, but he came a week or so ago—Martin wasn't clear on the time frame—looking for a boat to rent on a weekly basis. Martin didn't have anything for him, but made a few calls and directed him to other marinas in the area that allow live-aboards."

"Pretty accommodating dockmaster," Tony said doubtfully.

"Good business practice," Brad said with a shrug.

"And he felt sorry for Kublin. Apparently your guy didn't look good. He's emaciated, like he's sick or something."

"He is sick," June said. "He's dying of pancreatic cancer."

"You left that little detail out of your story," Tony said, exchanging a glance with Brad.

"Does it matter?" she asked.

"Desperate men do desperate things," Tony said grimly. "Especially escapees from a nuthouse."

"This is making more sense," Brad said. "So your guy is on his way out and on a mission to clear his name."

"Which makes him even more dangerous, if you ask me," Tony said. "Nothing to lose."

"Although, according to the dockmaster, your guy didn't act nuts at all. The fact that Kublin was such a nice guy made Martin want to help him."

"So, Ms. Latham, what now?" Brad asked. "I assume you want to check to see if he's at any of these other marinas."

"Yes, please," June said, her hopes shooting skyward. "Oh, my God. What if we actually find him?" She glanced from guard to guard. "Wouldn't that be awesome?"

Already working the keypad on a cell phone, Brad didn't respond.

"Don't get too excited," Tony said, but he cracked a tiny smile for the first time as he met her gaze. Maybe she was winning him over.

"You got an address?" he asked Brad.

"Holidaze Marina is our first stop. Take a left onto Overseas Highway."

June could hardly sit still on the drive. She found it even harder to wait in the car while Brad went inside the office to show the photo. But by the time they'd canvassed three other marinas, driving farther and farther south in the Keys, with Brad and Tony switching off who went in to ask the questions, her enthusiasm had dimmed.

Outside the Bitter End Marina, June watched Tony trudge back to the limo. She knew by his grim expression that once again they'd struck out.

"No luck," she said, not asking a question, when Tony slid in the passenger seat.

"Something," Tony said. "Something strange."

Strange? "What?" June asked, scooting forward to hear Tony's report.

"Someone else was here last week asking about this same guy."

"Who?" Brad asked.

"Law enforcement of some kind," Tony said. "The dockmaster said the guy flashed a badge, but he didn't bother to read it."

"Did the dockmaster recognize Kublin's photo?" Brad asked.

"No, and I tried to jog his memory with mentioning how emaciated Kublin looked now, but the man was certain he hadn't seen anyone like that around his docks."

"So someone else is looking for Kublin," June said. Could Dean have come down here and failed to mention it to her? No way. A trip to Key Largo took too much time, and she could pretty much account for what he'd been doing hour by hour lately. Except today.

"It's the shooter," Tony said. "Looking for Kublin. He's already covered the same ground we are."

"So the shooter is a cop?" Brad wondered.

"Either that or has false credentials," Tony said.

"Or maybe someone's trying to return Kublin to the mental hospital," June suggested, hating the idea of a bad cop, but wondering if this was something else Dean had hidden from her.

"What's next?" Tony asked.

Brad consulted his list. "The Salty Dog Saloon, a waterfront tavern where locals hang out and maintain an exchange for rentals."

Tony nodded. "The dockmaster here mentioned the Salty Dog to our inquiring badge, so it's likely he's already paid a visit."

"So wouldn't it be safe for me to go in?" June asked, eager to at least stretch her legs. She hadn't stepped out of the limo in hours. "You're certain we weren't followed from Miami and there'd be no reason for the sniper to come here again."

Brad and Tony exchanged another one of their meaningful glances. Tony shrugged, which she took as a grudging okay.

"If you put on the vest," Brad said.

June reached for the protection but realized it had to go under her blouse or she'd look way too weird. She looked up as a dark privacy window slid into place, blocking the view of the backseat from the front.

Fifteen minutes later, feeling like a stuffed sausage, June followed Brad into the dimly lit Salty Dog Saloon. With Tony walking so closely behind her, she decided she was a stuffed-sausage sandwich.

"Wait here," Tony ordered. She remained by the door while her bodyguards checked out the room, determining if the Salty Dog was safe for her.

As her eyes adjusted to the dim light, she counted ten or twelve patrons gathered around a weathered bar. Wooden panels covered the walls, making the room even darker. Old arcade games, even an ancient pinball machine, hugged the perimeter. She heard the distinctive sound of a cue stick hitting a hard ball, and in a separate room spotted two billiard tables, a game in progress at one. The place was quiet for a local watering hole, but it was Saturday afternoon. The room would probably be jumping in a couple of hours.

She looked for a ladies' room. She wasn't leaving here without using one.

Her bodyguards returned and nodded an okay. The bartender approached when Brad sat at the bar. June went with him, but remained standing. It felt good to put weight on her feet again, to feel as if she were participating in the search. Tony stood by her side, surveying the room constantly.

Brad showed his license and the photo to the bar-

keep, explained Kublin was sick and they were looking for him because he needed help. The bartender,
a man in his fifties with a deeply lined face, his long
blond hair secured in a ponytail, retrieved a small
flashlight from under the bar to illuminate the photo.
He squinted and nodded.

"Yeah, he was here, looking for a boat to rent. I remember because a cop of some kind was here a day
or so later looking for him, just like you guys."

June edged forward so she could better hear.

"Did the guy in the photo hook up with anyone for
a place to stay?" Brad asked.

The barkeep shrugged. "Like I told the cop, I sent
him to Marathon. I got a buddy down there with five
or six houseboats he rents out and most always has a
vacancy since they're not in the best shape."

"Did he go down there?" June asked.

Brad gave her a quelling look. One that said he
was asking the questions. June resisted the urge to
roll her eyes.

"I got no idea, ma'am."

"Can you call him and find out?" Brad asked.

The bartender squinted at a calendar of half-naked
women suspended from a wall near the bar. "Nah.
He's delivering a boat down to the Caymans. I don't
expect him back for a few more days. If he doesn't
decide to chill in the islands."

"Could you give me the address of these houseboats?" Brad asked.

The bartender grabbed a pen and scribbled some-

SHARON HARTLEY   351

thing on a cocktail napkin. "I gave this info to that cop fellow, too," he said. "Before you ask, I don't know if he went down to Marathon, either."

"Thanks," Brad said.

Realizing they were about to return to the limo, June said, "I need to use the bathroom."

"In the back," the barkeep said.

Brad knocked on a door with a large-busted female silhouette. "Anyone in there?" When there was no response, he went in and quickly exited. "All clear."

When safely back in the limo, June removed the vest. "I'm decent," she said, and her guards lowered the privacy window.

Tony was behind the wheel again, and Brad turned to face her.

"It's a long drive to Marathon," Tony said.

"We'd have to spend the night," Brad added.

"So you've already discussed it?" June asked.

"Yes, ma'am," Brad said. "Your uncle has authorized the expense."

"You were right about Kublin coming to the Keys," Tony said. "But Marathon is a long way from Miami and not a good base of operation for his mission there."

"It's our only lead," June said.

"That's a fact," Brad agreed. "Your decision."

"I hope we don't find Kublin's body," Tony muttered.

"Let's go," she said. Dean thought she was hiding from life? Not this time.

CHAPTER TWENTY-TWO

DEAN WAITED IMPATIENTLY for the concierge desk to pick up at the Enclave. June hadn't answered her cell or her home number. He'd texted her three times. She didn't work on Saturdays. If she'd gone down to the pool for a swim, she'd be back by now.

Where the hell was she? And why wasn't she answering her phone?

"Concierge," said a cultured voice. "This is Magda."

"This is Detective Hammer, Magda. Do you know where June is?"

"She left this morning in a limo," Magda said. "Her uncle sent the car."

Dean released a breath. *Thank God.* "Do you know where she went?"

"Key Largo. Don't worry. She'll be home tonight."

"Thanks." Dean disconnected, realizing instantly what June was up to. Strange that she wasn't picking up, but at least she was far away from the sniper.

"Damn, a houseboat," Sanchez said as he maneuvered the Crown Vic toward five or six other police vehicles at an active scene along Indian Creek. Circulating blue and red lights flashed around them. "I didn't know there were any houseboats left in South Florida."

Refocusing on the scene, Dean noted that a crowd of fifty to sixty citizens had gathered, some spilling into the roadway.

"Damn loony lookers," Sanchez muttered as he braked to a stop.

Dean exited the Crown Vic without speaking. He glanced across Collins Avenue toward the parade of thirty-story buildings looming over this section of Miami Beach.

Each rooftop contained a perfect spot for a sniper to hide.

Midbeach, the department called this section of the city. These oceanfront high-rises began their lives as luxury hotels, but most had now been converted into condominiums. Residents who could afford the expense kept huge yachts docked in protected Indian Creek, a narrow waterway directly across Collins Avenue. Access to the ocean or Biscayne Bay was maybe a thirty-to-forty-minute gas-guzzling journey away.

And yes, a floating home or two still remained here, leftovers from the past. The sniper's latest victim waited for him inside this faded pink aluminum-sided houseboat swarming with law enforcement. A wooden sign with etched script letters, Casita Rosita, hung over the front door. This square-shaped hunk of junk looked nothing like a boat and probably hadn't left the dock since the owner tied it up decades ago.

Dean and Sanchez pulled on latex gloves and covered their shoes with paper booties before entering. Dean looked for and didn't find a bullet hole anywhere in the facade.

Thankful he no longer feared this corpse could be

June, he stepped inside the houseboat. Squatting, Dr. Owen Fishman hovered over the body.

"Good morning, Hawk," Fishman said, turning his head, nodding.

"Morning, Doc," Dean replied. "What have we got?"

The ME stood and Dean stared into the wide-open but very dead eyes of Al Kublin.

"Damn," Sanchez muttered. "Isn't that Kublin?"

"You know our victim?" Fishman asked.

"Been looking for him," Dean said, still focused on Kublin's body. The man was thin, almost anorexic. Dark blood spread across his sunken chest. The kill shot had been to the center mass of the body.

"Well, someone else found him first. Single gunshot wound just like the hit on North Beach. Death was immediate."

Dead nodded. Maybe quick was better than the long, slow, painful demise that Kublin had been up against. The man might even have welcomed it. Had that been the reason for the phone call last night? Had Kublin known the sniper had tracked him down again and wanted to make certain the cops kept digging for the truth?

"Time of death?" Dean asked.

Fishman shook his head. "Hasn't been long. You'll have to wait for the exact time."

"Who found the body?" Dean asked.

A female uniformed officer stepped forward. Her badge read S. Jones. "Dispatch received report of a gunshot around four p.m.," Officer Jones said. "I was first on the scene and called it in. Looked like he opened the door to exit, got whacked and was thrown back by the impact."

Dean nodded. The sniper was getting bolder, taking a shot in the afternoon with plenty of civilians around. Desperation? Or maybe once he found his target, he didn't want to take a chance on losing him again.

"Have you done a canvass?" Dean asked.

"Nobody saw a thing. Anyone who heard the gunshot knew immediately what the sound was."

"Who owns this boat?"

Jones consulted her notepad. "William Amos, a resident in the Paradise Club, a condo at Fifty-third and Collins. He rents out to tourists weekly." She looked up. "Amos is nervous because he knows short-term rentals are illegal in the city and now won't talk to us without his attorney present."

"We need to set that up immediately," Dean said. "I want to find out how long Kublin has been here."

"He probably rented this place after the hit on North Beach," Sanchez suggested.

"Probably," Dean said. "Has the body been moved?"

"I turned him over to check for an exit wound," Fishman said. "But he's lying where he fell."

"Just so you know," Dean said to Fishman, "on autopsy you'll find this guy has got advanced pancreatic cancer."

"That explains his weight." Fishman made a grim face. "Someone did this guy a favor, then."

"Maybe," Dean said. "But I sure wanted to talk to him first."

Whatever Kublin knew had died with him. Dean took a last look at the corpse. It was a damn shame if this man had been set up and wrongly convicted. Had Kublin hastened his death in a last effort to prove his innocence and that of June's parents?

"I'm sick of this shooter always being one step ahead of me," Dean murmured.

He moved to the front door and gazed east across Collins to the condo canyon, focusing on roofs, computing the trajectory of the shot. Sanchez joined him.

"I'd say our sniper took his shot from the Alexandrine," Dean said to his partner, who was also looking up.

"Agreed," Sanchez said.

"What do you say we mosey over there and take a look?"

Dean ignored the questions thrown at him by journalists as he and Sanchez exited the houseboat and hurried across the street. The department's public relations officer would tell the media anything they needed to know.

On the southbound side of Collins next to the waterway, four lanes of traffic had been funneled to one by the police activity, creating a long line of vehicles full of impatient commuters. Horns blared every few seconds. On the northbound side, curious drivers slowed and ogled the scene.

"Citizens hoping to see some gore," Sanchez muttered when they reached the east side of Collins.

Dean's cell rang before he could respond. He answered immediately, not checking the caller ID. *This had better be June.*

"Hammer," he barked.

"Well, you're in a good mood," Sheila said.

"Sorry." Dean slowed his steps. "I'm at a new crime scene, a murder."

"Ouch. I won't keep you, then. I have the name of that witness you wanted."

"Go ahead," Dean said, trying to suppress the excitement churning in his gut, certain of the name Sheila would reveal.

"A state Fish and Wildlife officer, one Donald Gillis, was the primary witness against Al Kublin," Sheila reported.

Dean realized he was holding his phone tightly enough to break the plastic or a finger. He relaxed his grip. Shit. He'd been right. Gillis, June's contact at Fish and Wildlife, was the sniper, the dirty cop. Dean's thoughts swirled around what this meant for his case. For June.

"Gillis testified to seeing Kublin at the scene and found him in possession of the accelerant that the fire marshal proved started the fire," Sheila continued. "Thanks to Gillis, evidence against Kublin was overwhelming, and his attorney barely mounted a defense. Kublin didn't even have a lame alibi. The jury returned a guilty verdict in two hours."

"Thanks, Sheila. I owe you that drink."

"Don't worry about it, Hawk. Just solve your new murder so I can convict the asshole, whoever he is."

"You got it." Dean disconnected and told Sanchez, "Our shooter is Donald Gillis."

"The Fish and Wildlife guy?" Sanchez said.

"Bingo. We'll need hard proof to arrest a fellow law-enforcement officer. We'll start tailing him when we're done here." Dean looked up again. "Which probably won't take long. If I know Gillis, we won't find squat on top of that roof."

JUNE STEPPED INTO a blast of stale but very cold air when she entered her sparse room in the Marathon Motel behind Tony. While he checked out the bathroom, she tossed a plastic bag from a local drugstore onto the bed and moved to adjust the temperature on the ancient AC unit. The night's lodging had been chosen with security in mind, not amenities.

Tony opened the closet, then knelt to check beneath the bed. "All clear," he reported.

"Hard to hide in a room this size," she said.

"You still want to make a call?"

"I need to let the police officer I'm working with know someone else wants to find Kublin."

"Does your cop contact know what you're doing today?"

"No," she admitted. "He wanted me to hide behind four walls."

Tony nodded. "To keep you safe."

"Yes."

"Sounds like a good man," Tony said. "Okay. When we're secure here, I'll return and give you my cell. Keep this door locked and chained until you hear our knock."

When Tony left, she pulled back the bedspread, arranged three pillows against the wall and settled herself to wait. She didn't turn on the television, craving silence to cure a headache caused by heat and frustration.

Once in Marathon, they'd found the houseboats with no problem, but the manager had never seen Kublin. No one in the area had. They'd canvassed other marinas until offices closed. After selecting what her security team determined an easy-to-defend motel, Tony made a quick trip into the drugstore to purchase a few necessities, since none of them had planned for an overnight trip.

June reached for the bag and dumped the contents onto the bed. Tony had bought toothpaste, toothbrush and, thank you very much, aspirin. She held up a blue T-shirt featuring a bright yellow sun with *I Heart Florida Keys* in the center. She didn't want to sleep in her clothes, since she had to wear them tomorrow. She only liked to sleep nude when Dean was in the bed with her.

She'd had to argue with Brad and Tony to get her own room, but they'd relented, deciding they could alternate watches outside her door. At least they wouldn't be hovering over her bed all night.

After she called Dean, she and her guards would share the pizza and pasta Brad ordered in for dinner. The food would be delivered to the office so not even the delivery guy would know where their rooms were. Seemed like overkill to her, but whatever. Her security team was in charge. At least the meal wasn't a repeat of lunch, fast-food burgers and fries ordered at a drive-in window.

She closed her eyes. The whole trip had been a waste other than learning someone else was looking for Kublin. Had to be the sniper.

When she heard the rhythm of Brad's special knock, June checked through the peephole. He stood alone, so she opened the door.

"Here's my phone," Brad said. "Don't tell anyone exactly where you are."

"THERE HE IS," Dean said to Sanchez, raising his binoculars.

Agent Gillis emerged from his residence carrying a black duffel bag, one large enough to conceal a sniper rifle. After confirming with a phone call that Gillis was inside, Dean and Sanchez had positioned themselves where they couldn't be seen and waited. Fortunately it had only taken an hour for their suspect to move.

Gillis strode toward his vehicle as if he had a purpose in mind.

"Brand-new top-of-the-line Lexus," Sanchez said. "I'm working for the wrong department."

"He didn't purchase that luxury sedan based on his salary," Dean said, eyeballing Gillis's residence through the binocs. The neighborhood might be middle-class, but the home had been remodeled beyond the median price of other structures. Gillis was too smart to flaunt his illegal profits by moving to an expensive area. Wondering what he'd find on the inside with a warrant, Dean returned his attention to the silver Lexus. "Let him get to the end of the street before you follow."

The Fish and Wildlife agent placed the duffel in the trunk and backed out of the driveway.

When Gillis turned left at a stop sign, Sanchez accelerated out of their hiding place behind a large live oak. They'd exchanged Dean's Crown Vic for a different vehicle at the motor pool, one Gillis wouldn't recognize. Dean had transferred equipment, including his own sniper rifle, from one trunk to the other.

They followed at a safe distance through the residential area in southwest Miami-Dade County to the Palmetto Expressway.

"Whenever you're tailing a suspect, try to stay at least two cars back," Dean instructed Sanchez. "Otherwise you take a chance of getting spotted."

"How long are we going to surveil him?" Sanchez asked.

"Until the phone taps get approved," Dean said. "We're lucky he's on the move. Nothing more boring than a stakeout with the target hunkered down for the evening."

"Where do you think he's going?"

"No clue, but my gut tells me that something is about to break."

Gillis drove a legal speed until taking the turnoff for the Dolphin Expressway. He exited the Dolphin fifteen minutes later and turned in the direction of the Miami River, always staying within the speed limit. The area changed from residential to small businesses and then turned rougher, industrial. Not too many people around, since it was late on a Saturday afternoon, but it wasn't yet dark. Anything could happen.

"He's headed to the river," Sanchez said.

Dean agreed, thinking Gillis had either found another shipping company to use or gone into business on his own.

Sanchez stayed out of sight when Gillis parked in front of a two-story building on the south bank of the Miami River. No signage. Dean raised his binoculars, certain the structure had huge doors and loading docks on the other side to off-load cargo from a freighter.

Gillis exited the Lexus without checking his surroundings—obviously not worried about a tail—unlocked the door and stepped inside.

"So we wait?" Sanchez asked.

"You wait. I'll confirm what I think is on the other side and look for a window to get a glimpse of the interior. If you don't hear from me in fifteen minutes, call for backup."

"Got it," Sanchez said.

Dean jogged toward the river and quickly determined his assumptions correct. Although no boat was tied up at this dock, there were freighters across the water and at neighboring wharfs. He looked cautiously around the corner of the building and spotted the huge roll-up doors he expected.

One of them was partially open at the bottom. No visible light on the inside.

Dean edged along the structure until he reached the opening. He paused and listened. Nothing. He squatted and looked inside. A dark void.

He stared into the interior. Should he chance it? Was this taking an unnecessary risk? He placed his phone on vibrate and secured his weapon. Lying belly down on the asphalt, he rolled inside.

Clear of the door, he leaped to his feet and darted left, keeping his back against the wall. Alert for any sound or sign of Gillis, he waited for his eyes to adjust. Knowing he'd be visible if Gillis turned on a light, Dean crouched behind a forklift.

Light streamed from around a closed door in the opposite corner of the warehouse. Probably the office. Likely where he'd find Gillis.

The room was a huge square containing pallets, machinery and boxes for containerized freight. Dean wiped sweat from his eyes and realized it was damn hot in here, at least ninety-five degrees. Shit, maybe a hundred. Nobody could remain in here long without cooking. That was why the freight door was cracked open.

He heard a rustle to his left deeper in the structure

and swiveled his head to look. Not rats. Sound was too high. But something was moving. He edged his way closer and heard a feeble squawk, then another. Sounded like June's macaw, Lazarus.

Dean felt the sides of a large wire cage and peered into the gloom. Maybe a hundred parrots were crammed into a thirty-by-thirty space, miserably huddled together, listlessly staring at him. He didn't see any food. The water dish was empty. Several dead birds lay on the floor of the cage.

He smothered a curse, understanding in that instant why June waged her battle against bird smugglers. This treatment was beyond cruel.

The office door opened and light flooded the interior of the structure. Dean dropped low.

Gillis emerged from the office with a cell phone plastered to his ear. He raised his voice, sounding angry. Dean couldn't make out the words, but damn if Gillis didn't move in his direction. Dean relocated, moving quickly but quietly, keeping out of sight.

Gillis terminated his call and made another, staring into the bird cage.

The cell phone on Dean's belt vibrated. Shit. Was Gillis calling him? Why? Dean didn't dare twitch to check caller ID.

Gillis's call connected. He walked away from the cage, spoke briefly in the tone people use when leaving a message and pocketed his phone. Returning to the cage, he stared inside again, hands on his hips.

"Where the hell are you?" he muttered.

Wondering if he'd find a voice mail from Gillis on his cell phone, Dean watched Gillis turn on a hose and spray the birds with water. The ones with any energy roused themselves, flapped their wings and began to screech in earnest.

Dean itched to slam his fist into Gillis's smug face. What a hypocrite this jerk was. An officer sworn to protect wild animals was using them to make a profit, torturing them in the process. No telling how many helpless creatures he'd murdered. Dean knew of five humans, for sure.

Gillis trickled water into the birds' water dish, but in this heat Dean knew it would evaporate within an hour. He couldn't leave these birds like this. Or they'd soon be added to Gillis's kill list.

Gillis turned off the hose and moved to the open freight door. He received a phone call after two steps.

"June," he said. "Where are you? I've been trying to reach you."

Gillis slammed the freight door shut, the rumbling noise drowning out his next words. He moved back toward the office, out of Dean's earshot.

CHAPTER TWENTY-THREE

"I'm in the Keys," June told Agent Gillis. "Just a little trip to get away. What's up? I got several messages from you." No point in telling Gillis what she'd been doing. Like Dean, he'd think it a waste of time.

"Well, I need your help, June. I've got a rescue for you," Gillis said.

"Oh, no. What happened?"

"I intercepted a batch of smuggled gray parrots and one of them requires your tender, loving care. Can you meet me tonight to take him?"

"Sorry. I won't be home until tomorrow."

After a pause, Gillis said, "That'll work. Can you take a detour and meet me in Everglades National Park on your way north? I'm working a special assignment in the park tomorrow."

"On a Sunday?"

"I switched with a buddy. It's his wedding anniversary. Lucky guy," he added, with a hint of melancholy.

Stung at the thought of Gillis's own dead wife, her ersatz aunt Janice, her mother's best friend, June glanced at Brad. What was another hour or two? Her protectors were being paid well. Besides, she needed something useful to do after the frustration of this trip. How would Lazarus react to a roommate? Smiling, missing her aviary, she said, "Sure, but it'll have to be early. I need to get back and feed Lazarus."

"Early is perfect." Gillis gave her directions where he'd be working tomorrow morning and they disconnected.

Before returning Gillis's call, she'd listened to multiple messages from Dean on her home phone. Sounded as though he really wanted to talk to her. To apologize? Probably not, but he'd seemed agitated because he couldn't get through on the cell. There must have been a break in the case. Had he found Kublin? Or maybe the shooter. Now, wouldn't that be great?

When she'd called Dean back, he didn't answer his cell, which was strange. She left a message, reassuring him she was fine, that she was in the Keys. He'd know what that meant, so mentioned someone else had also been searching for Kublin, she'd explain everything when she got home, that they needed to talk. And didn't they ever! Then she'd called Gillis. Sweet of the agent to think of her for his rescue.

She'd have to tell him Dean's new theory when she saw him. He'd be thrilled to learn that his best friends had been innocent after all.

DEAN PHONED SANCHEZ as soon as Gillis left the warehouse. The rookie answered immediately.

"I was about to call for backup," Sanchez said. "Gillis returned to his vehicle."

"If I'm not back by the time he leaves, follow him," Dean barked, searching for the catch on the freight door.

"What about you?"

"Just stay with Gillis. I'm fine." Dean found the release and disengaged the door. "Don't lose him."

Dropping the phone into his pocket, Dean jerked up the freight door. He welcomed the blast of fresh air that met him as he stepped outside. His shirt was drenched in sweat. Leaving the door wide-open to cool off the parrots, he hurried back to the front of the warehouse. The Lexus remained in place. Dean jogged a route to his partner so Gillis couldn't spot him.

"Damn, Hawk," Sanchez said when Dean entered the vehicle. "Did you jump in the river for a swim?"

"It was a furnace inside that warehouse," Dean said. He found Tropical Bird Society's emergency number and placed a call, hoping someone would answer. What were the odds someone would respond to a bird emergency on a Saturday night?

"TBS Rescue. Jared speaking."

Of course. Dean almost laughed at the image of June's friend, the one who didn't like him, waiting by the phone.

"Gillis is on the move," Sanchez said.

Watching Gillis drive away, Dean gave Jared the details of the parrots in distress, painting a gruesome picture and emphasizing the need for a rapid response, and disconnected. No way could he get the department involved. There would be too many questions to answer, and those birds didn't have time to wait for a warrant, especially on a weekend. He'd left the warehouse door open. Jared understood he had to claim he heard the birds squawking in distress and acted as a Good Samaritan to help mistreated animals.

Sanchez shot him a look. "Parrots again?"

"Don't ask," Dean said.

The legalities of all this was the bitch. He didn't have probable cause for an arrest, because he'd entered the warehouse illegally. The case would never stand up to a good lawyer. Besides, what was the case? A bunch of sick birds. Might not even be a felony. As June said, nobody took animal smuggling seriously.

He needed to gather evidence to prove Gillis was a murdering sniper or else the scum would walk. He'd no doubt flee with money in offshore accounts before a solid case could be built.

Remembering the call he missed when Gillis was too close for him to answer it, Dean checked his messages and discovered a voice mail from June. He closed his eyes, relieved to hear her voice. Ten minutes ago she'd been alive and, thank God, still in the Keys, a long distance from Gillis. And in the care of two bodyguards from the Protection Alliance? What the... He listened as she explained how her guards had stashed her phone to block the signal.

He'd heard of the Alliance. They were hypersecretive but had a professional reputation. He hadn't wanted June to leave her apartment, but maybe this was better.

She'd called Gillis after him, and Dean wondered if she'd told the sniper her location. Alliance operatives would have cautioned against that, so maybe not. Although knowing June, she might ignore them.

Would Gillis drive down to find her? According to June's message, Gillis had searched in the Keys for Kublin. June didn't know Kublin was dead. And why had she called Gillis right after phoning him?

Dean snapped his phone onto his belt. Too many questions. June was out of reach, but no matter. He'd stick to Gillis until he heard from her again and not let the bastard anywhere near her.

He dreaded telling June her parents had been murdered by their best friend. Even worse, that it was Gillis who was trying to kill her.

At 6:00 A.M. Dean stretched long in an attempt to relieve cramped muscles, then blew out a hot breath. He rotated his neck one way, then the other, wincing at the cracking sound.

No way to get comfortable. He hated all-night stakeouts but wasn't budging from Gillis's residence until the man went on the move again, which shouldn't be long. At five thirty a light had gone on inside the house.

Dean rubbed his face, feeling the scratch of his morning beard. No chance of falling asleep on his watch. Not with Sanchez in the backseat snoring louder than the gun range during a competition. He'd told the rookie he could go home, but the kid wasn't having any of that and took the first watch while Dean slept. Or tried to. He probably caught an hour, but kept worrying the rookie would nod off and let Gillis sneak off into the night.

Dean took a sip of cold coffee, which made him hungry, but the only thing left to eat was a soggy-french fry. At a particularly loud snort from the back-seat, he remembered how he'd chafed at the idea of training a newbie. Amazing how he'd actually enjoyed the process of watching the kid grow and learn. Sanchez was a stand-up guy and would make a first-rate cop. No, he was already a good cop. Dean hadn't expected Sanchez to remain with him all night to watch Gillis. From the one-sided conversation, he knew the blushing bride wasn't happy about that decision.

Would June be understanding about the need to work all night? Was she the type of woman who could be a cop's wife? That life was tough. His sister was Exhibit A of how rough it could be. His mom, too, although for a different reason. Did June have what it took to put up with constant uncertainty, not knowing whether your man was coming home, of his foul mood when he did from the stress of the job?

Two years ago, he'd have bet a million dollars his sister had the right stuff, and would have lost that bet. He didn't know what went on in the dissolution of Kat's marriage, but he knew his sister had loved her cop husband with her whole heart. Probably still did.

Did June love him that much? Hell, did she love him at all? They'd never said those magic words to each other, the words that women all craved to hear. Words he wouldn't mind hearing himself.

Mostly they just peeled off each other's clothes and argued afterward. Maybe that was all she wanted, all she needed. Not him, though. He wanted more, a lot more. He needed the whole package with June, including marriage and a couple of kids.

He should have told her. What made it so hard?

Perhaps because she was barely speaking to him. He ought to be grateful she'd even returned his calls. She'd sounded friendly enough in the message, but who the hell ever knew what June was thinking? Still, she'd had sense enough to secure protection for her trip to the Keys. Hadn't she once told him she could take care of herself?

Shit. Maybe he did try to control people. He'd have to think about that. Was June a real-life lesson in sensitivity training who'd made him aware of his faults?

He saw movement behind the curtains in Gillis's front room.

"Time to roll, Sanchez," Dean barked.

Sanchez bolted up in the seat, his face contorted in wide-eyed confusion. "What the—"

"Gillis is on the move."

Dean cursed when he recognized the gun case in Gillis's right hand. No question this time. Remington M24, the same weapon he used.

They tailed Gillis to the Florida Turnpike, where he drove south. He made a pit stop in Florida City, so Dean and Sanchez did the same, refueling at one of the many gas stations, believing they were headed into the Keys.

But Gillis turned west.

Several miles behind Gillis on a straight, flat road, Dean watched the Lexus through his binoculars. Gillis drove through the entrance to Everglades National Park without stopping. When Sanchez approached the station's overhang, no ranger was on duty. Dean instructed Sanchez to wait.

"We'll lose him," Sanchez complained.

"He'll recognize the car," Dean said. "There's no one else out here this early."

Tension hummed in the vehicle as Dean brought up a map of the park on the laptop.

"Do you think he's working?" Sanchez asked.

"Could be. Fish and Wildlife monitors the wildlife out here."

Sanchez nodded. "And that's why he brought the weapon?"

"Maybe," Dean muttered, not convinced. His gut still told him Gillis had a human target in mind for that rifle.

Studying the map, he realized there weren't many locations in the sea-level Everglades to set up a hide. Gillis needed height. Where would he find it?

ANXIOUS TO GET HOME, June and her protectors were on the road long before dawn, before even the fast-food joints opened. At five they grabbed breakfast at a drive-through in Islamorada. Brad and Tony eyed every vehicle with suspicion.

With nothing else to do, June worried about Lazarus

on the long drive north. She'd left him plenty of food and water just in case, but she usually cleaned his enclosure twice a day. The macaw knew her routine and would get antsy when she didn't return. Maybe it was just as well, though. Lazarus was healed. It was time for him to move to his new home.

Just as it was time for her to move on, too.

She longed to talk to Dean, to set things right with him. She needed to know how he felt. Could he let go of his need to control her once the case was over? Or would she scare him away with talk of love?

Tough. He was a big boy. Yeah, he was big, all right. She bit her lip at her thoughts. She imagined the grin on his too-handsome face when she told him he'd been right about her hiding from the world in her uncle's penthouse. He'd be all smug and superior, and then she'd hit him with the fact that she loved him.

Would her big boy scoot out the door, not even telling her to set the alarm on the way?

Well, she'd just have to see. This girl wasn't hanging back scared and timid on the pool deck anymore. She was diving into the cold water without a wet suit and relishing every single chill. The idea was frightening but exhilarating.

The journey would be a lot more fun if Dean came with her, even with his guns and ammo in tow. She sighed, realizing she'd used his hunting as another excuse to push him away.

"Will the park be open this early?" Brad asked from

the front seat when they approached the entrance. It was growing light, but the sun hadn't yet risen. One of her favorite times of day.

"The park is open twenty-four hours a day, but there probably won't be anyone to take our money, since it's off-season. Not many people want to fight the mosquitoes, humidity and heat."

"Sounds delightful," Tony said.

June laughed. Maybe the Everglades were an acquired taste.

When Tony braked to a stop at the park entrance station, they found a sign telling them to enter and enjoy the park, but not to approach the alligators.

June stared out the windows as the limo zoomed toward Royal Palm, where Gillis waited for her. Grasslands extended to the horizon, the emerging sun painting them a burnished gold. A flock of white ibis took to wing over the peaceful tropical prairie. She'd forgotten how much she loved the Everglades and its abundance of birds.

"Audubon studied the birds near here in 1832," she said. "He fell in love with the place."

"Your uncle mentioned you were some kind of bird nut," Tony said.

"Wouldn't you love to see what this area looked like a hundred and fifty years ago?" she asked.

Brad nodded, also staring at the view. "It's so tranquil. Feels as if nothing bad could possibly happen."

Tony snorted. "Yeah, well, I've seen a photo of a gator and a python eating each other alive out there."

ANXIETY CHURNED IN Dean's gut when they arrived at Royal Palm, the area with services closest to the park's entrance. They'd lost sight of Gillis's Lexus. It was what Dean wanted, but he hated rolling the dice.

After studying the map, he didn't think Gillis would drive the thirty-seven miles to Flamingo. Yeah, Flamingo was isolated, but also had a marina, and fishermen were known to set out early. Plus, he'd be trapped down there if things went bad. There were other exits to lakes and ponds, a hiking trail through a hammock, but no stops with any facilities or elevation. He doubted Gillis planned to climb a tree even if there were one large enough.

No. Gillis was waiting at Royal Palm, the location where he could make the quickest exit and disappear.

"Pull off," he instructed Sanchez. "I want to approach on foot."

Sanchez parked on the edge of the road.

"I need you to wait here," Dean instructed his partner. "Call me on the cell if another vehicle approaches. Text if I don't answer."

"Got it."

"Keep your eyes and ears open. If you hear gunfire, call for backup."

Dean retrieved his rifle from the trunk and moved toward the parking lot, remaining in the cover of vegetation. Did this decision fall under the category of risky behavior? No question about it.

But he had a bad feeling about today. June's message said she'd be home this morning. Only one road out of the Keys, and that road led to Florida City, the gateway to this park.

He remained off the road and approached from an angle where he couldn't be seen, soon spotting Gillis's lone vehicle. Dean knew immediately where Gillis lay in wait—on top of the pink building that housed restrooms and a closed gift shop. Moving to the side opposite the parking area, near the swampy habitat where gators waited for their prey, Dean scanned the roof for any sign of the agent, knowing Gillis wouldn't be watching this direction. The roof featured a parapet, so he'd have to position his weapon over the edge in order to take his shot, which would make it easier to spot him.

Dean's phone vibrated. "Yeah?" he whispered.

"A limo is approaching," Sanchez reported.

June. But he wasn't in position. Praying the Protection Alliance was as good as their reputation and she wouldn't step out of the vehicle until he was ready, Dean moved to the side of the structure and prepared to make his own shot.

"I DON'T LIKE THIS," Tony announced.

"What?" June asked. They were on the access road to Royal Palm and should arrive any minute.

"The isolation," Tony replied. "Who is this guy you're meeting?"

"He was my parents' best friend. He's law enforcement."

"Doesn't feel right," Tony said, exchanging a glance with Brad.

"Look," June said. "We're not alone."

The limo rumbled by a blue car parked on the side of the road. She couldn't see inside the tinted glass.

Tony drove into a parking lot and didn't stop. Gillis's Lexus was the only vehicle, parked close to a pink one-story building with restrooms and vending machines.

"I'd like to use the ladies' room," June said.

"Don't get out of the car, June," Brad ordered.

"What is wrong with you guys?" June asked. "You're—"

"Stay low," Tony said in a hard voice.

Obeying, June felt her heart hammering inside her chest, the guards' sudden caution making her nervous. But this was crazy.

Tony circled the parking lot and braked to a stop close to where they had entered. "Where's your friend?"

June raised her head and scanned the area. Where was Gillis? He should have heard their approach. But of course he didn't know she was in this long, black vehicle.

"He wouldn't recognize the limo. Maybe he's waiting in the car," she suggested.

"I didn't see him when we drove by," Tony said.

"Maybe he stretched out on the seat and fell asleep," Brad said. "It's damn early."

"Or he's out on Anhinga Trail," June said.

Tony removed June's phone from the box, checked for a signal and handed it to her. "Call him."

WORKING WITH QUICK, sure movements, Dean had nearly completed assembling his weapon when a phone rang. The sound came from the roof.

The limo was idling on the other side of the parking lot. No way could anyone inside hear that ring. No one had emerged from the vehicle. Probably because June's guards wondered why the hell Gillis hadn't shown himself.

Good men.

"Yeah, June?" Gillis answered.

Dean watched the roof. Couldn't see anything, but could easily hear the bastard in the early-morning quiet.

"I'm out on the trail," Gillis said. "Wood storks are nesting out here. Really. You have to see it. Yeah, okay. I'll be right back. Oh, I've unlocked the facilities if you need to make a pit stop." Gillis laughed at some comment from June. "Yeah, coffee does that every time. See you in a few."

Assembly completed, Dean came to his feet. He brought the scope to his eye. If a guard emerged first, Gillis wouldn't take him out, because June could drive away. Gillis would wait until June became visible. He'd kill her, eliminate the guards and disappear forever.

Focused on his target, Dean began to breathe in a controlled rhythm, timing each breath to slow his heart rate. He needed a steady hand to keep his aim true.

He'd only have one shot.

"He'll be here in five minutes," June said to her guards. "Can I please use the bathroom? He unlocked it for us."

"You're sure about this guy?" Brad asked.

"Yes," June replied, sick of the tension. She just wanted to get the injured bird and go home. "I've known him for years."

"Let me go first," Brad said.

Brad exited the limo and moved toward the structure, a gun in his hand. She shook her head. Crazy paranoia over Agent Gillis.

After a few minutes, Brad looked back and nodded. June opened her door and stepped into the quiet morning, smelling the tangy brine of the nearby mangroves. She heard the sweet call of a cardinal and felt herself relax.

In the cover of a tree, Dean heard a car door open, but he didn't dare look away from his focus through the scope. No movement on the roof. Another door opened. Dean waited for Gillis to show himself.

The barrel of a rifle slid onto the edge of the roof. The top of Gillis's skull became visible. Dean knew he could take the kill shot. He wanted to. He could blow the bastard's brains out, rid the world of the scum forever.

But June would never get the answers she needed.

A hand gripped the weapon. A long finger approached the trigger. At the bottom of his breath, Dean took the shot.

The rifle broke into pieces in a blur of blood. The barrel kicked up into the air and dropped to the ground.

A woman screamed. June.

So did a man. In pain. Gillis.

Dean turned toward the limo. One of the guards lay on top of June. The other one was in a shooting stance with his weapon focused on him.

"Police," Dean shouted, raising his arms into the air.

Sanchez roared their unmarked car into the parking lot, yelling, "Police. Drop your weapon," over the PA system. The guard relaxed his stance.

"June?" Dean shouted, moving in that direction.

"Dean?"

When he heard her voice, he broke into a run. She shoved her bodyguard aside and ran to meet him. Gathering her close, Dean breathed in the essence of her and swore he'd never let her go again.

"I love you," she said fiercely, her words hot against his cheek.

He closed his eyes. "God, I love you."

A week later

WITH THE SUN sinking low behind her, June stared at the granite headstones carved with her parents' names. This was the first time she'd visited their resting place since the funeral. Dean stood beside her, an arm around her shoulders. She liked this spot. It seemed peaceful.

She'd just explained to her mom and dad what had really happened ten years ago and apologized for not believing in them. Maybe this conversation would seem silly to most people, but she knew Dean understood.

"So, Gillis is rotting in jail," she told them. "Dean says he'll never get out, but probably won't get the death penalty."

"I said I didn't know," Dean corrected. "But he's confessed to everything, including the murder of his wife, so the death penalty might be off the table."

"Aunt Janice apparently discovered he'd framed you," June added. "So he had to kill her, too, making it look like natural causes."

Dean squeezed her shoulder.

"It's still so hard to believe," she said. "I trusted Gillis. He was always concerned for my well-being. He even asked me to forgive my parents."

"What he was doing was keeping tabs on you in case you wanted to reopen the arson case."

"And that never once occurred to me," she said.

"Good thing. As long as the truth stayed buried, he let things ride. When Kublin escaped, Gillis decided he had to get rid of all the old players so he could quit worrying."

"I wasn't a player," June said. "Just a lonely little girl. Remember the bunting rescue?"

"Oh, I think I recall that little adventure," Dean said.

"Gillis had a rifle with him that day. I think he planned to shoot me then if he'd gotten the chance."

Dean pulled her into an embrace, and June leaned into his protective warmth, wrapping her arms around his waist. She felt safe, whole, as if the fragments of her life that disintegrated after the fire had finally merged back together.

She fingered the engagement ring on her left hand. She'd finally flown free of the past.

"Are we done here?" Dean asked softly.

"Almost." June stepped away and turned to the graves again. "I'm in the process of moving out of Uncle Mike's penthouse and in with Dean. I know what you're thinking, but we're getting married." She held up her left hand and displayed the new diamond, the most beautiful piece of jewelry she'd ever owned. "See?"

"Is there where I should ask for your father's permission?" Dean asked in a mock-serious tone.

She gently elbowed him in the ribs. "He's a good man," June said to the graves, "even if he's too cocky and shoots birds."

"I also shoot bad guys," Dean added helpfully.

"Yes, he does," June agreed, reaching for his hand. "He's saved my life in so many ways, and I know you'd love him as much as I do."

Dean kissed the top of her head.

"I'm sorry you'll never meet him," she whispered. "Or our children."

"Three children," Dean stated.

"Maybe four," June corrected.

"Whatever you say." Dean shrugged. "Thanks to some sensitivity training, I'm a changed man."

* * * * *